OLYMPIAD TRAINER

FOR MATHEMATICS

Standard - II

- Useful for Olympiads and other competitive exams like IPM, Wisdom etc.
- Ample number of questions on every topic.
- Helpful and informative explanations.
- Model Question Papers

By

Mrs. Kajal Sugandhi

N0013

OLYMPIAD TRAINER (STD. I : MATHEMATICS) **ISBN 978-93-5164-538-2**

First Edition : **June 2015**

Published By :

NIRALI PRAKASHAN

Abhyudaya Pragati, 1312, Shivaji Nagar,
Off J.M. Road, PUNE – 411005
Tel - (020) 25512336/37/39, Fax - (020) 25511379
Email : niralipune@pragationline.com

PREFACE

It gives me immense pleasure to present this book for **Mathematics Olympiads For Standard II.** Maths is a subject that has applications in all other subjects. Maths is needed for mundane everyday jobs as well as in highly technical fields. Therefore every parent wishes his or her child to excel in Maths.

Olympiad exams encourage children to apply the basic principles of Maths in situations that we encounter in every day life.

This book for Standard II students has been prepared keeping in mind the basic mathematical concepts that the students are tested for in the Olympiads. Maximum efforts have have been made to see that the chapters are simplified and elaborated so that the child gets a better understanding of the concepts and the problems based on them. The main purpose of this book is to give thorough practise of all the possible questions to the child so that it becomes easier for him/her to ace the exams.

This book will not only help in preparing for the Olympiads but also for other competitive exams and regular academics.

The model papers included in the book recreate the exam like environment. Explanations are given for each and every question which I am sure will clear the doubts from the minds of the students.

Utmost care has been taken while preparing this book but any error that might have crept in by oversight is deeply regretted.

I take this opportunity to express my deep gratitude to my family members, especially my mother-in- law, Mrs. Geeta Sugandhi who has been my pillar of support without whose encouragement and strong belief in my abilities, this book would not have been possible.

I am thankful to Shri Dineshbhai Furia, Shri Jignesh Furia and the entire staff of Nirali Prakashan for their co-operation in bringing out this book.

Every valuable suggestion and constructive criticism that would help in the improvement of the book will be highly appreciated.

Author

12th June 2015 **Kajal Sugandhi**

CONTENTS

1.	Number Sense	1 – 8
2.	Computation Operation	10 – 24
3.	Fractions	26 – 36
4.	Length, Mass and Volume	38 – 50
5.	Time and Money	52 – 67
6.	Geometry	69 – 72
7.	Patterns	74 – 77
	Model Paper I	79 – 83
	Model Paper II	85 – 91
	Explanation	93 – 192

•••

MATHEMATICS – STANDARD II

Chapter 1
NUMBER SENSE

Topics: Number and number names till 1000, place values, ascending and descending order of numbers, greater than, less than, equal to, expanded form, before, after and between numbers, smallest 1-digit number, smallest 2 digit number, smallest 3- digit number, largest 1-digit number, largest 2-digit number, largest 3- digit number, Abacus.

Choose the Correct Answer

1. Four hundred and fifty eight is written in numbers as -

   (A) 485 (B) 458 (C) 488 (D) None of these

2. When written in words, 793 is same as

   (A) Seven hundred and ninety three

   (B) Seven hundred and ninety

   (C) Seven hundred and nineteen

   (D) None of these

3. What is six hundred and two in numeral?

   (A) 620 (B) 600 (C) 602 (D) None of these

4. In number 846, the place value of digit 8 is

   (A) 80 (B) 8 (C) 88 (D) 800

5. In 463, the digit 6 is in _____ place.

   (A) Tens (B) Ones (C) Hundreds (D) Thousand

6. Place value of 3 in 603 is

   (A) 33 (B) 3 (C) 30 (D) 300

7. 800 and 80 and 8 makes

(A) 808 (B) 880 (C) 888 (D) 88

8. 397 = 3 hundred + 9 tens + _____ones

(A) 3 (B) 9 (C) 6 (D) 7

9. 900 + 40 + 2 is same as

(A) 902 (B) 940 (C) 942 (D) None of these

10. 546 = 500 + x + 6

(A) 40 (B) 54 (C) 46 (D) 56

11. 192 = 1 hundred + ____ tens + 2 ones

(A) 1 (B) 9 (C) 2 (D) 3

12. 137 can be written as

(A) 100 + 3 + 7 (B) 1 + 30 + 7 (C) 100 + 30 + 7 (D) 1 + 3 + 7

13. In number 943, the place value of digit 3 is

(A) 30 (B) 3 (C) 300 (D) 33

14. Arrange the numbers in box to make the smallest three – digit number?

4	1	9

(A) 194 (B) 149 (C) 941 (D) None of these

15. Which is the greatest number?

742	396
147	923

(A) 923 (B) 147 (C) 742 (D) 396

16. The largest of the given numbers is

(A) 746 (B) 147 (C) 764 (D) 396

17. Which of the following will make the sentence true?

(A) 1,423 > 1,923 (B) 2,664 < 1,080

(C) 2,396 > 1,249 (D) 1,184 < 1,049

18. Which one presents the number 2,306 below?

(A) 2,000 + 36 (B) 2,000 + 300 + 6

(C) 2,000 + 30 + 6 (D) 2,000 + 300 + 60

19. Fill in the appropriate number

(A) 22 (B) 32 (C) 42 (D) None of these

20. Which of the following is smallest?

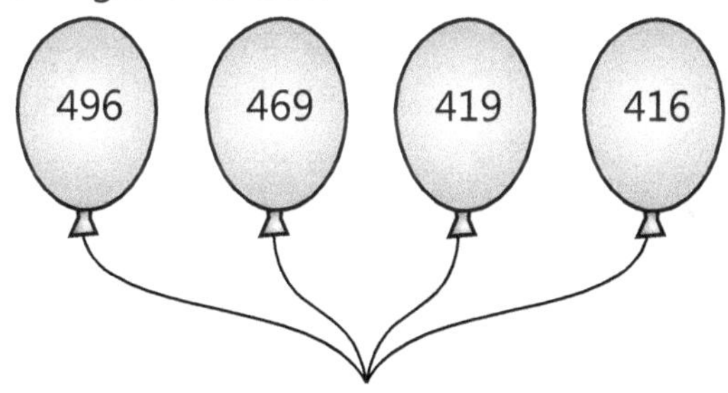

(A) 469 (B) 496 (C) 419 (D) 416

21.

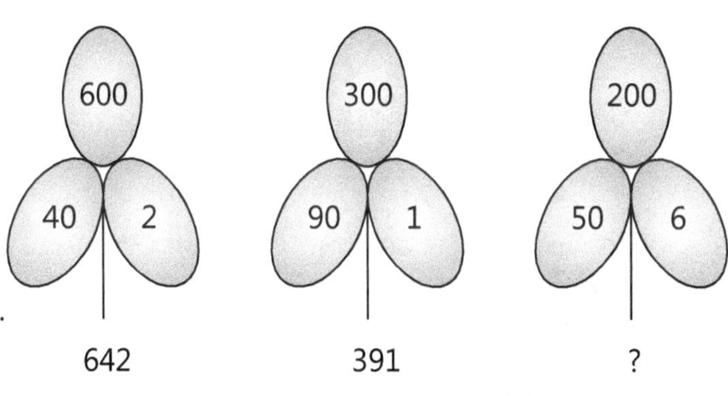

(A) 256 (B) 265 (C) 526 (D) 652

22. One more than smallest three digit number is

(A) 121 (B) 100 (C) 111 (D) 101

23. Largest two digit number is

(A) 999 (B) 99 (C) 9 (D) 90

24. Smallest two digit number is

    (A) 10 (B) 11 (C) 01 (D) 19

25. Largest three digit number is

    (A) 900 (B) 999 (C) 090 (D) 909

26. Smallest three digit number is

    (A) 110 (B) 011 (C) 100 (D) 101

27. Largest one digit number is

    (A) 3 (B) 9 (C) 1 (D) 0

28.

13		88		28	
	46		38		78

Which box am I in?

I am a two digit number, I have 8 in ones place, I am less than 40 and more than 30

(A) 88 (B) 78 (C) 38 (D) 28

29.

I am 3 digit number, I have 5 in tens place, I am less than 360 and more than 350. Which flower am I?

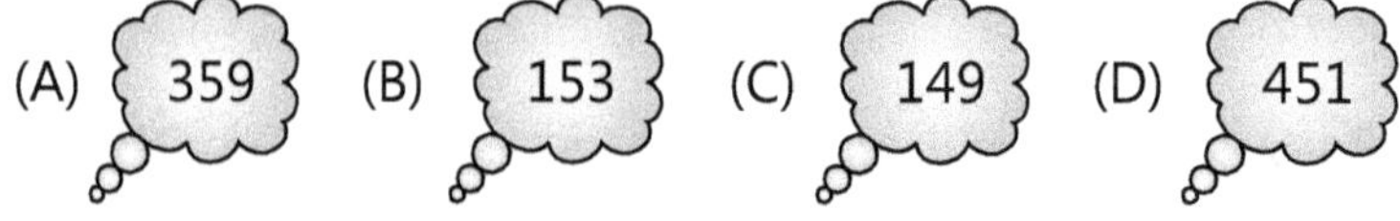

30. Find the odd one out.

(A) 448 – 446
(B) 394 – 392
(C) 760 – 756
(D) 214 – 212

31. Find odd one out

(A) 455 – 450
(B) 870 – 865
(C) 220 – 215
(D) 284 – 186

32. Given figure belongs to which basket?

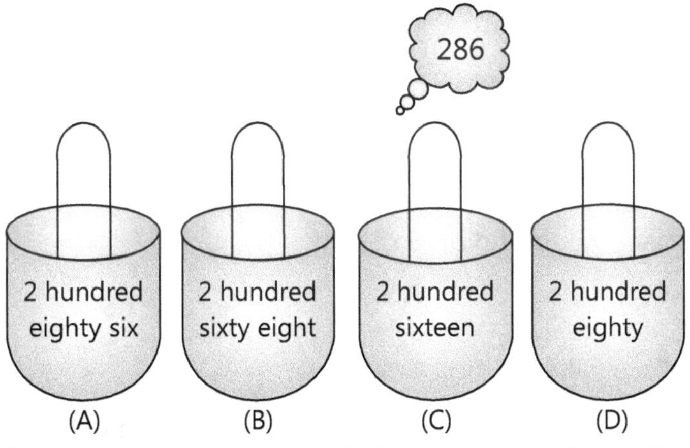

33. Raj was putting number cards in order when he noticed he was missing some cards

?	288	?	?

Which set of numbers are missing?

(A) 200, 300, 400
(B) 201, 202, 203
(C) 287, 289, 290
(D) 291, 292, 293

34. Which 2 numbers can balance the scale?

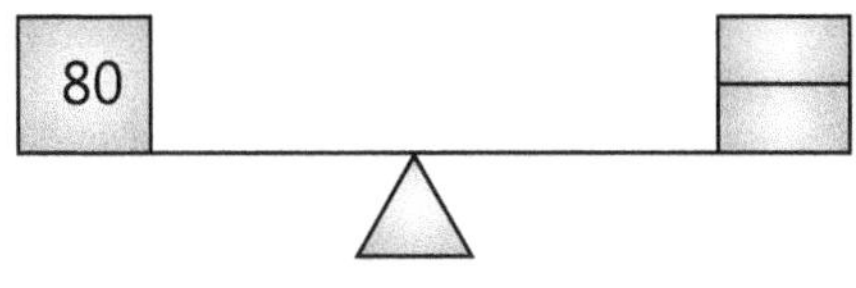

(A) 50 and 30
(B) 28 and 41
(C) 72 and 19
(D) 29 and 56

35. Which 2 numbers can balance the scale?

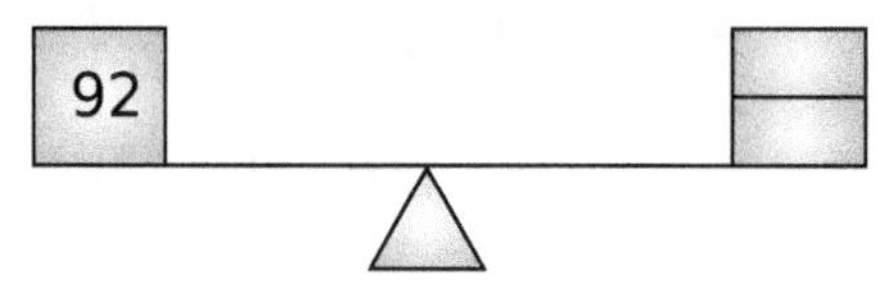

(A) 52 and 40 (C) 41 and 17

(B) 23 and 86 (D) 63 and 33

36. Four hundred and seventy four is written in numbers as

(A) 470 (B) 474 (C) 477 (D) 407

37. Six hundred and sixty six is written in numbers as

(A) 666 (B) 660 (C) 606 (D) 066

38. In number 486, the place value of digit 6 is

(A) 60 (B) 06 (C) 600 (D) 66

39. In number 392, the place value of digit 9 is

(A) 99 (B) 90 (C) 09 (D) 92

40. 4 8 2 Arrange the number squares to make the smallest three-digit number?

(A) 428 (B) 284 (C) 248 (D) 824

41. Which of the following symbol will make the sentence true?

Eight hundred and two ☐ 828

(A) < (B) > (C) = (D) ≤

42. Which is more than 16 tens?

(A) 168 (B) 20 (C) 99 (D) 17

43. Which is more than 20 tens?

(A) 22 (B) 202 (C) 30 (D) None of these

44. Study the number chain

Which number is more than 300 but less than 400?

(A) 200 (B) 316 (C) 442 (D) None of these

45. 399 comes just before

(A) 300 (B) 400 (C) 390 (D) None of these

46. 400 and 40 and 4 makes

(A) 4404 (B) 440 (C) 404 (D) 444

47. What number does the abacus show?

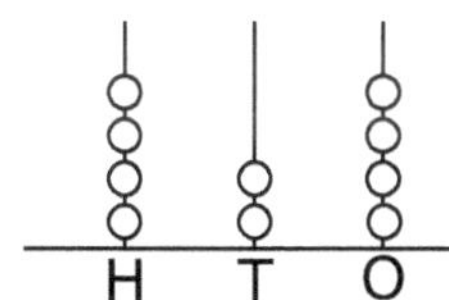

(A) 244 (B) 425 (C) 424 (D) None of these

48. Which of the following shows the correct relation?

(A) 486 < 482 (B) 392 <392 (C) 562 > 438 (D) 179 > 233

49. Which of the following shows the correct relation?

(A) 893 < 493 (B) 672 > 344 (C) 606 < 146 (D) 733 < 642

50. Which of the following object is shorter than 20 cm?

(A) A bed (B) A pencil (C) A table (D) A car

51. 500 ones is same as

(A) 50 ten (B) 5 hundred (C) Both (A) & (B) (D) None of these

52. 800 ones is same as

(A) 800 (B) 80 ones (C) 80 (D) None of these

53. 6 tens is

(A) 60 (B) 60 tens (C) 6 ones (D) 6

54. 4 tens is

    (A) 40 tens (B) 40 (C) 44 ones (D) 44

55. 486 = 400 + B + 6. So "B" is

    (A) 80 (B) 48 (C) 30 (D) 3

56. 392 = A + 90 + 2. So "A" is

    (A) 39 (B) 92 (C) 300 (D) 3

57. One more than largest one digit number is

    (A) 90 (B) 99 (C) 10 (D) None

58. One more than largest two digit number is

    (A) 900 (B) 100 (C) 909 (D) 999

...

ANSWERSHEET

1.	Ⓐ Ⓑ Ⓒ Ⓓ	2.	Ⓐ Ⓑ Ⓒ Ⓓ	3.	Ⓐ Ⓑ Ⓒ Ⓓ	4.	Ⓐ Ⓑ Ⓒ Ⓓ
5.	Ⓐ Ⓑ Ⓒ Ⓓ	6.	Ⓐ Ⓑ Ⓒ Ⓓ	7.	Ⓐ Ⓑ Ⓒ Ⓓ	8.	Ⓐ Ⓑ Ⓒ Ⓓ
9.	Ⓐ Ⓑ Ⓒ Ⓓ	10.	Ⓐ Ⓑ Ⓒ Ⓓ	11.	Ⓐ Ⓑ Ⓒ Ⓓ	12.	Ⓐ Ⓑ Ⓒ Ⓓ
13.	Ⓐ Ⓑ Ⓒ Ⓓ	14.	Ⓐ Ⓑ Ⓒ Ⓓ	15.	Ⓐ Ⓑ Ⓒ Ⓓ	16.	Ⓐ Ⓑ Ⓒ Ⓓ
17.	Ⓐ Ⓑ Ⓒ Ⓓ	18.	Ⓐ Ⓑ Ⓒ Ⓓ	19.	Ⓐ Ⓑ Ⓒ Ⓓ	20.	Ⓐ Ⓑ Ⓒ Ⓓ
21.	Ⓐ Ⓑ Ⓒ Ⓓ	22.	Ⓐ Ⓑ Ⓒ Ⓓ	23.	Ⓐ Ⓑ Ⓒ Ⓓ	24.	Ⓐ Ⓑ Ⓒ Ⓓ
25.	Ⓐ Ⓑ Ⓒ Ⓓ	26.	Ⓐ Ⓑ Ⓒ Ⓓ	27.	Ⓐ Ⓑ Ⓒ Ⓓ	28.	Ⓐ Ⓑ Ⓒ Ⓓ
29.	Ⓐ Ⓑ Ⓒ Ⓓ	30.	Ⓐ Ⓑ Ⓒ Ⓓ	31.	Ⓐ Ⓑ Ⓒ Ⓓ	32.	Ⓐ Ⓑ Ⓒ Ⓓ
33.	Ⓐ Ⓑ Ⓒ Ⓓ	34.	Ⓐ Ⓑ Ⓒ Ⓓ	35.	Ⓐ Ⓑ Ⓒ Ⓓ	36.	Ⓐ Ⓑ Ⓒ Ⓓ
37.	Ⓐ Ⓑ Ⓒ Ⓓ	38.	Ⓐ Ⓑ Ⓒ Ⓓ	39.	Ⓐ Ⓑ Ⓒ Ⓓ	40.	Ⓐ Ⓑ Ⓒ Ⓓ
41.	Ⓐ Ⓑ Ⓒ Ⓓ	42.	Ⓐ Ⓑ Ⓒ Ⓓ	43.	Ⓐ Ⓑ Ⓒ Ⓓ	44.	Ⓐ Ⓑ Ⓒ Ⓓ
45.	Ⓐ Ⓑ Ⓒ Ⓓ	46.	Ⓐ Ⓑ Ⓒ Ⓓ	47.	Ⓐ Ⓑ Ⓒ Ⓓ	48.	Ⓐ Ⓑ Ⓒ Ⓓ
49.	Ⓐ Ⓑ Ⓒ Ⓓ	50.	Ⓐ Ⓑ Ⓒ Ⓓ	51.	Ⓐ Ⓑ Ⓒ Ⓓ	52.	Ⓐ Ⓑ Ⓒ Ⓓ
53.	Ⓐ Ⓑ Ⓒ Ⓓ	54.	Ⓐ Ⓑ Ⓒ Ⓓ	55.	Ⓐ Ⓑ Ⓒ Ⓓ	56.	Ⓐ Ⓑ Ⓒ Ⓓ
57.	Ⓐ Ⓑ Ⓒ Ⓓ	58.	Ⓐ Ⓑ Ⓒ Ⓓ	59.	Ⓐ Ⓑ Ⓒ Ⓓ	60.	Ⓐ Ⓑ Ⓒ Ⓓ
61.	Ⓐ Ⓑ Ⓒ Ⓓ	62.	Ⓐ Ⓑ Ⓒ Ⓓ	63.	Ⓐ Ⓑ Ⓒ Ⓓ	64.	Ⓐ Ⓑ Ⓒ Ⓓ
65.	Ⓐ Ⓑ Ⓒ Ⓓ	66.	Ⓐ Ⓑ Ⓒ Ⓓ	67.	Ⓐ Ⓑ Ⓒ Ⓓ	68.	Ⓐ Ⓑ Ⓒ Ⓓ
69.	Ⓐ Ⓑ Ⓒ Ⓓ	70.	Ⓐ Ⓑ Ⓒ Ⓓ	71.	Ⓐ Ⓑ Ⓒ Ⓓ	72.	Ⓐ Ⓑ Ⓒ Ⓓ
73.	Ⓐ Ⓑ Ⓒ Ⓓ	74.	Ⓐ Ⓑ Ⓒ Ⓓ	75.	Ⓐ Ⓑ Ⓒ Ⓓ	76.	Ⓐ Ⓑ Ⓒ Ⓓ
77.	Ⓐ Ⓑ Ⓒ Ⓓ	78.	Ⓐ Ⓑ Ⓒ Ⓓ	79.	Ⓐ Ⓑ Ⓒ Ⓓ	80.	Ⓐ Ⓑ Ⓒ Ⓓ
81.	Ⓐ Ⓑ Ⓒ Ⓓ	82.	Ⓐ Ⓑ Ⓒ Ⓓ	83.	Ⓐ Ⓑ Ⓒ Ⓓ	84.	Ⓐ Ⓑ Ⓒ Ⓓ
85.	Ⓐ Ⓑ Ⓒ Ⓓ	86.	Ⓐ Ⓑ Ⓒ Ⓓ	87.	Ⓐ Ⓑ Ⓒ Ⓓ	88.	Ⓐ Ⓑ Ⓒ Ⓓ
89.	Ⓐ Ⓑ Ⓒ Ⓓ	90.	Ⓐ Ⓑ Ⓒ Ⓓ	91.	Ⓐ Ⓑ Ⓒ Ⓓ	92.	Ⓐ Ⓑ Ⓒ Ⓓ
93.	Ⓐ Ⓑ Ⓒ Ⓓ	94.	Ⓐ Ⓑ Ⓒ Ⓓ	95.	Ⓐ Ⓑ Ⓒ Ⓓ	96.	Ⓐ Ⓑ Ⓒ Ⓓ
97.	Ⓐ Ⓑ Ⓒ Ⓓ	98.	Ⓐ Ⓑ Ⓒ Ⓓ	99.	Ⓐ Ⓑ Ⓒ Ⓓ	100.	Ⓐ Ⓑ Ⓒ Ⓓ

Chapter 2
COMPUTATION OPERATION

Topics covered : Addition of two digits and three digits (with and without carrying over), Word problems on addition (with and without carrying over), missing addends.

Subtraction of two digits and three digits (with and without borrowing), word problems on subtraction (with and without borrowing), missing subtrahend, missing minuend.

Multiplication tables 2 to 9.

Multiplication of single-digit numbers,multiplication of 2-digit numbers by single-digit numbers. (With and without carryover)

Multiplication of 3-digit numbers by single-digit number, multiplication of 2-digit numbers by 2 digit (With and without carryover)

Multiplication word problems missing multiplicand, missing multiplier.

Division, (dividend, divisor and quotient) missing dividend, missing divisor,

division of single-digit numbers by a single-digit, division of 2-digit number by single- digit number and 3-digit by single digit.

Points to Remember

1.
```
    23 → Addend 1
+   41 → Addend 2
---------
    64 → Sum
```

2. If any of the addend is missing we subtract the another addend from the sum.

3. 48 → Minuend – 27 → Subtrahend 21 → Difference	If minuend is missing we add subtrahend and difference. If subtrahend is missing we subtract difference from minuend.

4. If multiplicand is missing we divide the product by multiplier. If multiplier is missing we divide the product by multiplicand.

5. In a division sum if the dividend is missing we multiply divisor and quotient.

   In a division sum if the divisor is missing, we divide dividend by quotient.

Division rule : If any number is divided by 1, the answer is the number itself.

Key words for subtraction: how many more, how many less, difference, how many left. Key words for addition : in all, altogether, total, sum.

Choose the correct answer

1. Reema has 406 stamps. She has 220 more stamps than Seema. How many stamps does Seema have?

   (A) 406 + 220 (C) 406 x 120

   (B) 406 – 220 (D) 406 ÷ 120

2. Maya has 518 stamps. She has 346 more stamps than Jaya. How many stamps does Jaya have?

   (A) 518 × 346 (C) 518 – 346

   (B) 518 ÷ 346 (D) None of these

3. Radhika has 814 papers. She has 179 more papers than Anamika. How many papers does Anamika have?

   (A) 814 + 178 (C) 814 – 178

   (B) 814 ÷ 178 (D) None of these

4. Sum of two numbers is 543. If one of the numbers is 422, then the other number is

   (A) 322 (B) 43 (C) 121 (D) None of these.

5. Sum of two numbers is 900. If one of the numbers is 473,then the other number is

   (A) 472 (B) 724 (C) 427 (D) None of these.

6. Sum of two numbers is 896. If one of the numbers is 141,then the other number is

   (A) 757 (B) 754 (C) 755 (D) 577

7. If ❀ + ❀ + ❀ = 9 then ❀ =

(A)4 (B) 3 (C) 2 (D) 5

8. If □ + □ + □ + □ = 20, then □ =

(A) 4 (B) 2 (C) 5 (D) None of these

9. If □ + □ = 8, then □ =

(A) 8 (B) 2 (C) 4 (D) None of these.

10. Divide the number by 4 and the result is 5. The number is

(A) 9 (B) 12 (C) 20 (D) None

11. Divide a number by 3 and the result is 6. The number is

(A) 9 (B) 3 (C) 18 (D) 2

12. Divide a number by 5 and the result is 9. The number is

(A) 14 (B) 4 (C) 45 (D) None

13. Multiply a number by 6 and the number you get is 18. The number is

(A) 6 (B) 24 (C) 3 (D) 12

14. Multiply a number by 5 and the number you get is 30. The number is

(A) 25 (B) 6 (C) 35 (D) None

15. Multiply a number by 2 and the answer you get is 10. The number is

(A) 5 (B) 12 (C) 8 (D) None

16. $20 \times ? = 10 + 30$. The missing number is

(A) 22 (B) 40 (C) 2 (D) None

17. $5 \times ? = 15 + 5$. The missing number is

(A) 9 (B) 20 (C) 4 (D) 1

18. $2 \times ? = 9 + 7$. The missing number is

(A) 2 (B) 8 (C) 16 (D) None

19. $? \times 7 = 15 + 6$. The missing number is

(A) 21 (B) 2 (C) 3 (D) None

20. $30 \div ? = 2 \times 5$

(A) 10 (B) 3 (C) 27 (D) None

21. $40 \div ? = 4 \times 5$

(A) 38 (B) 20 (C) 2 (D) None

22. Which of the following is correctly matched?

(A) $4 \times 8 = 36$ (C) $4 + 8 = 8$

(B) $4 \div 8 = 2$ (D) $8 - 4 = 4$

23. Which number box shows the maximum value?

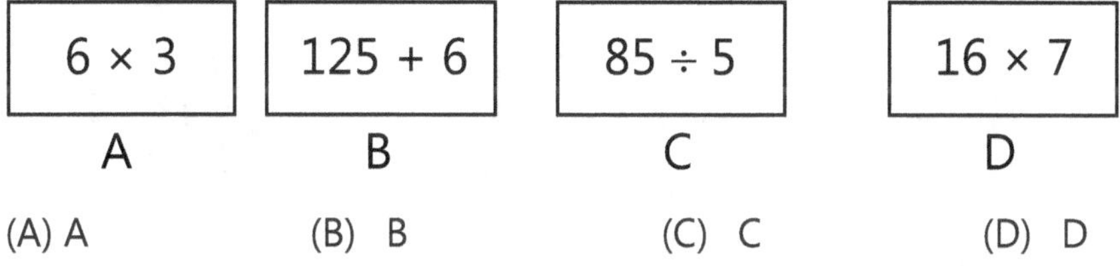

(A) A (B) B (C) C (D) D

24. Which number box shows the maximum value?

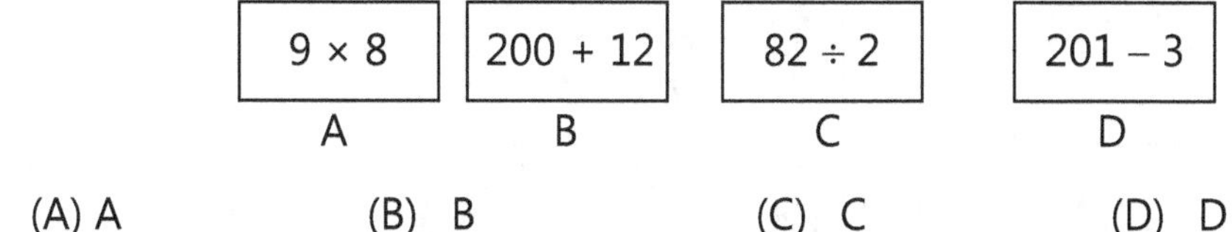

(A) A (B) B (C) C (D) D

25. There were 490 students in a school. If 246 of them were girls and the rest were boys, how many boys were there?

(A) $490 + 246$ (B) 90×246 (C) $490 \div 246$ (D) $490 - 246$

26. There were 840 passengers in a train. If 492 of them were men and the rest were women. How many women were there?

(A) 840 + 492 (B) 840×492 (C) $840 \div 492$ (D) 840 – 492

27. Rahul needs 800 pages for writing,. He had 460 pages with him. How many more pages he must buy?

(A) 1260 pages (B) 800 pages (C) 340 pages (D) None of these

28. Which picture shows how four children should share twelve balls equally?

(A)

(B)

(C)

(D) None of these

29. Which picture shows how 8 balloons are equally distributed among 2 children?

(A)

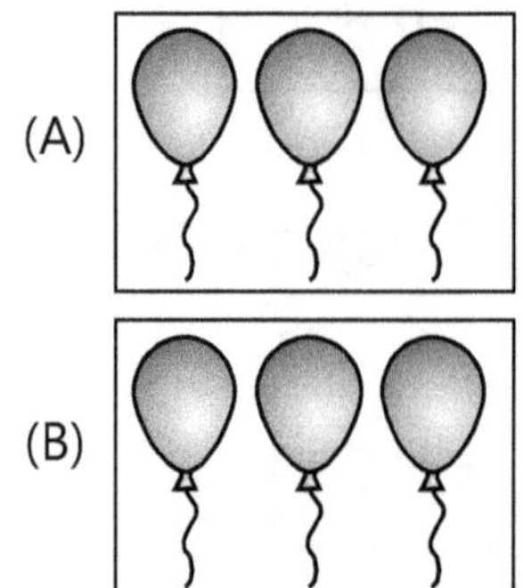

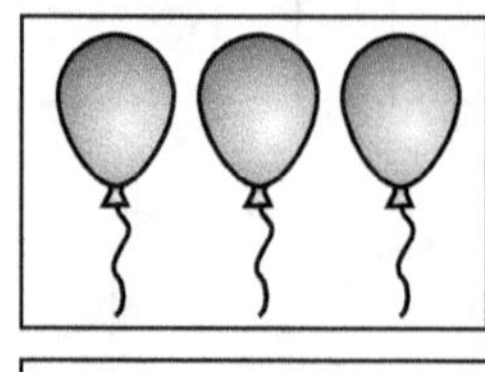

(B)

(C)

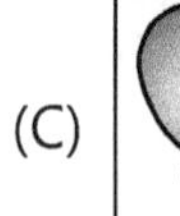

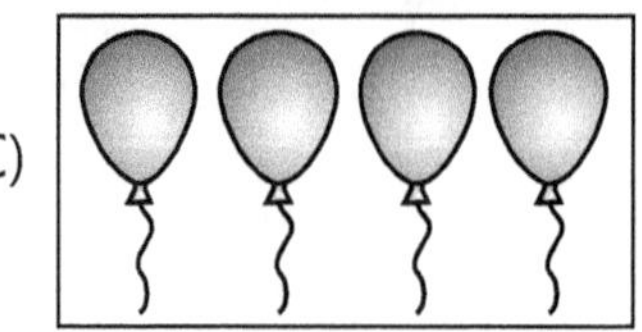

(D) None of these

30. Sahil baked some cakes. He sold 80 cakes and had 5 cakes left. How many cakes did Sahil bake?

(A) 55 (B) 85 (C) 80 (D) 50

31. There are 200 eggs in a box. 164 eggs were broken during transferring. How many eggs were left unbroken?

(A) 30 (B) 20 (C) 36 (D) None of these

32. Sum of 396 and 489 is

(A) 934 (B) 885 (C) 746 (D) None of these

33. 348 more than 244 is same as

(A) 672 (B) 592 (C) 762 (D) None of these

34. What must be added to 70 tens to make 10 hundred?

(A) 200 (B) 300 (C) 40 tens (D) None of these

35. What must be added to 60 tens to make 90 tens?

(A) 3 tens (B) 30 tens

(C) 300 tens (D) None of these

36. What must be added to 20 tens to make 80 tens?

(A) 10 tens (B) 60 tens (C) 2 hundred (D) None of these

37. Which sentence correctly shows

○⊗ ○⊗ ○⊗ ○⊗ ○○

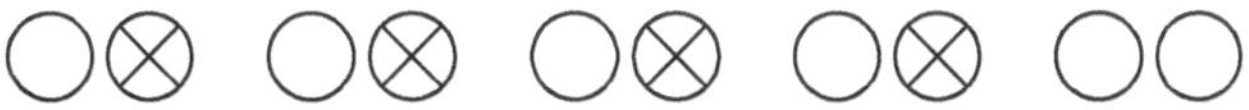

(A) $6 - 4 = 2$ (C) $10 - 6 = 4$

(B) $10 - 4 = 6$ (D) $4 + 6 = 10$

38. Which sentence correctly shows

(crossed)△ △ △ (crossed)△ △ △ △ (crossed)△ △ △ △

(A) $8 - 3 = 5$ (B) $11 - 3 = 8$

(C) $3 + 5 = 8$ (D) None of these

39. Radhika has 208 stamps. She has 100 stamps more than Radha. How many stamps does Radha have?

(A) 108 (B) 100 (C) 308 (D) None of these.

40. Mohan has 50 pens. He has 15 pens more than Sohan. How many pens does Sohan have?

(A) 65 (B) 35 (C) 55 (D) None of these

41. Ramesh has 40 story books. He has 12 more story books than Sham. How many does Sham have?

(A) 40×12 (B) $40 + 12$ (C) $40 - 12$ (D) None of these

42. Sum of two numbers is 500. If one of the number is 200, Then the other number is

(A) 300 (B) 700 (C) 200 (D) None of these

43. Sum of two numbers is 450.If one of the numbers is 178, the other number is

(A) 500 (B) 628 (C) 272 (D) None of these

44. Fill in the box to make the addition correct?

$$\begin{array}{r} 5\ 4\ 3 \\ +\ 1\ \square\ 1 \\ \hline 6\ 8\ 4 \end{array}$$

(A) 4 (B) 3 (C) 7 (D) 8

45. Fill in the box

$$\begin{array}{r} 3\ 2\ 3 \\ +\ \square\ 6\ 4 \\ \hline 9\ 8\ 7 \end{array}$$

(A) 3 (B) 6 (C) 9 (D) None of these

46.

If  +  + = 6 then  =

(A) 2 (B) 3 (C) 4 (D) 5

47.

If  + = 12 then  =

(A) 4 (B) 3 (C) 5 (D) None of these

48. Fill in the box

$$\begin{array}{r} 8\ 4\ 9 \\ -\ 3\ 3\ \square \\ \hline 5\ 1\ 3 \end{array}$$

(A) 6 (B) 3 (C) 9 (D) None of these

49. Fill in the box

$$\begin{array}{r} 5\ 5\ 8 \\ -\ 4\ \square\ 1 \\ \hline 1\ 2\ 7 \end{array}$$

(A) 3 (B) 4 (C) 7 (D) None of these

50. Which is the most suitable multiplication sentence for the following picture?

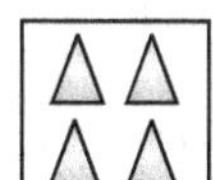 

(A) 4×6 (B) 7×6 (C) 4×5 (D) None of these

51. Rahul puts 30 balls equally in 6 boxes. How many balls are there in each box?

(A) 5 (B) 180 (C) 36 (D) None of these

52. The given triangles are divided into groups of 2. Which number sentence helps you to get the number of groups?

△△ △△ △△ △△ △△

(A) 10 ÷ 5 = 2 (B) 10 ÷ 2 = 5 (C) 10 ÷ 10 = 1 (D) None of these

53. Ram has 8 jars. Each jar contains 2 beads. How many beads are there altogether?

(A) 8 + 2 (B) 8 × 2 (C) 8 ÷ 2 (D) 8 – 2

54. There were 546 students in a school. If 249 of them were boys and the rest of them were girls, how many girls were there?

(A) 546 + 249 (B) 546 x 249 (C) 546 - 249 (D) 546 ÷ 249

55. Which of the following is not matched correctly?

(A) 3 × 8 = 24 (B) 3 + 8 = 12 (C) 8 × 2 = 16 (D) 8 + 2 = 10

56.

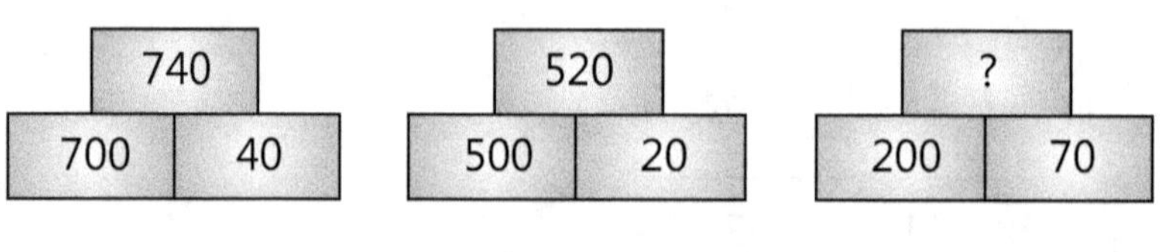

(A) 720 (B) 270 (C) 200 (D) 700

57. Which symbol should be put in the box to make number sentence correct

24 □ 6 = 4

(A) × (B) + (C) ÷ (D) –

58. Which number box shows the maximum value?

3 × 9	30 ÷ 5	35 × 4	100 + 5
A	B	C	D

(A) A (B) B (C) C (D) D

59. Divide a number by 2 and the quotient is 9.So the number is

(A) 18 (B) 8 (C) 11 (D) 7

60. Divide a number by 4 and the quotient is 6.So the number is

(A) 14 (B) 20 (C) 24 (D) 10

61. Find the missing number 5, 10, 15, 20, ----------, 30, 35

(A) 29 (B) 35 (C) 22 (D) 25

62. Multiply a number by 5 and the product you get is 45. The number is

(A) 7 (B) 4 (C) 6 (D) 9

63. Multiply a number by 4 and the number you get is 20. The number is

(A) 4 (B) 5 (C) 3 (D) 6

64. $10 \times$ ____ $= 30 + 40$. The missing number is

(A) 70 (B) 7 (C) 60 (D) 40

64. $5 \times$ ____ $= 20 + 30$. The missing number is

(A) 5 (B) 20 (C) 10 (D) 50

66. Taking 200 away from 210 gives

(A) 10 (B) 200 (C) 210 (D) None of these

67. Taking 6 hundred away from 602 gives

(A) 10 (B) 6 (C) 2 (D) None of these

68. $3 + 3 + 3 + 3 + 3$ is same as

(A) 3×5 (B) 3×3 (C) 3×8 (D) None of these

69. $4 + 4 + 4 + 4 + 4$ is same as

(A) 16 (B) 4 (C) 10 (D) None of these

70. 100 more than sum of 144 and 201 is

(A) 301 (B) 445 (C) 244 (D) None of these

71. How many fives are there in sum of 25 and 25?

(A) 11 (B) 10 (C) 5 (D) None of these

72. How many fives are there in sum of 15 and 25?

(A) 5 (B) 10 (C) 8 (D) None of these

73. 100 more than sum of 182 and 346 is

(A) 628 (B) 446 (C) 282 (D) None of these

74. ______ groups of 3 is same as 30

(A) 20 (B) 10 (C) 15 (D) None of these

75. ______ groups 4 is same as 24.

(A) 10 (B) 4 (C) 6 (D) None of these

76. Which of the following is same as 342?

(A) 284 + 340 (B) 200 + 142 (C) 1000 – 934 (D) None of these

77. Which of the following is same as 439?

(A) 128 + 300 (B) 563 + 124 (C) 342 – 234 (D) None of these

78. 7 ____ 8 = 20 – 5. What is the missing sign?

(A) + (B) – (C) × (D) ÷

79. 21 _____ 3 = 6 x 3 which sign is missing?

(A) + (B) – (C) ÷ (D) ×

80. $40 \div ? = 5 \times 2$

(A) 5 (B) 10 (C) 4 (D) None of these

81. $30 \div ? = 6 \times 5$

(A) 1 (B) 30 (C) 10 (D) None of these

82. Which of the following is correct?

(A) $4 + 4 + 4 + 4 + 4 = 16$ (B) $4 \times 6 = 24$

(C) $18 - 4 = 12$ (D) $40 \div 4 = 8$

83. Mona did this subtraction problem. Which addition problem shows that she got the right answer?

$$\begin{array}{r} 94 \\ -32 \\ \hline 62 \end{array}$$

(A) $\begin{array}{r} 32 \\ +94 \\ \hline \end{array}$ (B) $\begin{array}{r} 62 \\ +32 \\ \hline \end{array}$ (C) $\begin{array}{r} 94 \\ +62 \\ \hline \end{array}$ (D) $\begin{array}{r} 32 \\ +32 \\ \hline \end{array}$

84. Radha has these balls. She gives three balls to each of her four friends. How many balls will be left for Radha?

(A) 6 (B) 8 (C) 10 (D) None of these

85. Rishika had some cookies. After she ate 3 of them, 12 cookies were left. Which number sentence tells how many cookies Rishika had?

(A) $15 - 3 = 12$ (B) $15 + 3 = 18$

(C) $12 - 3 = 9$ (D) None of these

86. Radhika had some chocolates. After she ate 6 of them, 8 chocolates were left. Which number sentence tells how many chocolates Radhika had?

(A) $2 + 6 = 8$ (B) $8 - 2 = 6$

(C) $14 - 6 = 8$ (D) None of these

87. There were 8 frogs in a pond. Each frog had 4 legs. How many frog legs were there all altogether?

(A) 12 (B) 4 (C) 32 (D) None of these

88. Which of the following number sentence is correct?

(A) $8 \times 4 = 72$ (B) $8 + 8 + 8 + 8 = 32$

(C) $64 \div 8 = 6$ (D) $90 - 8 = 62$

89. Study the number machine shown. What operation is used to change the IN numbers to the OUT numbers.

NUMBER MACHINE

IN	OUT
8 and 4	32
6 and 4	24
9 and 5	45
7 and 1	7
5 and 4	20

(A) Addition (B) Subtraction (C) Multiplication (D) Division

90. Study the number machine shown. What operation is used to change to IN number to OUT NUMBER?

NUMBER MACHINE

IN	OUT
6 and 2	8
10 and 8	18
5 and 6	11
2 and 5	7
5 and 4	9

(A) Addition (B) Subtraction (C) Multiplication (D) Division

91. Rahul did this subtraction problem. Which addition problem shows he got the right answer?

$$\begin{array}{r} 75 \\ -22 \\ \hline 53 \end{array}$$

(A) $\begin{array}{r} 53 \\ +22 \\ \hline \end{array}$ (B) $\begin{array}{r} 22 \\ +75 \\ \hline \end{array}$ (C) $\begin{array}{r} 22 \\ +21 \\ \hline \end{array}$ (D) $\begin{array}{r} 22 \\ +22 \\ \hline \end{array}$

92. A man was carrying balloons but wind blew 6 balloons away. He has 12 balloons left. How many did he start with?

(A) 6 (B) 18 (C) 10 (D) None of these

93. Your friend just gave you 12 pencils, now you have 20. How many did you have before your friend gave you 12 more?

(A) 10 (B) 8 (C) 22 (D) None of these

94. Find the number

95 **add** 38 **subtract** 32 = ?

(A) 133 (B) 101 (C) 89 (D) None of these

95. John drew 80 circles and 49 triangles on a piece of paper. How many fewer triangles than circles he drew?

(A) 129 (B) 31 (C) 100 (D) None of these

...

ANSWERSHEET

1.	Ⓐ Ⓑ Ⓒ Ⓓ	2.	Ⓐ Ⓑ Ⓒ Ⓓ	3.	Ⓐ Ⓑ Ⓒ Ⓓ	4.	Ⓐ Ⓑ Ⓒ Ⓓ
5.	Ⓐ Ⓑ Ⓒ Ⓓ	6.	Ⓐ Ⓑ Ⓒ Ⓓ	7.	Ⓐ Ⓑ Ⓒ Ⓓ	8.	Ⓐ Ⓑ Ⓒ Ⓓ
9.	Ⓐ Ⓑ Ⓒ Ⓓ	10.	Ⓐ Ⓑ Ⓒ Ⓓ	11.	Ⓐ Ⓑ Ⓒ Ⓓ	12.	Ⓐ Ⓑ Ⓒ Ⓓ
13.	Ⓐ Ⓑ Ⓒ Ⓓ	14.	Ⓐ Ⓑ Ⓒ Ⓓ	15.	Ⓐ Ⓑ Ⓒ Ⓓ	16.	Ⓐ Ⓑ Ⓒ Ⓓ
17.	Ⓐ Ⓑ Ⓒ Ⓓ	18.	Ⓐ Ⓑ Ⓒ Ⓓ	19.	Ⓐ Ⓑ Ⓒ Ⓓ	20.	Ⓐ Ⓑ Ⓒ Ⓓ
21.	Ⓐ Ⓑ Ⓒ Ⓓ	22.	Ⓐ Ⓑ Ⓒ Ⓓ	23.	Ⓐ Ⓑ Ⓒ Ⓓ	24.	Ⓐ Ⓑ Ⓒ Ⓓ
25.	Ⓐ Ⓑ Ⓒ Ⓓ	26.	Ⓐ Ⓑ Ⓒ Ⓓ	27.	Ⓐ Ⓑ Ⓒ Ⓓ	28.	Ⓐ Ⓑ Ⓒ Ⓓ
29.	Ⓐ Ⓑ Ⓒ Ⓓ	30.	Ⓐ Ⓑ Ⓒ Ⓓ	31.	Ⓐ Ⓑ Ⓒ Ⓓ	32.	Ⓐ Ⓑ Ⓒ Ⓓ
33.	Ⓐ Ⓑ Ⓒ Ⓓ	34.	Ⓐ Ⓑ Ⓒ Ⓓ	35.	Ⓐ Ⓑ Ⓒ Ⓓ	36.	Ⓐ Ⓑ Ⓒ Ⓓ
37.	Ⓐ Ⓑ Ⓒ Ⓓ	38.	Ⓐ Ⓑ Ⓒ Ⓓ	39.	Ⓐ Ⓑ Ⓒ Ⓓ	40.	Ⓐ Ⓑ Ⓒ Ⓓ
41.	Ⓐ Ⓑ Ⓒ Ⓓ	42.	Ⓐ Ⓑ Ⓒ Ⓓ	43.	Ⓐ Ⓑ Ⓒ Ⓓ	44.	Ⓐ Ⓑ Ⓒ Ⓓ
45.	Ⓐ Ⓑ Ⓒ Ⓓ	46.	Ⓐ Ⓑ Ⓒ Ⓓ	47.	Ⓐ Ⓑ Ⓒ Ⓓ	48.	Ⓐ Ⓑ Ⓒ Ⓓ
49.	Ⓐ Ⓑ Ⓒ Ⓓ	50.	Ⓐ Ⓑ Ⓒ Ⓓ	51.	Ⓐ Ⓑ Ⓒ Ⓓ	52.	Ⓐ Ⓑ Ⓒ Ⓓ
53.	Ⓐ Ⓑ Ⓒ Ⓓ	54.	Ⓐ Ⓑ Ⓒ Ⓓ	55.	Ⓐ Ⓑ Ⓒ Ⓓ	56.	Ⓐ Ⓑ Ⓒ Ⓓ
57.	Ⓐ Ⓑ Ⓒ Ⓓ	58.	Ⓐ Ⓑ Ⓒ Ⓓ	59.	Ⓐ Ⓑ Ⓒ Ⓓ	60.	Ⓐ Ⓑ Ⓒ Ⓓ
61.	Ⓐ Ⓑ Ⓒ Ⓓ	62.	Ⓐ Ⓑ Ⓒ Ⓓ	63.	Ⓐ Ⓑ Ⓒ Ⓓ	64.	Ⓐ Ⓑ Ⓒ Ⓓ
65.	Ⓐ Ⓑ Ⓒ Ⓓ	66.	Ⓐ Ⓑ Ⓒ Ⓓ	67.	Ⓐ Ⓑ Ⓒ Ⓓ	68.	Ⓐ Ⓑ Ⓒ Ⓓ
69.	Ⓐ Ⓑ Ⓒ Ⓓ	70.	Ⓐ Ⓑ Ⓒ Ⓓ	71.	Ⓐ Ⓑ Ⓒ Ⓓ	72.	Ⓐ Ⓑ Ⓒ Ⓓ
73.	Ⓐ Ⓑ Ⓒ Ⓓ	74.	Ⓐ Ⓑ Ⓒ Ⓓ	75.	Ⓐ Ⓑ Ⓒ Ⓓ	76.	Ⓐ Ⓑ Ⓒ Ⓓ
77.	Ⓐ Ⓑ Ⓒ Ⓓ	78.	Ⓐ Ⓑ Ⓒ Ⓓ	79.	Ⓐ Ⓑ Ⓒ Ⓓ	80.	Ⓐ Ⓑ Ⓒ Ⓓ
81.	Ⓐ Ⓑ Ⓒ Ⓓ	82.	Ⓐ Ⓑ Ⓒ Ⓓ	83.	Ⓐ Ⓑ Ⓒ Ⓓ	84.	Ⓐ Ⓑ Ⓒ Ⓓ
85.	Ⓐ Ⓑ Ⓒ Ⓓ	86.	Ⓐ Ⓑ Ⓒ Ⓓ	87.	Ⓐ Ⓑ Ⓒ Ⓓ	88.	Ⓐ Ⓑ Ⓒ Ⓓ
89.	Ⓐ Ⓑ Ⓒ Ⓓ	90.	Ⓐ Ⓑ Ⓒ Ⓓ	91.	Ⓐ Ⓑ Ⓒ Ⓓ	92.	Ⓐ Ⓑ Ⓒ Ⓓ
93.	Ⓐ Ⓑ Ⓒ Ⓓ	94.	Ⓐ Ⓑ Ⓒ Ⓓ	95.	Ⓐ Ⓑ Ⓒ Ⓓ	96.	Ⓐ Ⓑ Ⓒ Ⓓ
97.	Ⓐ Ⓑ Ⓒ Ⓓ	98.	Ⓐ Ⓑ Ⓒ Ⓓ	99.	Ⓐ Ⓑ Ⓒ Ⓓ	100.	Ⓐ Ⓑ Ⓒ Ⓓ

Chapter 3
FRACTIONS

Topics : Numerator, dividing line, denominator, half, one-third, one-fourth, three – fourth

Points to Remember

Equal parts of a whole are called fractions.

Two halves make one whole.

One-third is one of the three equal parts of a whole.

A quarter is one of the four equal parts of a whole.

Two quarters make a half.

The number above the line is called the numerator.

The number below the line is called the denominator of the fraction.

Denominator is always equal to the number of parts in the figure.

Numerator is always the shaded part only.

While adding fractions, we add only numerators not denominators.

E.g. : $\frac{2}{9}+\frac{3}{9}=\frac{5}{9}$ (we add only numerators 2 and 3. 9 = denominator remains as it is)

While subtracting fractions, we subtract only the numerators and not the denominators

E.g. $\frac{7}{9}-\frac{2}{9}=\frac{5}{9}$ (subtract only numerators 7 and 2. 9 = denominator remains as it is)

If two fractions have the same denominator, then the fraction with the greater numerator is the greater fraction.

E.g. : $\frac{6}{10}<\frac{7}{10}$

Choose the correct answer

1. What part of this shape is shaded?

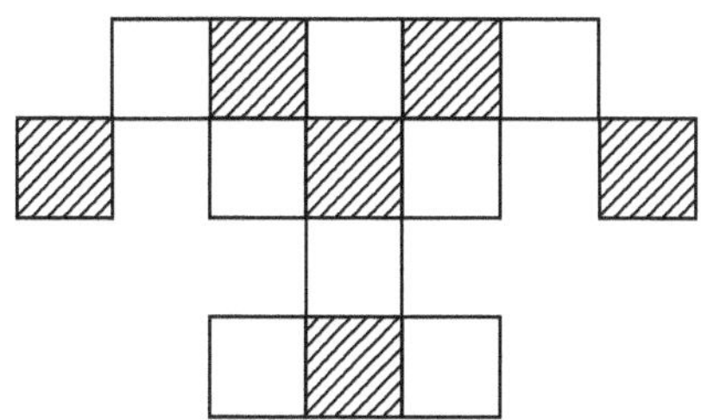

(A) $\frac{6}{14}$ (B) $\frac{6}{16}$ (C) $\frac{14}{6}$ (D) None of these

2. Which figure shows 3/5 shaded?

(A) 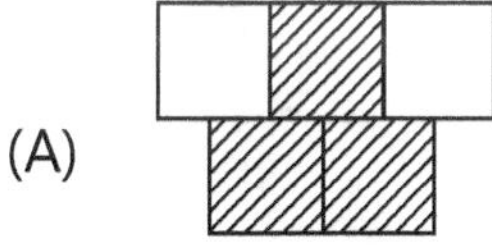

(B) 

(C) 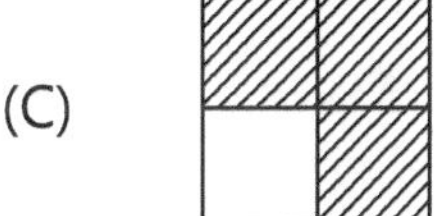

(D) None of these

3.

(i) 

(ii) 

(iii) 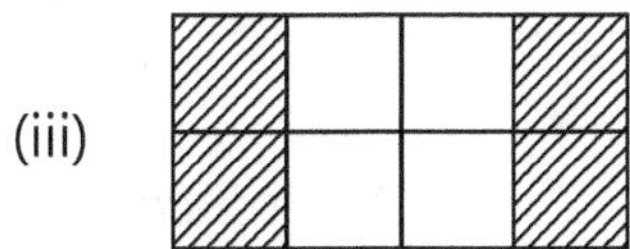

(iv) 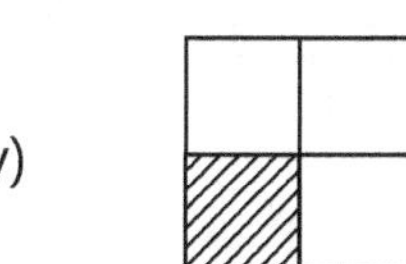

Which two figures are equally shaded?

(A) i & ii (B) i & iv (C) iii & i (D) None of these

4. How many $\frac{1}{4}$ make one whole?

(A) 3 (B) 2 (C) 4 (D) None of these

5. How many $\frac{1}{2}$ make one whole?

(A) 4 (B) 3 (C) 2 (D) None of these

6. How many $\frac{1}{4}$ make $\frac{3}{4}$?

(A) 3 (B) 2 (C) 9 (D) None of these

7. Which is the greatest fraction?

(A) $\frac{7}{13}$ (B) $\frac{2}{13}$ (C) $\frac{10}{13}$ (D) $\frac{11}{13}$

8. Which of the following fractions are arranged from largest to smallest?

(A) $\frac{4}{14}, \frac{1}{14}, \frac{2}{14}$ (B) $\frac{4}{14}, \frac{1}{14}, \frac{2}{14}$

(C) $\frac{1}{14}, \frac{8}{14}, \frac{7}{14}$ (D) $\frac{8}{14}, \frac{7}{14}, \frac{4}{14}$

9. Which of the following has $\frac{4}{5}$ of its contents shaded?

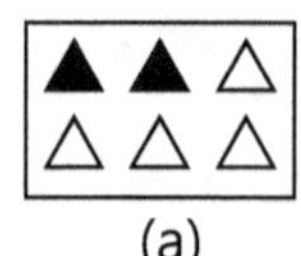
(a)

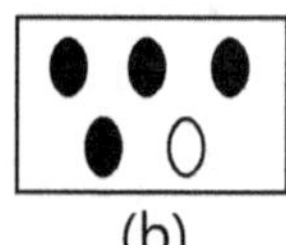
(b)

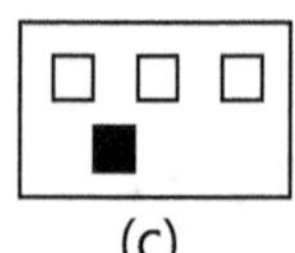
(c)

(A) a (B) b (C) b (D) None of these

10. Which of the following shows $\frac{2}{5}$ of their content circled?

(A) ⓧ X ⓧ
X X X

(B) X ⓧ ⓧ
X X

(C) X X X
ⓧ X

(D) ⓧ ⓧ X
X X X X

11.

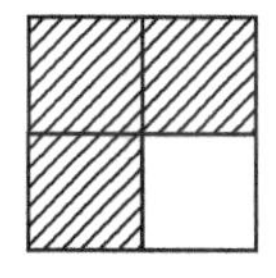 is the same as

(A) $\frac{1}{4}$ (B) $\frac{2}{4}$ (C) $\frac{3}{4}$ (D) $\frac{4}{4}$

12. Which is the greatest fraction?

(A) $\frac{3}{8}$ (B) $\frac{4}{8}$ (C) $\frac{1}{8}$ (D) $\frac{5}{8}$

13. $\frac{4}{9} + \frac{3}{9} =$

(A) $\frac{8}{9}$ (B) $\frac{5}{9}$ (C) $\frac{7}{9}$ (D) $\frac{6}{9}$

14. $\frac{4}{13} + \frac{6}{13} =$

(A) $\frac{11}{13}$ (B) $\frac{9}{13}$ (C) $\frac{10}{13}$ (D) $\frac{8}{13}$

15. Rahul cut a pizza into 10 equal pieces. He ate 4 pieces. What fraction of pizza he has eaten?

(A) $\frac{6}{10}$ (B) $\frac{4}{10}$ (C) $\frac{10}{10}$ (D) $\frac{5}{10}$

16. Reema cut a cake into 6 equal pieces. She has given each part to her friends. What fractions of each cake her each friend got?

(A) $\frac{1}{6}$ (B) $\frac{2}{6}$ (C) $\frac{3}{6}$ (D) $\frac{4}{6}$

17. Sonali cut a pizza into 10 equal pieces. She has given each part to her friends. What fraction of each cake her each friend got?

(A) $\frac{6}{10}$ (B) $\frac{4}{10}$ (C) $\frac{1}{10}$ (D) $\frac{7}{10}$

18. $\frac{3}{8}$ and ______ make 1 whole

(A) $\frac{4}{8}$ (B) $\frac{7}{8}$ (C) $\frac{5}{8}$ (D) None of these

19. $\frac{7}{12}$ and ______ make 1 whole

(A) $\frac{3}{12}$ (B) $\frac{4}{12}$ (C) $\frac{5}{12}$ (D) None of these

20. Vijay drew a circle. He coloured $\frac{3}{9}$ of circle green and $\frac{4}{9}$ yellow

He coloured the rest blue. What fraction of the circle did he colour blue?

(A) $\frac{2}{9}$ (B) $\frac{1}{9}$ (C) $\frac{3}{9}$ (D) None of these

21. Sangita cut a cake into 12 equal pieces. She gave $\frac{3}{12}$ pieces to Ram $\frac{2}{12}$ pieces to Geeta & rest she had. What fraction of piece of cake did she eat?

(A) $\frac{7}{12}$ (B) $\frac{3}{12}$ (C) $\frac{4}{12}$ (D) None of these

22. A puzzle has 12 equal pieces. Radha has 4 pieces of the puzzle. What fraction of pieces does she need to complete the puzzle?

(A) $\frac{8}{12}$ (B) $\frac{4}{12}$ (C) $\frac{6}{12}$ (D) None of these

23. Joe cut a cake into 7 equal slices. 3/7 of the cake he ate.

How much cake was left?

(A) $\frac{4}{7}$ (B) $\frac{2}{7}$ (C) $\frac{5}{7}$ (D) $\frac{1}{7}$

24. Kamal had a loaf of brown bread. He had given $\frac{4}{8}$ of it to his sister and ate $\frac{2}{8}$ of it. What fraction of the bread was left?

(A) $\frac{4}{8}$ (B) $\frac{2}{8}$ (C) $\frac{3}{8}$ (D) None of these

25. Anil bought 15 fruits. 6 of them were bananas and 4 of them were apples. The rest were mangoes. What fraction of the fruits were mangoes?

(A) $\frac{5}{15}$ (B) $\frac{4}{15}$ (C) $\frac{6}{15}$ (D) None of these

26. Bina drew a picture. She coloured $\frac{3}{9}$ of the picture in green and $\frac{1}{9}$ in red.

She did not colour the rest of the picture. What fraction of picture was left uncoloured?

(A) $\frac{4}{9}$ (B) $\frac{1}{9}$ (C) $\frac{5}{9}$ (D) None of these

Direction (Q. 27 – Q. 28)

Mr. Sharma bought 2 similar cakes. Meena ate $\frac{4}{7}$ of the cake and Mona ate $\frac{2}{7}$ of another cake.

27. Who ate more?

(A) Meena (B) Mona (C) Both ate same

(D) Meena ate 2/7 of the cake less than Mona.

28. Who ate less?

(A) Meena (B) Mona (C) Both ate same

(D) Mona ate 2/7 of the cake more than Meena

Direction (Q. 29 – Q. 31)

Study the figure given below and answer the following questions.

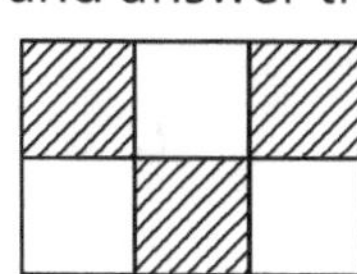

29. The parts of figure not shaded is

(A) $\frac{3}{6}$ (B) $\frac{3}{2}$ (C) $\frac{1}{3}$ (D) $\frac{2}{3}$

30. The parts of the figure that is shaded is

(A) $\frac{1}{3}$ (B) $\frac{3}{6}$ (C) $\frac{1}{6}$ (D) None of these

31. How many equal parts are there altogether in the figure?

(A) 1 (B) 2 (C) 6 (D) 4

Direction (Q. 32 – Q. 34)

32. A bread is cut into 7 equal parts. Anvita ate 3 such parts.

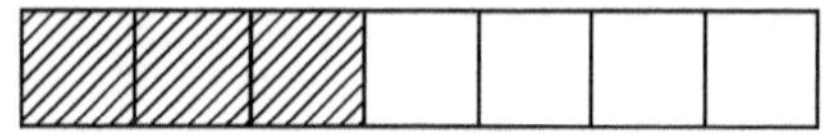

How many parts are left?

(A) 3 (B) 2 (C) 1 (D) 4

33. Fraction of bread left is

(A) $\frac{3}{7}$ (B) $\frac{4}{7}$ (C) $\frac{2}{7}$ (D) None of these

34. Fraction of bread that is eaten by Anvita

(A) $\frac{2}{7}$ (B) $\frac{3}{7}$ (C) $\frac{1}{7}$ (D) $\frac{4}{7}$

35. 3/7 and ________ make a whole

(A) $\frac{1}{7}$ (B) $\frac{2}{7}$ (C) $\frac{4}{7}$ (D) None of these

36. Which is the smallest fraction?

(A) $\frac{2}{6}$ (B) $\frac{4}{6}$ (C) $\frac{3}{6}$ (D) $\frac{5}{6}$

37. Which is the largest fraction?

(A) $\frac{7}{9}$ (B) $\frac{6}{9}$ (C) $\frac{5}{9}$ (D) $\frac{3}{9}$

38. Which shaded fraction is the smallest?

(A) 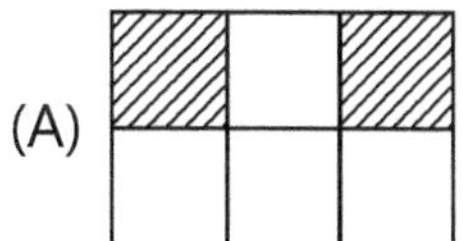 (B) 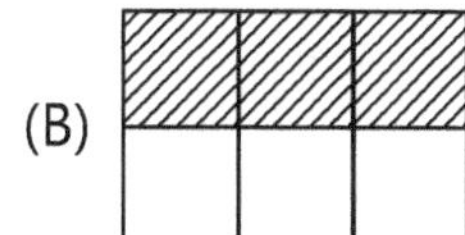

(C) 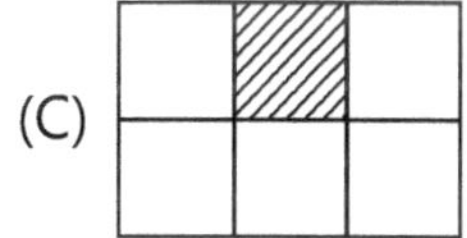 (D) 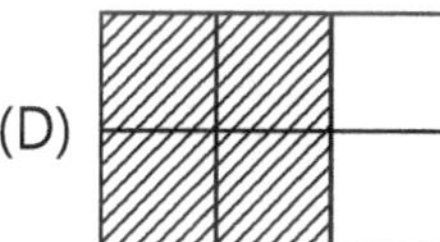

39. Which shaded fraction is the largest?

(A) 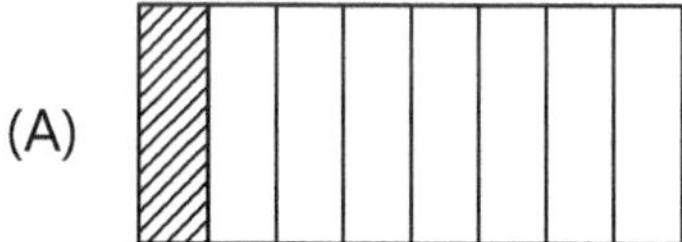 (B) 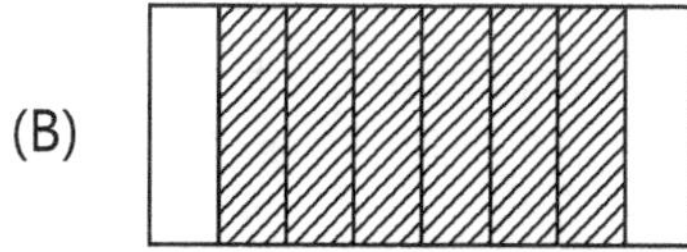

(C) 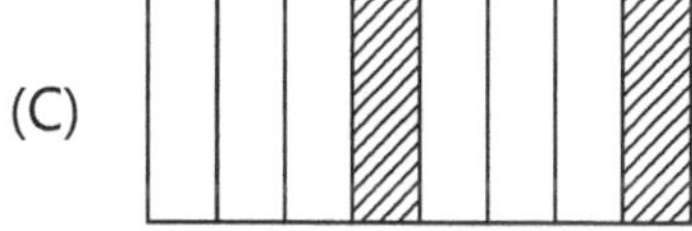 (D) 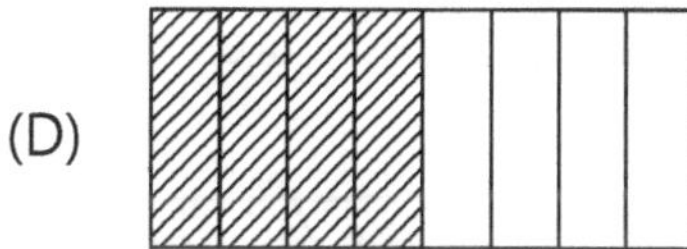

40. $\frac{4}{10} + \frac{5}{10} = ?$

(A) $\frac{9}{10}$ (B) $\frac{9}{20}$ (C) $\frac{1}{10}$ (D) None of these

41. $\frac{2}{9}$ is the same as 2 out of ____ equal parts of a whole.

(A) 4 (B) 2 (C) 9 (D) None of these

42. $\frac{6}{13}$ is the same as ____ out of 13 equal parts of a whole.

(A) 13 (B) 6 (C) 7 (D) None of these

43. $\frac{2}{7}$ is the same as ____ out of 7 equal parts of a whole.

(A) 7 (B) 5 (C) 2 (D) 4

44. Which of the following fraction is the same as $\frac{7}{9}$?

(A) $\frac{3}{6}+\frac{1}{6}$ (B) $\frac{3}{9}+\frac{5}{9}$ (C) $\frac{2}{9}+\frac{5}{9}$ (D) None of these

45. ________ is the other name of $\frac{1}{2}$?

(A) One quarter (B) Half (C) Both A and B (D) None of these

46. What is the other name of $\frac{1}{4}$?

(A) One quarter (B) Half (C) Both A and B (D) None of these

47. What fractions of the figures are squares here?

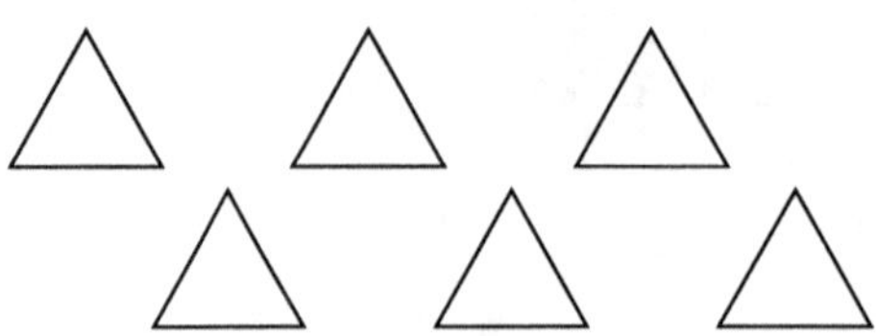
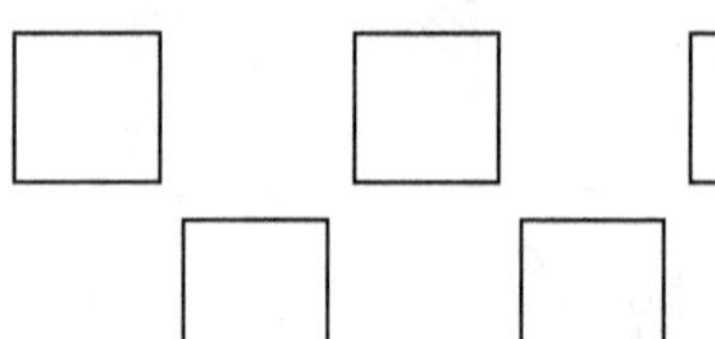

(A) $\frac{5}{6}$ (B) $\frac{5}{11}$ (C) $\frac{6}{11}$ (D) None of these

48. What fraction of the figures are star here?

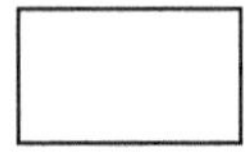
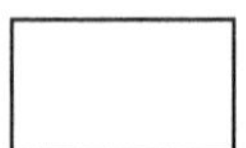

(A) $\frac{2}{3}$ (B) $\frac{3}{5}$ (C) $\frac{2}{5}$ (D) None of these

49. $\frac{1}{2}+\frac{1}{2}$ is the same as

(A) 1 (B) $\frac{3}{4}$ (C) $\frac{1}{4}$ (D) None of these

50. $\frac{1}{4}+\frac{1}{4}$ is same as

(A) 1 (B) $\frac{2}{4}$ (C) $\frac{3}{4}$ (D) None of these

51. $\frac{1}{4}+\frac{1}{4}+\frac{1}{4}$ is the same as

(A) $\frac{1}{2}$ (B) 1 (C) $\frac{3}{4}$ (D) None of these

52. $\frac{13}{20}+\frac{?}{20}=\frac{17}{20}$ .What will come in the place of (?) ?

(A) 13 (B) 4 (C) 17 (D) None of these

53. $\frac{4}{13}+\frac{x}{13}=\frac{10}{13}$ .What will come at the place of (x)?

(A) 10 (B) 4 (C) 5 (D) 6

54. $\frac{10}{17}-\frac{a}{17}=\frac{8}{17}$ .What will come in the place of (A)?

(A) 2 (B) 8 (C) 10 (D) None of these

55. $\frac{5}{11}+\frac{?}{11}=\frac{10}{11}$ .What will come in the place of (?) above?

(A) 10 (B) 5 (C) 11 (D) None of these

56. How many halves will make one whole?

(A) 2 (B) 3 (C) 1 (D) None of these

57. How many quarters make a whole?

(A) 2 (B) 3 (C) 1 (D) 4

58. Which of the following is same as one whole?

(A) $\frac{3}{7}$ (B) $\frac{4}{7}$ (C) $\frac{7}{7}$ (D) $\frac{2}{7}$

59. Which of the following is same as one whole?

(A) $\frac{3}{11}$ (B) $\frac{6}{11}$ (C) $\frac{2}{11}$ (D) $\frac{11}{11}$

60. Put the correct sign $\frac{7}{8} \square \frac{3}{8}$

(A) $>$ (B) $<$ (C) $=$ (D) None of these

...

ANSWERSHEET

1.	Ⓐ Ⓑ Ⓒ Ⓓ	2.	Ⓐ Ⓑ Ⓒ Ⓓ	3.	Ⓐ Ⓑ Ⓒ Ⓓ	4.	Ⓐ Ⓑ Ⓒ Ⓓ
5.	Ⓐ Ⓑ Ⓒ Ⓓ	6.	Ⓐ Ⓑ Ⓒ Ⓓ	7.	Ⓐ Ⓑ Ⓒ Ⓓ	8.	Ⓐ Ⓑ Ⓒ Ⓓ
9.	Ⓐ Ⓑ Ⓒ Ⓓ	10.	Ⓐ Ⓑ Ⓒ Ⓓ	11.	Ⓐ Ⓑ Ⓒ Ⓓ	12.	Ⓐ Ⓑ Ⓒ Ⓓ
13.	Ⓐ Ⓑ Ⓒ Ⓓ	14.	Ⓐ Ⓑ Ⓒ Ⓓ	15.	Ⓐ Ⓑ Ⓒ Ⓓ	16.	Ⓐ Ⓑ Ⓒ Ⓓ
17.	Ⓐ Ⓑ Ⓒ Ⓓ	18.	Ⓐ Ⓑ Ⓒ Ⓓ	19.	Ⓐ Ⓑ Ⓒ Ⓓ	20.	Ⓐ Ⓑ Ⓒ Ⓓ
21.	Ⓐ Ⓑ Ⓒ Ⓓ	22.	Ⓐ Ⓑ Ⓒ Ⓓ	23.	Ⓐ Ⓑ Ⓒ Ⓓ	24.	Ⓐ Ⓑ Ⓒ Ⓓ
25.	Ⓐ Ⓑ Ⓒ Ⓓ	26.	Ⓐ Ⓑ Ⓒ Ⓓ	27.	Ⓐ Ⓑ Ⓒ Ⓓ	28.	Ⓐ Ⓑ Ⓒ Ⓓ
29.	Ⓐ Ⓑ Ⓒ Ⓓ	30.	Ⓐ Ⓑ Ⓒ Ⓓ	31.	Ⓐ Ⓑ Ⓒ Ⓓ	32.	Ⓐ Ⓑ Ⓒ Ⓓ
33.	Ⓐ Ⓑ Ⓒ Ⓓ	34.	Ⓐ Ⓑ Ⓒ Ⓓ	35.	Ⓐ Ⓑ Ⓒ Ⓓ	36.	Ⓐ Ⓑ Ⓒ Ⓓ
37.	Ⓐ Ⓑ Ⓒ Ⓓ	38.	Ⓐ Ⓑ Ⓒ Ⓓ	39.	Ⓐ Ⓑ Ⓒ Ⓓ	40.	Ⓐ Ⓑ Ⓒ Ⓓ
41.	Ⓐ Ⓑ Ⓒ Ⓓ	42.	Ⓐ Ⓑ Ⓒ Ⓓ	43.	Ⓐ Ⓑ Ⓒ Ⓓ	44.	Ⓐ Ⓑ Ⓒ Ⓓ
45.	Ⓐ Ⓑ Ⓒ Ⓓ	46.	Ⓐ Ⓑ Ⓒ Ⓓ	47.	Ⓐ Ⓑ Ⓒ Ⓓ	48.	Ⓐ Ⓑ Ⓒ Ⓓ
49.	Ⓐ Ⓑ Ⓒ Ⓓ	50.	Ⓐ Ⓑ Ⓒ Ⓓ	51.	Ⓐ Ⓑ Ⓒ Ⓓ	52.	Ⓐ Ⓑ Ⓒ Ⓓ
53.	Ⓐ Ⓑ Ⓒ Ⓓ	54.	Ⓐ Ⓑ Ⓒ Ⓓ	55.	Ⓐ Ⓑ Ⓒ Ⓓ	56.	Ⓐ Ⓑ Ⓒ Ⓓ
57.	Ⓐ Ⓑ Ⓒ Ⓓ	58.	Ⓐ Ⓑ Ⓒ Ⓓ	59.	Ⓐ Ⓑ Ⓒ Ⓓ	60.	Ⓐ Ⓑ Ⓒ Ⓓ
61.	Ⓐ Ⓑ Ⓒ Ⓓ	62.	Ⓐ Ⓑ Ⓒ Ⓓ	63.	Ⓐ Ⓑ Ⓒ Ⓓ	64.	Ⓐ Ⓑ Ⓒ Ⓓ
65.	Ⓐ Ⓑ Ⓒ Ⓓ	66.	Ⓐ Ⓑ Ⓒ Ⓓ	67.	Ⓐ Ⓑ Ⓒ Ⓓ	68.	Ⓐ Ⓑ Ⓒ Ⓓ
69.	Ⓐ Ⓑ Ⓒ Ⓓ	70.	Ⓐ Ⓑ Ⓒ Ⓓ	71.	Ⓐ Ⓑ Ⓒ Ⓓ	72.	Ⓐ Ⓑ Ⓒ Ⓓ
73.	Ⓐ Ⓑ Ⓒ Ⓓ	74.	Ⓐ Ⓑ Ⓒ Ⓓ	75.	Ⓐ Ⓑ Ⓒ Ⓓ	76.	Ⓐ Ⓑ Ⓒ Ⓓ
77.	Ⓐ Ⓑ Ⓒ Ⓓ	78.	Ⓐ Ⓑ Ⓒ Ⓓ	79.	Ⓐ Ⓑ Ⓒ Ⓓ	80.	Ⓐ Ⓑ Ⓒ Ⓓ
81.	Ⓐ Ⓑ Ⓒ Ⓓ	82.	Ⓐ Ⓑ Ⓒ Ⓓ	83.	Ⓐ Ⓑ Ⓒ Ⓓ	84.	Ⓐ Ⓑ Ⓒ Ⓓ
85.	Ⓐ Ⓑ Ⓒ Ⓓ	86.	Ⓐ Ⓑ Ⓒ Ⓓ	87.	Ⓐ Ⓑ Ⓒ Ⓓ	88.	Ⓐ Ⓑ Ⓒ Ⓓ
89.	Ⓐ Ⓑ Ⓒ Ⓓ	90.	Ⓐ Ⓑ Ⓒ Ⓓ	91.	Ⓐ Ⓑ Ⓒ Ⓓ	92.	Ⓐ Ⓑ Ⓒ Ⓓ
93.	Ⓐ Ⓑ Ⓒ Ⓓ	94.	Ⓐ Ⓑ Ⓒ Ⓓ	95.	Ⓐ Ⓑ Ⓒ Ⓓ	96.	Ⓐ Ⓑ Ⓒ Ⓓ
97.	Ⓐ Ⓑ Ⓒ Ⓓ	98.	Ⓐ Ⓑ Ⓒ Ⓓ	99.	Ⓐ Ⓑ Ⓒ Ⓓ	100.	Ⓐ Ⓑ Ⓒ Ⓓ

Chapter 4

LENGTH, MASS & VOLUME

Length is measured in metres and centimeters.

100 centimetres = 1 metre

OR

100 cm = 1 m .

You can measure length accurately with the help of a ruler or a measuring tape. Your ruler is marked in centimeters or cm.

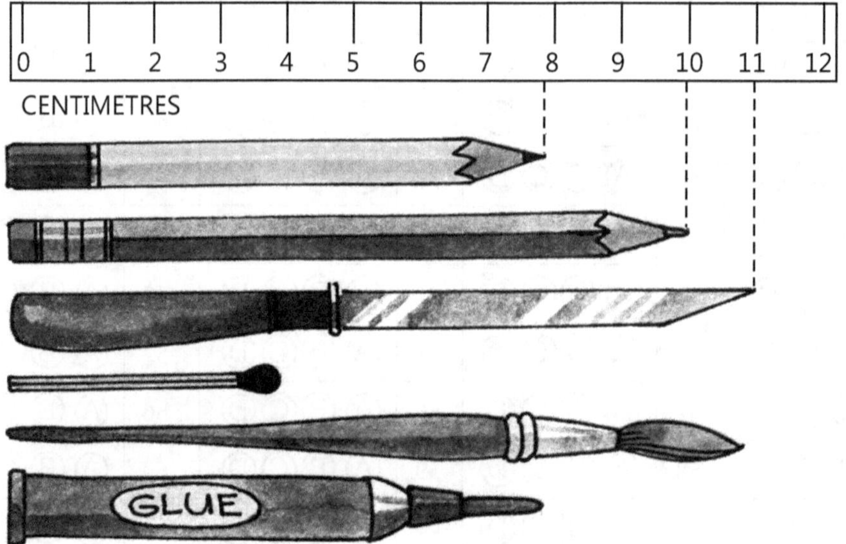

Length of the first pencil is 8 cm

Length of the second pencil is 10 cm

Length of the knife is 11 cm

Length of the matchstick is 4 cm

Length of the brush is 11 cm

Length of the glue is 8 cm

Addition of metres and centimeters.

4 metres 35 centimetres	8 m	42 cm
+ 3 metres 42 centimetres	+ 6 m	73 m
7 metres 77 centimetres	15 m	15 cm

Subtraction of metres and centimeters.

m	cm		m	cm		m	cm
						21	31
7	46		9	45		37	46
– 3	23		– 7	23		– 18	28
4	23		2	22		19	18

Weight

UNITS OF WEIGHT

Weight is measured in grams and kilograms.

1 kilogram = 1000 grams 1 kg = 1000 g

Smaller measures are used for smaller objects

Some small weights are

1 kilogram	=	1000 grams
half kilogram	=	500 g
quarter kilogram	=	250 g

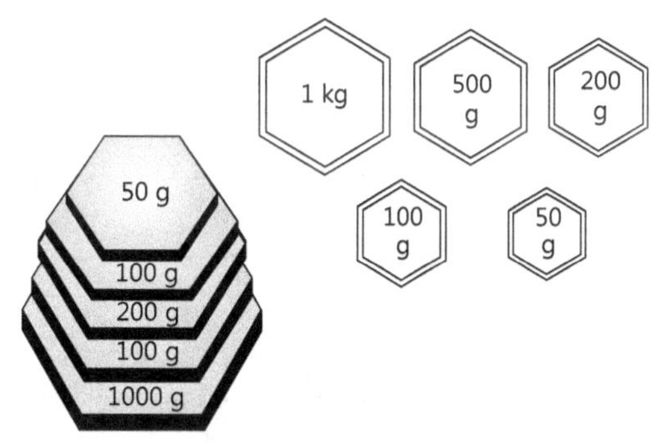

Addition and subtraction of weight.

	kg	g
	6	350
+	7	580
	13	930

	kg	g
	3	721
+	9	842
	13	563

	921 kg	649 g
–	36 kg	552 g
	885 kg	097 g

Capacity

How much milk do I contain?
MILK
1 LITRE
1. My capacity is 1 litre.
2. I can fill ten 100 mL cups or four 250 mL cups or two 500 mL cups.
100 mL
100 mL × 10 (cups = 1000 mL = 1L
250 mL
250 mL × 4 = 1000 mL = 1 L
500 mL
500 mL × 2 = 1000 mL = 1 L

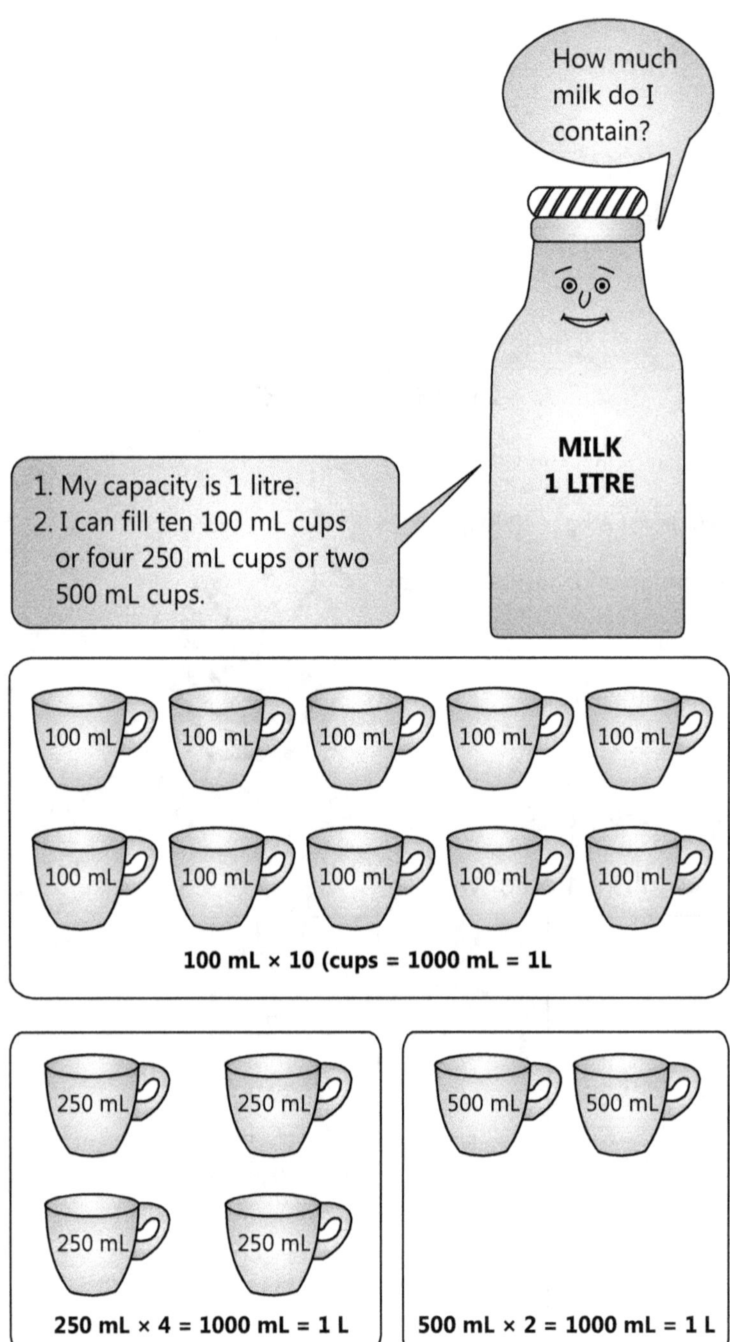

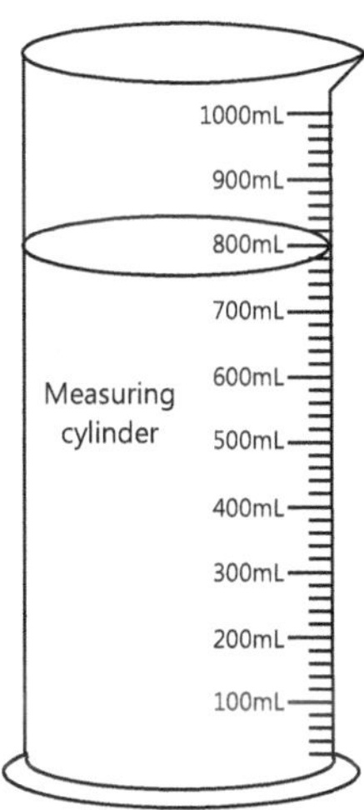

Measuring cylinders are used to measure capacity

Addition

305 litres 400 millitres
+ 252 litres 375 millitres
557 litres 775 millilitres

Subtraction

15 litres 500 millilitres
– 8 litres 250 millilitres
– 7 litres 250 millilitres

Choose the correct answer

1. Study the figure given below and answer the questions based on them (Q. 1 to Q. 5)

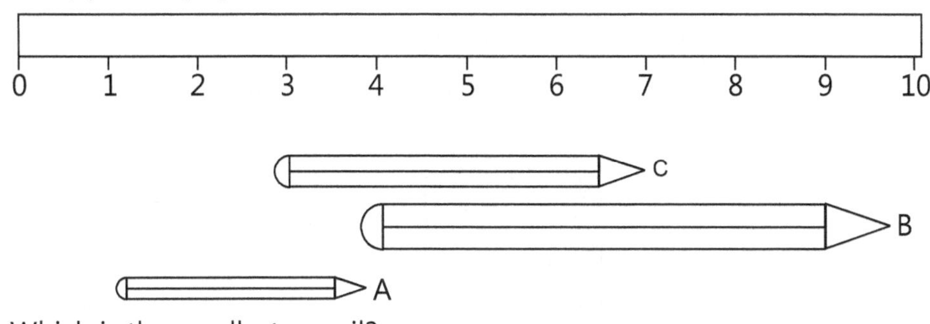

Which is the smallest pencil?

(A) A (B) B (C) C (C) None of these

2. Which is the longest pencil?

   (A) A (B) B (C) C (D) None of these

3. Length of pencil B is

   (A) 11 cm (B) 7 cm (C) 6 cm (D) None of these

4. Pencil A is shorter than pencil C by

   (A) 1 cm (B) 4 cm (C) 3 cm (D) None of these

5. How much longer is pencil B than pencil C?

   (A) 4 cm (B) 2 cm (C) 11 cm (D) None of these

6. Radha is 142 cm tall and Sham is 11 cm longer than Radha.

   How tall is Sham?

   (A) 11 cm (B) 153 cm (C) 142 cm (D) None of these

7. Mona has a ribbon of 80 cm. Sona has a ribbon which is 22 cm longer than Mona's ribbon How long is Sona's ribbon?

   (A) 22 cm (B) 58 cm (C) 102 cm (D) None of these

(Direction – Q-8 to Q-12)

Refer to the figure given here and answer following questions.

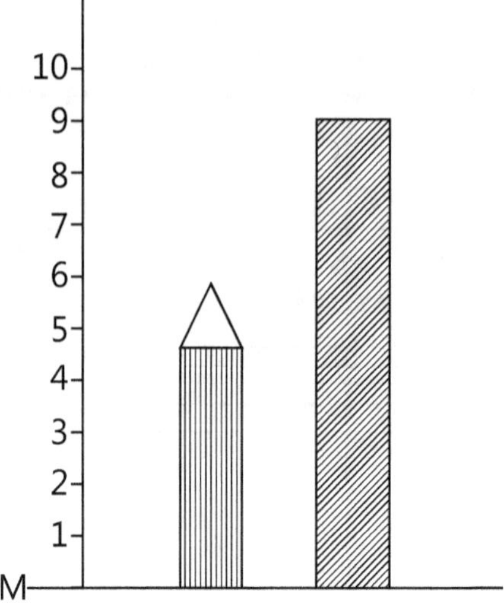

8. Height of the pencil is

(A) 6 m (B) 3 m (C) 4 m (D) None of these

9. Height of the block is

(A) 4 m (B) 2 m (C) 6 m (D) None of these

10. How much taller is block than the pencil?

(A) 4 m (B) 3 m (C) 2 m (D) None of these

11. How much less is the height of the pencil than that of the block?

(A) 4 m (B) 2 m (C) 8 m (D) None of these

12. Which of the following is true about the block?

(A) Its height is less than 7 m

(B) Its height is more than 7 m.

(C) Height of the block lies in between 2 m to 5 m.

(D) Height of the block is 2 m smaller than pencil.

13. Anita has a ribbon of 200 cm long. She cuts it into 2 pieces. If one piece is 45 cm long. What is the length of the other piece?

(A) 45 cm (B) 155 cm (C) 245 cm (D) None of these

14. A shopkeeper has 7 bags of wheat each having weight 10 kg. What is the total weight of wheat bags?

(A) 12 kg. (B) 70 kg (C) 120 kg (D) None of these

(Direction Q. 15 to Q. 18)

Jai cycled from his home to school and then to library.

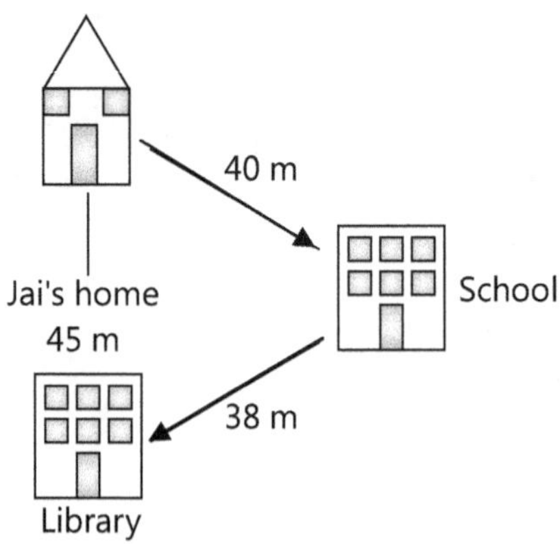

15. How much did Jai cycle from home to library?

(A) 45 m + 40 m (B) 45 m + 38 m

(C) 40 m + 38 m (D) None of these

16. What is the actual distance between his home and library?

(A) 83 m (B) 78 m (C) 85 m (D) None of these

17. What is the distance between school and library?

(A) 40 m (B) 45 m (C) 38 m (D) None of these

18. What is the distance between Jai's home and school?

(A) 40 m (B) 45 m (C) 38 m (D) None of these

19. Height of the tree is

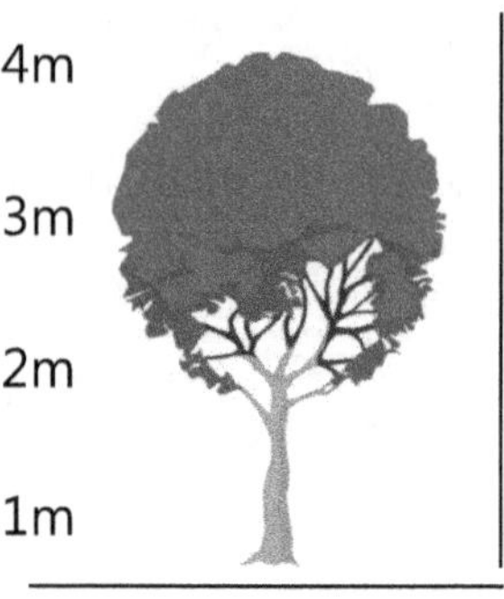

(A) 1 m (B) 12 m (C) 4 m (D) 6 m

20) Raja bought 100 litres of milk for a function. He used 74 litres. How much milk is left with him?

(A) 26 litres (B) 20 litres (C) 174 litres (D) None of these

(Direction Q-21 to Q – 23)

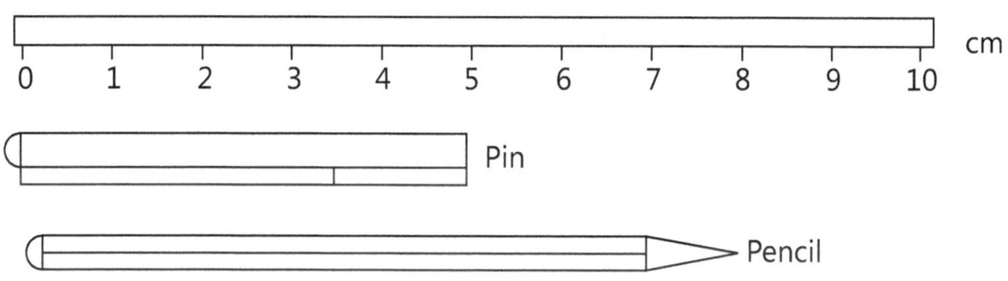

21. What is the length of the pin?

(A) 3 cm (B) 5 cm (C) 8 cm (D) None of these

22. What is the length of the pencil?

(A) 8 cm (B) 3 cm (C) 4 cm (D) None of these

23. Pencil is longer than the pin by

(A) 8 cm (B) 3 cm (C) 4 cm (D) None of these

24. Which is lightest among all four?

A	B	C	D
4 kg	6 kg	2 kg	3 kg

(A) A (B) B (C) C (D) D

25.

Apples	Bananas	Grapes	Fig.
3 kg	1 kg	4 kg	6 kg

Which is heaviest among the above four fruits?

(A) Apples (B) Bananas (C) Grapes (D) Fig.

26. Radha baked 4 cakes. The weight of 4 cakes is 12 kg. Each cake has the same weight what is the weight of each cake?

    (A) 4 kg. (B) 3 kg (C) 12 kg (D) None of these

27.

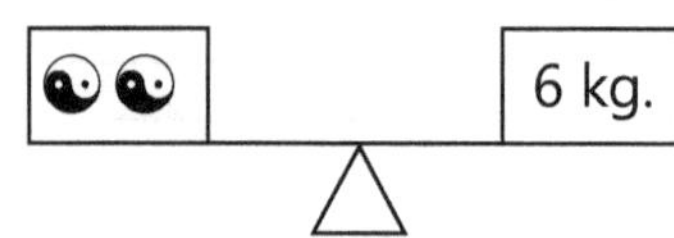

What is the weight of one ball ?

(A) 3 kg (B) 4 kg (C) 6 kg (D) None of these

28.

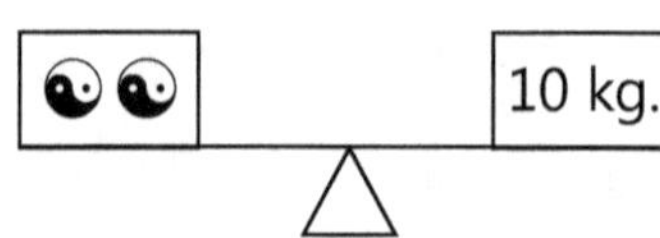

Weight of one ball is

(A) 10 kg (B) 6 kg (C) 5 kg (D) 4 kg

29.

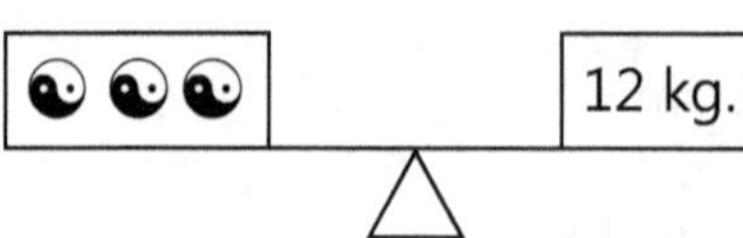

Weight of one ball is

(A) 4 kg (B) 3 kg (C) 16 kg (D) 6 kg

30.

+ + = 300gm

So =

(A) 100 g (B) 300 g (C) 150 g (D) 250 g

31.

▨ + ▨ + ▨ = 600 g

What is the weight of one block

(A) 100 g (B) 200 g (C) 300 g (D) None of these

32.

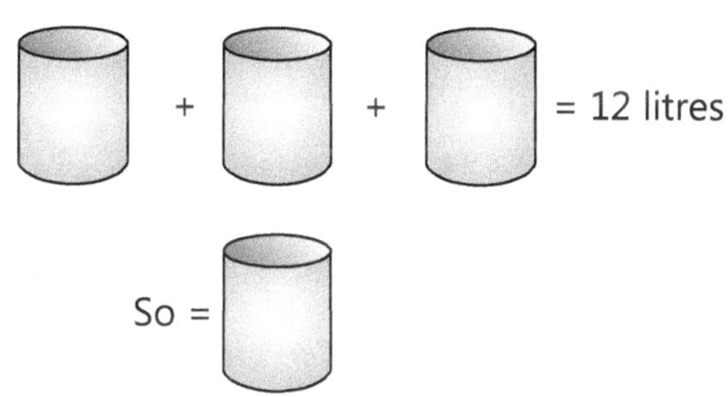

(A) 4 litres (B) 3 litres (C) 2 litres (D) None of these

33. Weight of 5 mangoes is 10 kg. What is the weight of 1 such mango?

(A) 15 kg (B) 50 kg (C) 2 kg (D) None of these

34. Weight of 4 potatoes is 12 kg. What is the weight of 1 potato ?

(A) 16 kg (B) 3 kg (C) 48 kg (D) None of these

35.

Wheat = 100 kg	Rice = 175 kg
Jawar = 150 kg	Bajra = 120 kg

Which is heaviest?

(A) Wheat (B) Jowar (C) Bajra (D) Rice

(Direction Q. 36 to Q. 40)

Salt 5 kg	Tea 10 kg	Sugar 6 kg

36 What is the weight of salt?

(A) 5 kg. (B) 10 kg (C) 15 kg. (D) 16 kg.

37. Which is the heaviest?

(A) Salt (B) Tea (C) Sugar (D) None of these

38. Which is the lightest?

(A) Tea (B) Salt (C) Sugar (D) None of these

39. How much is tea heavier than salt?

(A) 5 kg. (B) 6 kg (C) 15 kg (D) None of these

40. How much is sugar heavier than salt?

(A) 10 kg. (B) 6 kg (C) 1 kg (D) 5 kg.

41. Which of the choices can hold smallest quantity of liquid?

(A) Bucket (B) Teapot (C) Cup (D) Barrel

42. Which of the choices can hold maximum quantity of liquid?

(A) Barrel (B) Cup (C) Teapot (D) Bucket

43.

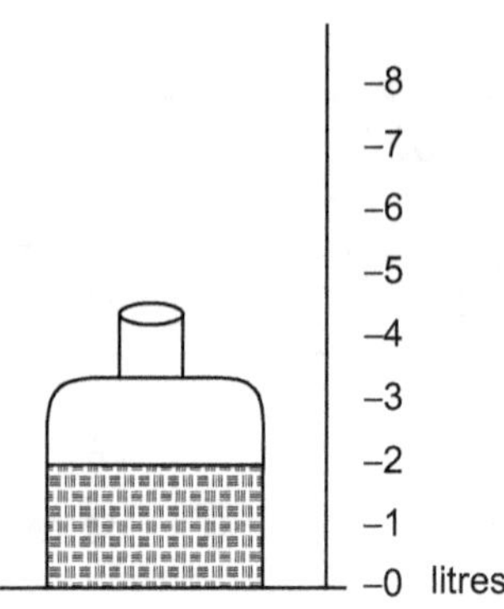

How many litres of water does the bottle contain?

(A) 1 litre (B) 4 litres (C) 2 litres (D) None of these

44. A tank contains 120 litres of water. Raja drained out 60 litres of water through tap from the tank. How much water is left?

(A) 30 litres (B) 40 litres (C) 180 litres (D) 60 litres

Direction Q. 45 to Q. 51.

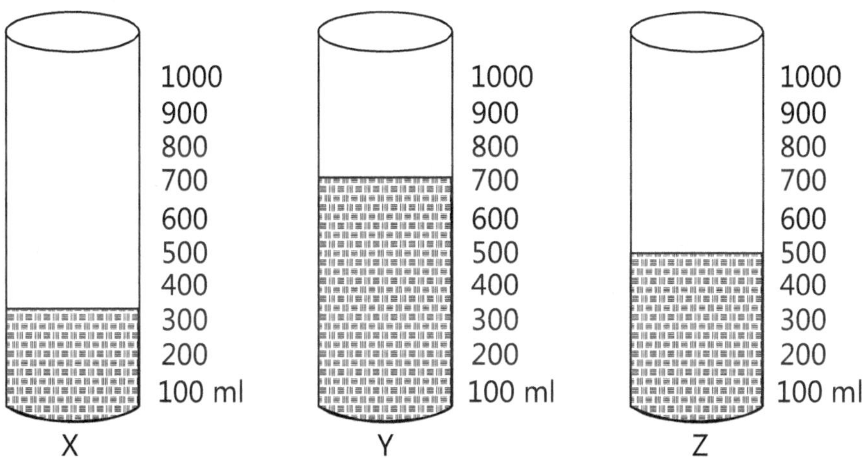

45. Which cylinder contains more than 600 ml of water?

(A) X (B) Y (C) Z (D) Both Z & Y

46. Which cylinder contains more than 400 ml of water?

(A) Z (B) Y (C) X (D) Both Y & Z

47. Which cylinder has half a litre of water?

(A) Y (B) Z (C) X (D) None of these

48. How much water is required to make the water in cylinder Y upto 1 litre ?

(A) 200 ml (B) 100 ml (C) 300 ml (D) 700 ml

49. How much water should be added to X cylinder to make it equal to the quantity in cylinder Z?

(A) 500 ml (B) 200 ml (C) 300 ml (D) None of these

50. How much water should be taken out from cylinder Z to make it 200 ml?

(A) 200 ml (B) 300 ml (C) 100 ml (D) None of these

51. Maximum water these containers can hold is

(A) 1 litre (B) 900 ml (C) 1000 ml (D) Both A and C

52. Ram bought 200 litres of paint . He used 110 litres for his house . How much paint is left with him?

(A) 310 litres (B) 200 litres (C) 110 litres (D) 90 litres

53. Seema drinks 4 litres of water daily. If she drinks same quantity of water each day, how much does she drink in 12 days?

(A) 8 litres (B) 3 litres (C) 16 litres (D) 48 litres

Direction Q 54 to Q 56)

Barrel 14 litres	Bucket 11 litres	Bottle 5 litres	Vase 2 litres

54. Which container can hold more water than bucket?

(A) Barrel (B) Bucket (C) Vase (D) Bottle

55. Which container can hold less than a bottle?

(A) Bucket (B) Barrel (C) Vase (D) Bottle

56. Which container can hold maximum quantity of water?

(A) Bottle (B) Barrel (C) Bucket (D) Vase

...

ANSWERSHEET

1.	Ⓐ Ⓑ Ⓒ Ⓓ	2.	Ⓐ Ⓑ Ⓒ Ⓓ	3.	Ⓐ Ⓑ Ⓒ Ⓓ	4.	Ⓐ Ⓑ Ⓒ Ⓓ
5.	Ⓐ Ⓑ Ⓒ Ⓓ	6.	Ⓐ Ⓑ Ⓒ Ⓓ	7.	Ⓐ Ⓑ Ⓒ Ⓓ	8.	Ⓐ Ⓑ Ⓒ Ⓓ
9.	Ⓐ Ⓑ Ⓒ Ⓓ	10.	Ⓐ Ⓑ Ⓒ Ⓓ	11.	Ⓐ Ⓑ Ⓒ Ⓓ	12.	Ⓐ Ⓑ Ⓒ Ⓓ
13.	Ⓐ Ⓑ Ⓒ Ⓓ	14.	Ⓐ Ⓑ Ⓒ Ⓓ	15.	Ⓐ Ⓑ Ⓒ Ⓓ	16.	Ⓐ Ⓑ Ⓒ Ⓓ
17.	Ⓐ Ⓑ Ⓒ Ⓓ	18.	Ⓐ Ⓑ Ⓒ Ⓓ	19.	Ⓐ Ⓑ Ⓒ Ⓓ	20.	Ⓐ Ⓑ Ⓒ Ⓓ
21.	Ⓐ Ⓑ Ⓒ Ⓓ	22.	Ⓐ Ⓑ Ⓒ Ⓓ	23.	Ⓐ Ⓑ Ⓒ Ⓓ	24.	Ⓐ Ⓑ Ⓒ Ⓓ
25.	Ⓐ Ⓑ Ⓒ Ⓓ	26.	Ⓐ Ⓑ Ⓒ Ⓓ	27.	Ⓐ Ⓑ Ⓒ Ⓓ	28.	Ⓐ Ⓑ Ⓒ Ⓓ
29.	Ⓐ Ⓑ Ⓒ Ⓓ	30.	Ⓐ Ⓑ Ⓒ Ⓓ	31.	Ⓐ Ⓑ Ⓒ Ⓓ	32.	Ⓐ Ⓑ Ⓒ Ⓓ
33.	Ⓐ Ⓑ Ⓒ Ⓓ	34.	Ⓐ Ⓑ Ⓒ Ⓓ	35.	Ⓐ Ⓑ Ⓒ Ⓓ	36.	Ⓐ Ⓑ Ⓒ Ⓓ
37.	Ⓐ Ⓑ Ⓒ Ⓓ	38.	Ⓐ Ⓑ Ⓒ Ⓓ	39.	Ⓐ Ⓑ Ⓒ Ⓓ	40.	Ⓐ Ⓑ Ⓒ Ⓓ
41.	Ⓐ Ⓑ Ⓒ Ⓓ	42.	Ⓐ Ⓑ Ⓒ Ⓓ	43.	Ⓐ Ⓑ Ⓒ Ⓓ	44.	Ⓐ Ⓑ Ⓒ Ⓓ
45.	Ⓐ Ⓑ Ⓒ Ⓓ	46.	Ⓐ Ⓑ Ⓒ Ⓓ	47.	Ⓐ Ⓑ Ⓒ Ⓓ	48.	Ⓐ Ⓑ Ⓒ Ⓓ
49.	Ⓐ Ⓑ Ⓒ Ⓓ	50.	Ⓐ Ⓑ Ⓒ Ⓓ	51.	Ⓐ Ⓑ Ⓒ Ⓓ	52.	Ⓐ Ⓑ Ⓒ Ⓓ
53.	Ⓐ Ⓑ Ⓒ Ⓓ	54.	Ⓐ Ⓑ Ⓒ Ⓓ	55.	Ⓐ Ⓑ Ⓒ Ⓓ	56.	Ⓐ Ⓑ Ⓒ Ⓓ
57.	Ⓐ Ⓑ Ⓒ Ⓓ	58.	Ⓐ Ⓑ Ⓒ Ⓓ	59.	Ⓐ Ⓑ Ⓒ Ⓓ	60.	Ⓐ Ⓑ Ⓒ Ⓓ
61.	Ⓐ Ⓑ Ⓒ Ⓓ	62.	Ⓐ Ⓑ Ⓒ Ⓓ	63.	Ⓐ Ⓑ Ⓒ Ⓓ	64.	Ⓐ Ⓑ Ⓒ Ⓓ
65.	Ⓐ Ⓑ Ⓒ Ⓓ	66.	Ⓐ Ⓑ Ⓒ Ⓓ	67.	Ⓐ Ⓑ Ⓒ Ⓓ	68.	Ⓐ Ⓑ Ⓒ Ⓓ
69.	Ⓐ Ⓑ Ⓒ Ⓓ	70.	Ⓐ Ⓑ Ⓒ Ⓓ	71.	Ⓐ Ⓑ Ⓒ Ⓓ	72.	Ⓐ Ⓑ Ⓒ Ⓓ
73.	Ⓐ Ⓑ Ⓒ Ⓓ	74.	Ⓐ Ⓑ Ⓒ Ⓓ	75.	Ⓐ Ⓑ Ⓒ Ⓓ	76.	Ⓐ Ⓑ Ⓒ Ⓓ
77.	Ⓐ Ⓑ Ⓒ Ⓓ	78.	Ⓐ Ⓑ Ⓒ Ⓓ	79.	Ⓐ Ⓑ Ⓒ Ⓓ	80.	Ⓐ Ⓑ Ⓒ Ⓓ
81.	Ⓐ Ⓑ Ⓒ Ⓓ	82.	Ⓐ Ⓑ Ⓒ Ⓓ	83.	Ⓐ Ⓑ Ⓒ Ⓓ	84.	Ⓐ Ⓑ Ⓒ Ⓓ
85.	Ⓐ Ⓑ Ⓒ Ⓓ	86.	Ⓐ Ⓑ Ⓒ Ⓓ	87.	Ⓐ Ⓑ Ⓒ Ⓓ	88.	Ⓐ Ⓑ Ⓒ Ⓓ
89.	Ⓐ Ⓑ Ⓒ Ⓓ	90.	Ⓐ Ⓑ Ⓒ Ⓓ	91.	Ⓐ Ⓑ Ⓒ Ⓓ	92.	Ⓐ Ⓑ Ⓒ Ⓓ
93.	Ⓐ Ⓑ Ⓒ Ⓓ	94.	Ⓐ Ⓑ Ⓒ Ⓓ	95.	Ⓐ Ⓑ Ⓒ Ⓓ	96.	Ⓐ Ⓑ Ⓒ Ⓓ
97.	Ⓐ Ⓑ Ⓒ Ⓓ	98.	Ⓐ Ⓑ Ⓒ Ⓓ	99.	Ⓐ Ⓑ Ⓒ Ⓓ	100.	Ⓐ Ⓑ Ⓒ Ⓓ

Chapter 5
TIME AND MONEY

Clocks tell time.

The long hand tells the **minutes**.

The short hand tells the **hour**.

Look at this clock.

The long hand points to 12.

The short hand points to 2.

This means that the time is 2 O' clock.

Look at the clock face.

The long hand is the minute hand.

The short hand is the hour hand.

The hour hand takes 1 hour to go from one number to the next.

It always travels like this

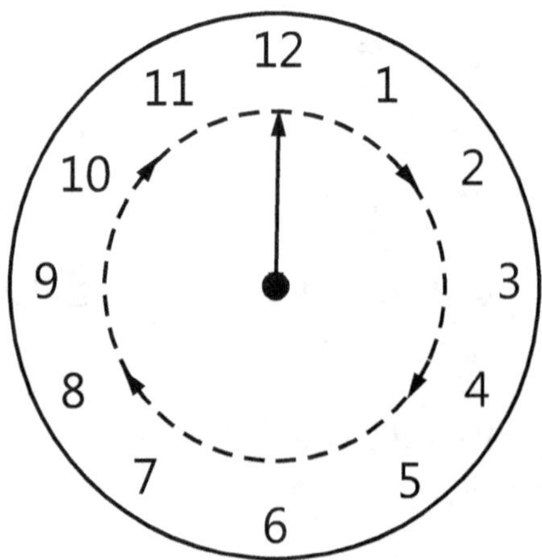

The hour hand takes 12 hours to go around all the 12 numbers on the clock.

There are 24 hours in one day.

So, the hour hand goes twice round the clock in one day.

The minute hand is much faster.

The minute hand takes 1 hour to go round all the 12 numbers on the clock.

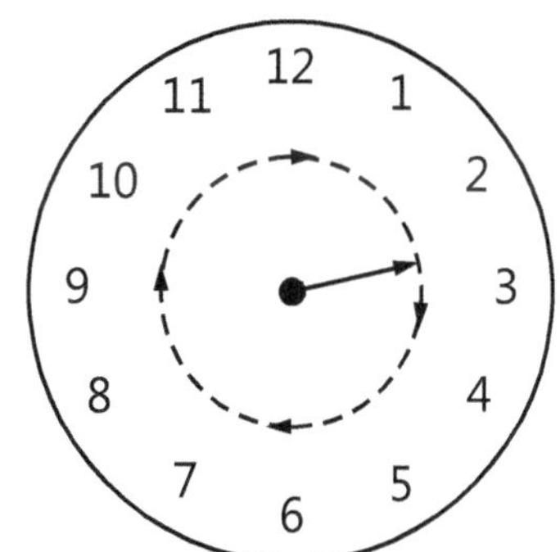

If it starts at 12 at 2 o' clock, it will reach 12 again at 3 o' clock.

There are 60 minutes in one hour.

The minute hand only takes 5 minutes to go from one number to the next.

Look at the time on these clocks.

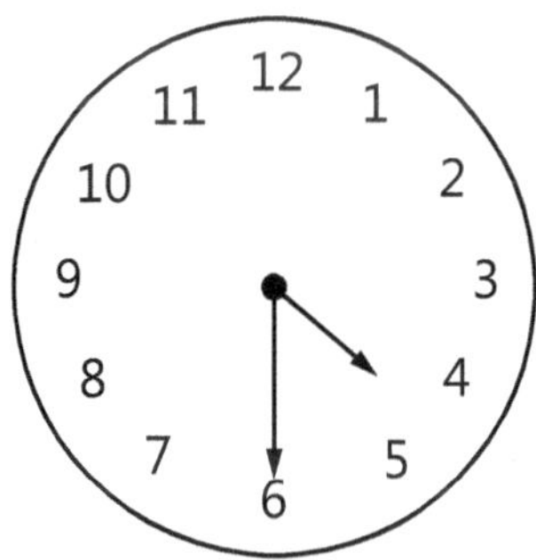

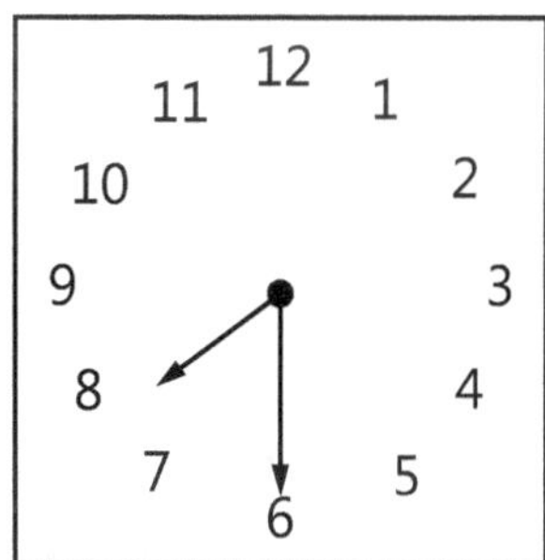

We see that when the time is 4:30 or 7:30. The minute hand has travelled half way round the clock.

So, when it is 4:30, we usually say **half-past 4**.

Look at these clocks.

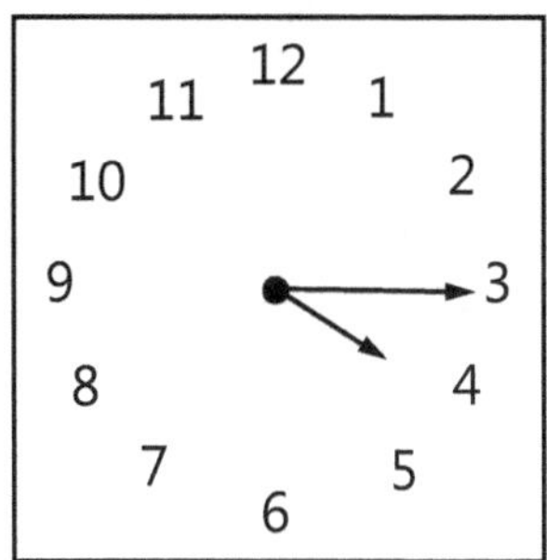

When the time is 4:15 or 7:15, we see that the minute hand has travelled a quarter of the way round the clock.

So, when it is 4:15, we say it is **a quarter past 4**.

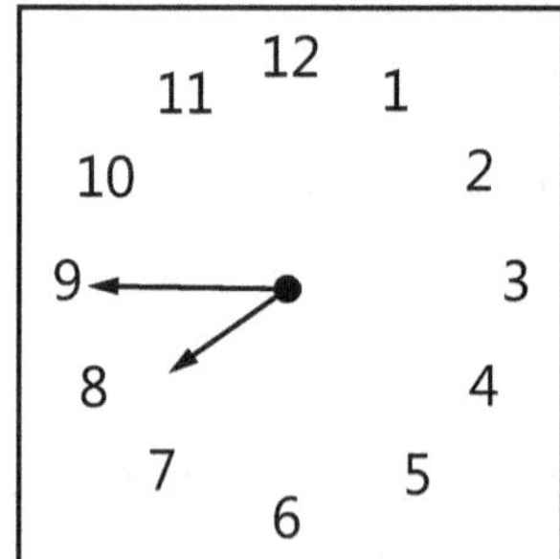

When the time is 4:45 or 7.45, we see that the minute hand only has a quarter way left to reach the end of the hour.

So, when it is 4 : 45, we say it is **a quarter to 5**.

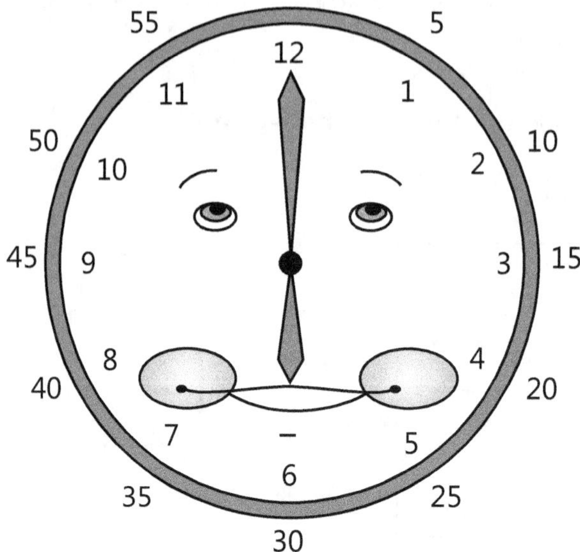

The minute hand goes round the clock once every hour - 24 times in one day!

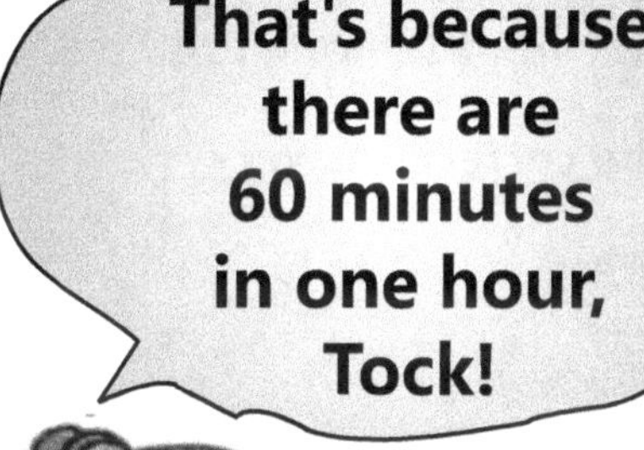

The minute hand is at 10, so it is 50 minutes past the hour. The hour hand is before 4, so it is past 3. The time is 3:50.

1 hour = 60 minutes,

1 minute = 60 seconds.

The hour hand takes 12 hours to complete one round.

The minute hand takes 1 hour to complete one round.

Some conversions :

1 day =24 hours;

1 week = 7 days;

1 month = 4 weeks;

1 year = 12 months;

1 year = 52 weeks;

1 year = 365 days.

The time from 12 midnight to 12 noon is noted as A.M. (Anti Meridian) and the time from 12 noon to 12 midnight as P.M. (Post Meridian)

Choose the correct answer

1. Direction Q. 1 to Q. 3

The hour hand is pointing at ________

(A) 15 (B) 3 (C) 8 (D) 40

2. The minute hand is pointing at ________ minutes.

(A) 40 (B) 8 (C) 80 (D) 35

3. What is the time in the clock?

(A) 3 min past 10 (B) 40 min past 3 (C) 4 min. past 30 (D) None of these

4. What time is the clock showing?

(A) 6 min past 2 (B) Half past 1 (C) 30 min past 1 (D) Both B and C

5. What time is the clock showing?

(A) 45 min past 4 (B) 5 min past 9 (C) 9 min past 5 (D) None of these

6. What time is the clock showing?

(A) 1:06 (B) 6 : 10 (C) 6:05 (D) 1:30

7. This time is _______ min after 9 O'clock

(A) 4 (B) 20 (C) 40 (D) None of these

8. Every morning my father goes for a walk at 6:00 _____

(A) A.M. (B) F.M. (C) S.M. (D) P.M.

9. Which clock correctly shows 6 O' clock?

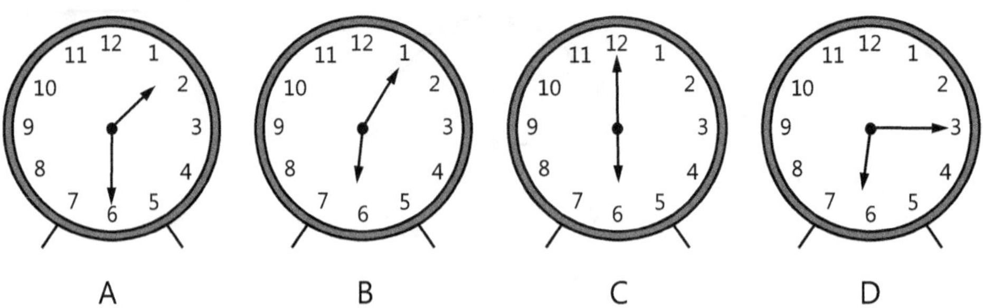

10. Dinesh comes back from school in the afternoon at 3 _______

(A) A.M. (B) S.M. (C) P.M. (D) F.M

11. My favourite cartoon 'TOM & JEERY' comes in the night at 8:30___

(A) A.M. (B) F.M. (C) S.M. (D) P.M.

12. 10:00 is an hour after

(A) 1:00 (B) 9:00 (C) 11:00 (D) 12:00

13. 6:00 is an hour after

(A) 7:00 (B) 5:00 (C) 4:00 (D) None of these

14. Ragini watched her favourite programme from 5:20pm to 5:50p.m.. How long did the programme last?

(A) 30 min (B) 20 min (C) 25 min (D) 35 min

15. Rani started studying at 4:05 pm and she finished at 4:55 pm. How long did she study?

(A) 60 min (B) 50 min (C) 55 min (D) 40 min.

16. Mohan left home at 6:00 in the morning and reached school at 6:45. How long did he take to reach school?

(A) 50 min (B) 45 min (C) 40 min (D) None of these

17. Tina went to see the movie at 4:15 pm and came back at 7:15 pm. How long did she watch the movie?

(A) 3 hrs 40 min (B) 1 hr 50 min (C) 3 hrs (D) None of these

18. Rina started walking to the beach at 6:00 pm. She went back home at 7:30 pm. How long did she walk?

(A) 30 min (B) 1 hr 50 min (C) 1 hr 30 min (D) 2 hr 55 min

19. Sneha's music classes started at 11:00 am. The class lasted for half an hour. When did the class end?

(A) 12:00 (B) 12:30 (C) 11:03 (D) 11:30

20. Rohit started jogging at 6:00 am. He jogged for 50 min. When did he stop?

(A) 5:56 pm (B) 5:10 pm (C) 6:50 pm (D) 6:50 am

21. Reema studied for 25 min. If she started at 4:10 pm when did she stop?

(A) 10:25 am (B) 4:25 pm (C) 4:35 pm. (D) 4:35 am

22. How long did the movie last ?

Movie started
1:00

Movie ended
3:30

(A) 1 hr 30 min (B) 2 hr 30 min (C) 1 hr 12 min (D) 3 hr 06 min

23. Kavita reached a mall at 9:30 am. She shopped there for 1 hour and left the mall. At what time did she leave the mall?

(A) 10:30 (B) 30 min past 10 (C) 9:10 (D) Both a and b

24. Ram went to his Olympiad classes at 3:00 pm. The class was for 1 hr 20 min. At what time did his class get over?

(A) 4:20pm (B) 4:20am (C) 4:30pm (D) None of these

25. The clock is 15 min fast. If the clock is showing 10:35 am. What is the actual time?

(A) 10:20 am (B) 10:50 am (C) 10:50 pm (D) 15:35 am

26. The clock is 20 min fast. If the clock is showing 11:40 pm, what is the actual time?

(A) 11:30 pm (B) 11:20 pm (C) 11:00 pm (D) 11:20 am

27. The clock is 10 min slow. If the clock is showing 2:30 pm, what is the actual time?

(A) 2:20 pm (B) 2:40 pm (C) 2:10 pm (D) 3:20

28. The clock is 18 min slow. If the clock is showing 3:35 am, what is the actual time?

(A) 3:17 am (B) 3:53 am (C) 3:53 pm (D) 5:35 am

29. What is the time if it is 15 min after 6 pm?

(A) 6:51 pm (B) 6:15pm (C) 6:15 am (D) 15:6 pm

30. What is the time if it is 20 min after 2 am?

(A) 2:20 am (B) 2:20 pm (C) 12:08 pm (D) Both (A) & (B)

31. What is the time if it is 18 min after 12 noon?

(A) 12:18 pm (B) 12:18 am (C) 12:08 pm (D) Both (A) & (B)

32. What is the time if it is 20 min after 12 midnight?

(A) 12:02 am (B) 12:02 pm (C) 12:20 am (D) 12:20 pm

33. 1 hour = _______ min

(A) 12 min (B) 60 min (C) 30 min (D) 6 min

34. 3 hour = _______ min

(A) 180 min (B) 60 min (C) 120 min (D) None of these

35. 1 min = _______ seconds

(A) 40 (B) 30 (C) 60 (D) 120

36. Which clock is showing 3 hours before 4 am?

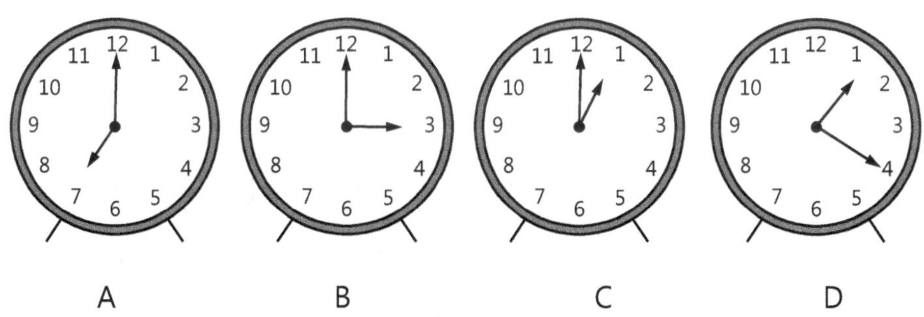

37. Seema watched her favourite programme from 4 pm to 7:30 p.m. How long did the programme last?

(A) 3.30 hrs (B) 3 hrs (C) 2 hrs (D) 2:30 hrs.

38. Bina went into the swimming pool at 6:30 am and came out at 8:00 am. How long did she swim?

(A) 1:20 hrs (B) 2:10 hrs (C) 7:30 hrs (D) 1:30 hrs.

39. At 2:10 pm the hour hand will be at

(A) 10 (B) 2 (C) 12 (D) 8

40. At 4:30 am the hour hand will be at

(A) 4 (B) 6 (C) 30 (D) 43

41. At 9:30 am the hour hand will lie between

(A) 3 and 4 (B) 9 and 10 (C) 8 and 9 (D) 10 and 11

42. At 6:45 am the hour hand will lie between

(A) 6 and 7 (B) 4 and 5 (C) 5 and 6 (D) 7 and 8

43. At 7:35 am the hour hand will lie between

(A) 5 and 6 (B) 6 and 7 (C) 7 and 8 (D) 6 and 3

44. Leena starts her homework at 1 pm and finishes at 5 pm. If she takes an hour off for lunch, how many hours does she study every day?

(A) 4 hours (B) 3 hours (C) 6 hours (D) 5 hours

45. Rajeshwari starts her homework at 6 am and finishes at 11 am. If she takes an hour off for breakfast how many hours does she study every day?

(A) 6 hours (B) 11 hours (C) 4 hours (D) 5 hours

46. Manisha left her house at 11:30 am. She takes one hour to reach her office. What time she will reach office?

(A) 12:30 am (B) 12:30 pm (C) 12:03 pm (D) 12:03 am

47. Rahul's school starts at 10.20 am. If the school works for 5 hours, then

at what time will the school get over?

(A) 5:20 am (B) 3:20 am (C) 3:20 pm (D) None of these

48. Rohan takes 30 minutes to complete one round of the park. How long will he take to complete 3 rounds?

(A) 60 min. (B) 90 min (C) 33 min (D) 93 min.

49. Meena takes 20 minutes to complete one round of the park. How long will she take to complete 3 rounds

(A) 30 min (B) 60 min (C) 1 hour (D) Both B and C

50. Monisha takes 60 minutes to complete one round of the park. How long will she take to complete 2 rounds?

(A) 160 minutes (B) 120 minutes (C) 2 hours (D) Both B and C

51. 1 Rupee = ______ paise

(A) 10 (B) 100 (C) (C) 1000 (D) 110

52. ₹ 2 . = _____ p.

(A) 250 (B) 200 (C) 120 (D) 210

53. ₹ 6 . = ______ p.

(A) 600 (B) 610 (C) 160 (D) 060

54. 300 p = ₹ _____

(A) 3 (B) 30 (C) 33 (D) 130

55. 700 p. = ₹ ______

(A) 70 (B) 07 (C) 17 (D) 71

56. ₹100 = ______

(A) Twenty notes of ₹ 10 (B) Five notes of ₹ 10

(C) Ten notes of ₹ 10 (D) Ten notes of ₹100

57. The sum of ₹ 20 and ₹ 12 is

(A) ₹ 32 (B) ₹ 22 (C) ₹ 42 (D) ₹ 52

58. Sum of ₹ 14 and ₹ 34 is

(A) ₹ 44 (B) ₹ 48 (C) ₹ 38 (D) None of these

59. Which of the following sets of coins gives you rupee 1?

(A) (25 p) (25 p) (25 p) (25 p)

(B) (10 p) (10 p) (10 p)

(C) (50 p) (10 p)

(D) (30 p) (30 p)

60. How money ₹ 10 do you need to make ₹ 40?

(A) 14 (B) 4 (C) 41 (D) 40

61. How many ₹ 5 do you need to make ₹35?

(A) 5 (B) 3 (C) 7 (D) 13

62. How many ₹ 2 coins do you need to make ₹ 8 ?

(A) 4 (B) 2 (C) 6 (D) 10

63. How many ₹ 2 coins do you need to make ₹ 14?

(A) 12 (B) 16 (C) 7 (D) 28

Direction Q. 64 to Q. 68

BALL	BOOK	PENCIL BOX	1 DOZEN ERASERS
₹ 10	₹ 40	₹ 25	₹ 20

64. Which is the most expensive of the four items?

(A) Ball (B) Book

(C) Pencil box (D) 1 dozen erasers

65. Which is the cheapest of the four?

(A) Pencil box (B) 1 dozen erasers (C) Book (D) Ball

66. If Manish has ₹ 10, which of the following articles he can buy?

(A) Book (B) Pencil box (C) Ball (D) 1 dozen erasers

67. If Raj has ₹ 45 what two things he can buy?

(A) Ball and book (B) Book and pencil box

(C) Pencil box and 1 dozen erasers (D) None of these

68. How much money is required to buy all of them?

(A) ₹ 95 (B) ₹ 85 (C) ₹ 75 (D) ₹ 70.

69. Which set of money is enough to buy a ₹ 36 book?

(A) ☐ 15 ₹ (B) ☐ 50 ₹

(C) ☐ 30 ₹ (D) ☐ 35 ₹

70. How many ₹ 10 will make ₹ 100?

(A) 10 (B) 11 (C) 5 (D) 20

71. How many ₹ 20 will make ₹ 100?

(A) 12 (B) 21 (C) 5 (D) 20

72. Harish bought a toy of ₹ 560. He gave the shopkeeper ₹ 600. How much money will the shopkeeper return back?

(A) 60 (B) 1,160 (C) 40 (D) None of these

73. Hema bought some books worth ₹ 310. She gave a 500 rupee note to the shopkeeper. How much money will the shopkeeper return?

(A) ₹ 910 (B) ₹ 190 (C) ₹ 19 (D) ₹ 10

74. How much money will Jigar get back if he paid ₹ 500 for a ₹ 425 toy car?

(A) ₹ 42 (B) ₹ 75 (C) ₹ 25 (D) ₹ 50

75. How much money will Khushi get back if she paid ₹ 500 for a ₹ 320 school bag?

(A) ₹180 (B) ₹ 18 (C) ₹ 80 (D) ₹ 810

76. How many ₹ 50 will make ₹ 100?

(A) 5 (B) 02 (C) 10 (D) 1

77. How many ₹ 50 will make ₹ 200 ?

(A) 5 (B) 4 (C) 2 (D) None of these

78. If Sushmita saves ₹ 5 from her pocket money every month, how much will she save at the end of a year?

(A) ₹ 60 (B) ₹ 5 (C) ₹ 12 (D) ₹17

79. If Radha saves ₹ 2 from her pocket money daily in the month of April, how much she will save at the end of the month?

(A) ₹ 30 (B) ₹ 32 (C) ₹ 60 (D) ₹ 62

80. If Riya saves ₹ 5 everyday from her pocket money in the month of September, how much she will save at the end of the month?

(A) ₹ 35 (B) ₹30 (C) ₹ 150 (D) ₹ 155

81. If Mohan saves ₹ 10 every month from his pocket money, how much he will save at the end of the September year?

(A) ₹ 22 (B) ₹ 32 (C) ₹ 120 (D) ₹ 20

82. Which could you do in about a minute?

(A) Read a page of the book (B) Take a bath

(C) Brush your teeth (D) None of these.

Direction (Q. 83 to Q. 85)

A pair of shoes costs ₹ 200 and a shirt costs ₹ 140.

83. How much will 3 similar pairs of shoes cost?

(A) ₹ 600 (B) ₹ 420 (C) ₹ 203 (D) ₹ 143

84. How much will 4 shirts cost?

(A) ₹ 560 (B) ₹ 144 (C) ₹ 100 (D) None of these

85 How much will one pair of shoes and a shirt cost?

(A) ₹ 40 (B) 340 (C) 240 (D) None of these

...

ANSWERSHEET

1.	Ⓐ Ⓑ Ⓒ Ⓓ	2.	Ⓐ Ⓑ Ⓒ Ⓓ	3.	Ⓐ Ⓑ Ⓒ Ⓓ	4.	Ⓐ Ⓑ Ⓒ Ⓓ
5.	Ⓐ Ⓑ Ⓒ Ⓓ	6.	Ⓐ Ⓑ Ⓒ Ⓓ	7.	Ⓐ Ⓑ Ⓒ Ⓓ	8.	Ⓐ Ⓑ Ⓒ Ⓓ
9.	Ⓐ Ⓑ Ⓒ Ⓓ	10.	Ⓐ Ⓑ Ⓒ Ⓓ	11.	Ⓐ Ⓑ Ⓒ Ⓓ	12.	Ⓐ Ⓑ Ⓒ Ⓓ
13.	Ⓐ Ⓑ Ⓒ Ⓓ	14.	Ⓐ Ⓑ Ⓒ Ⓓ	15.	Ⓐ Ⓑ Ⓒ Ⓓ	16.	Ⓐ Ⓑ Ⓒ Ⓓ
17.	Ⓐ Ⓑ Ⓒ Ⓓ	18.	Ⓐ Ⓑ Ⓒ Ⓓ	19.	Ⓐ Ⓑ Ⓒ Ⓓ	20.	Ⓐ Ⓑ Ⓒ Ⓓ
21.	Ⓐ Ⓑ Ⓒ Ⓓ	22.	Ⓐ Ⓑ Ⓒ Ⓓ	23.	Ⓐ Ⓑ Ⓒ Ⓓ	24.	Ⓐ Ⓑ Ⓒ Ⓓ
25.	Ⓐ Ⓑ Ⓒ Ⓓ	26.	Ⓐ Ⓑ Ⓒ Ⓓ	27.	Ⓐ Ⓑ Ⓒ Ⓓ	28.	Ⓐ Ⓑ Ⓒ Ⓓ
29.	Ⓐ Ⓑ Ⓒ Ⓓ	30.	Ⓐ Ⓑ Ⓒ Ⓓ	31.	Ⓐ Ⓑ Ⓒ Ⓓ	32.	Ⓐ Ⓑ Ⓒ Ⓓ
33.	Ⓐ Ⓑ Ⓒ Ⓓ	34.	Ⓐ Ⓑ Ⓒ Ⓓ	35.	Ⓐ Ⓑ Ⓒ Ⓓ	36.	Ⓐ Ⓑ Ⓒ Ⓓ
37.	Ⓐ Ⓑ Ⓒ Ⓓ	38.	Ⓐ Ⓑ Ⓒ Ⓓ	39.	Ⓐ Ⓑ Ⓒ Ⓓ	40.	Ⓐ Ⓑ Ⓒ Ⓓ
41.	Ⓐ Ⓑ Ⓒ Ⓓ	42.	Ⓐ Ⓑ Ⓒ Ⓓ	43.	Ⓐ Ⓑ Ⓒ Ⓓ	44.	Ⓐ Ⓑ Ⓒ Ⓓ
45.	Ⓐ Ⓑ Ⓒ Ⓓ	46.	Ⓐ Ⓑ Ⓒ Ⓓ	47.	Ⓐ Ⓑ Ⓒ Ⓓ	48.	Ⓐ Ⓑ Ⓒ Ⓓ
49.	Ⓐ Ⓑ Ⓒ Ⓓ	50.	Ⓐ Ⓑ Ⓒ Ⓓ	51.	Ⓐ Ⓑ Ⓒ Ⓓ	52.	Ⓐ Ⓑ Ⓒ Ⓓ
53.	Ⓐ Ⓑ Ⓒ Ⓓ	54.	Ⓐ Ⓑ Ⓒ Ⓓ	55.	Ⓐ Ⓑ Ⓒ Ⓓ	56.	Ⓐ Ⓑ Ⓒ Ⓓ
57.	Ⓐ Ⓑ Ⓒ Ⓓ	58.	Ⓐ Ⓑ Ⓒ Ⓓ	59.	Ⓐ Ⓑ Ⓒ Ⓓ	60.	Ⓐ Ⓑ Ⓒ Ⓓ
61.	Ⓐ Ⓑ Ⓒ Ⓓ	62.	Ⓐ Ⓑ Ⓒ Ⓓ	63.	Ⓐ Ⓑ Ⓒ Ⓓ	64.	Ⓐ Ⓑ Ⓒ Ⓓ
65.	Ⓐ Ⓑ Ⓒ Ⓓ	66.	Ⓐ Ⓑ Ⓒ Ⓓ	67.	Ⓐ Ⓑ Ⓒ Ⓓ	68.	Ⓐ Ⓑ Ⓒ Ⓓ
69.	Ⓐ Ⓑ Ⓒ Ⓓ	70.	Ⓐ Ⓑ Ⓒ Ⓓ	71.	Ⓐ Ⓑ Ⓒ Ⓓ	72.	Ⓐ Ⓑ Ⓒ Ⓓ
73.	Ⓐ Ⓑ Ⓒ Ⓓ	74.	Ⓐ Ⓑ Ⓒ Ⓓ	75.	Ⓐ Ⓑ Ⓒ Ⓓ	76.	Ⓐ Ⓑ Ⓒ Ⓓ
77.	Ⓐ Ⓑ Ⓒ Ⓓ	78.	Ⓐ Ⓑ Ⓒ Ⓓ	79.	Ⓐ Ⓑ Ⓒ Ⓓ	80.	Ⓐ Ⓑ Ⓒ Ⓓ
81.	Ⓐ Ⓑ Ⓒ Ⓓ	82.	Ⓐ Ⓑ Ⓒ Ⓓ	83.	Ⓐ Ⓑ Ⓒ Ⓓ	84.	Ⓐ Ⓑ Ⓒ Ⓓ
85.	Ⓐ Ⓑ Ⓒ Ⓓ	86.	Ⓐ Ⓑ Ⓒ Ⓓ	87.	Ⓐ Ⓑ Ⓒ Ⓓ	88.	Ⓐ Ⓑ Ⓒ Ⓓ
89.	Ⓐ Ⓑ Ⓒ Ⓓ	90.	Ⓐ Ⓑ Ⓒ Ⓓ	91.	Ⓐ Ⓑ Ⓒ Ⓓ	92.	Ⓐ Ⓑ Ⓒ Ⓓ
93.	Ⓐ Ⓑ Ⓒ Ⓓ	94.	Ⓐ Ⓑ Ⓒ Ⓓ	95.	Ⓐ Ⓑ Ⓒ Ⓓ	96.	Ⓐ Ⓑ Ⓒ Ⓓ
97.	Ⓐ Ⓑ Ⓒ Ⓓ	98.	Ⓐ Ⓑ Ⓒ Ⓓ	99.	Ⓐ Ⓑ Ⓒ Ⓓ	100.	Ⓐ Ⓑ Ⓒ Ⓓ

Chapter 6
GEOMETRY

Choose the correct answer

1. I have 6 faces, 12 edges and 8 corners. Who am I?

   (A) Cylinder (B) Cube (C) Cuboid (D) Both B and C

2. How many circles are there in the given figure?

   (A) 8 (B) 9 (C) 3 (D) None of these

3. This figure is made up of _______ triangles.

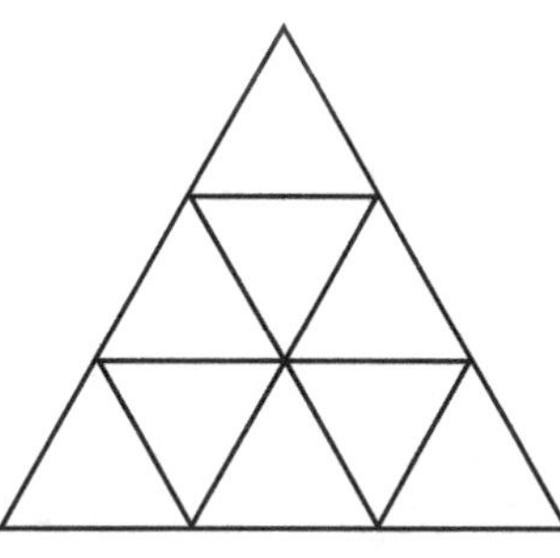

   (A) 11 (B) 9 (C) 10 (D) 13

4. How many squares are there in this figure?

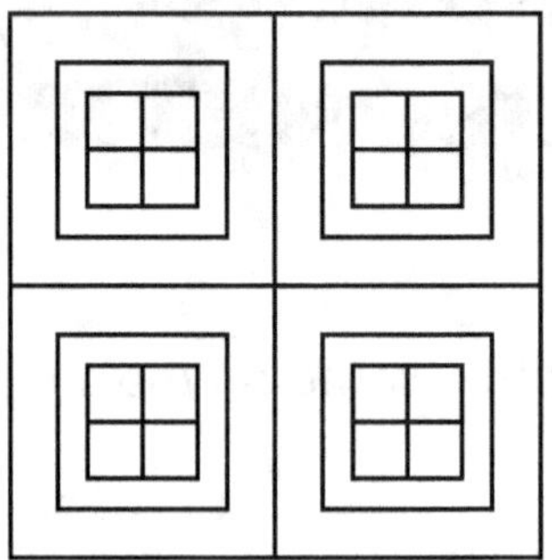

(A) 29 (B) 25 (C) 16 (D) None of these.

5. How many squares are there in the figure ?

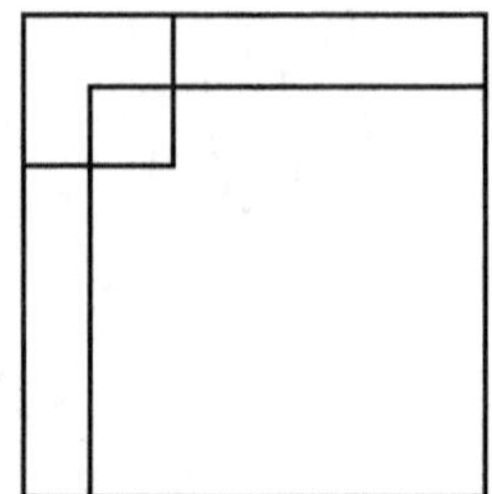

(A) 4 (B) 5 (C) 6 (D) None of these.

6. A cone has ______ faces.

(A) 1 (B) 2 (C) 3 (D) None of these.

7. A cylinder has ______ faces.

(A) 3 (B) 0 (C) 2 (D) None of these.

8. Solid (B) has _____ more faces than solid (A)

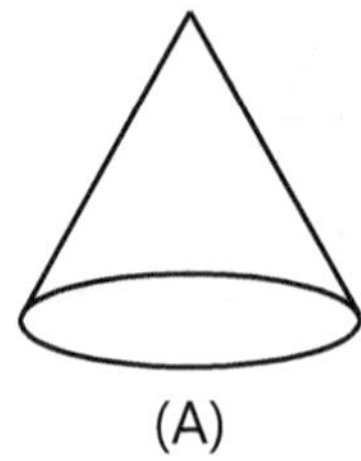

(A)

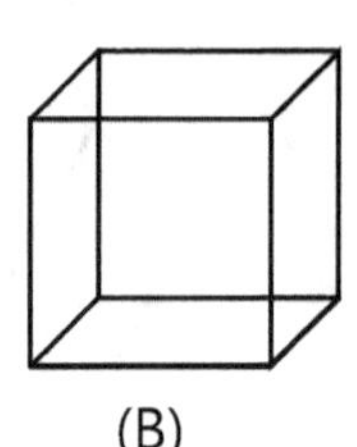

(B)

(A) 3 (B) 4 (C) 2 (D) None of these.

9. 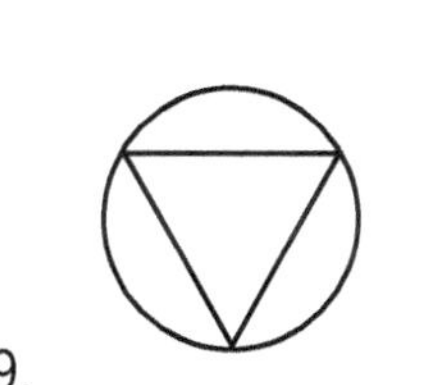 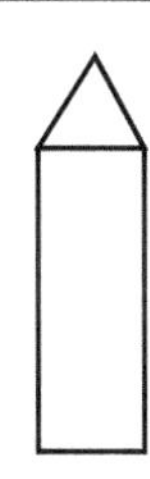  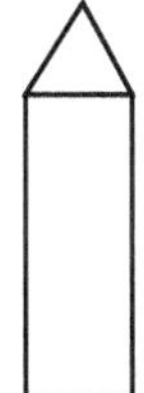  

How many triangles are used to make this figure?

(A) 3 (B) 6 (C) 4 (D) None of these.

10. If Johnny connects the points shown here with line segments. What shape will he make?

. A

. B

C .

(A) Rectangle (B) Circle (C) Triangle (D) Square

11. What two shapes can be joined without overlap to form the given kite?

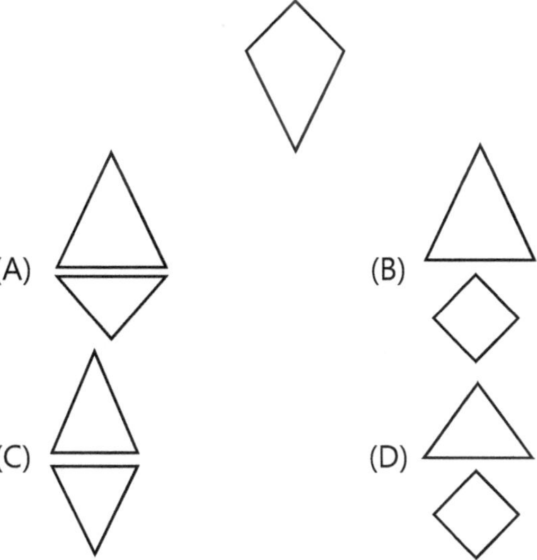

12. Which shape fits the missing part of the figure on the right?

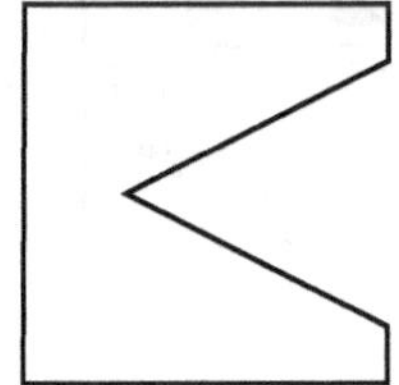

(A) 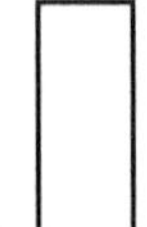 (B)  (C) 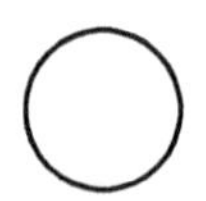 (D) 

13. How many circles can you make out of these?

(A) 4 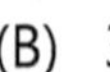 (B) 3 (C) 6 (D) None of these

14. How many squares are there in this figure?

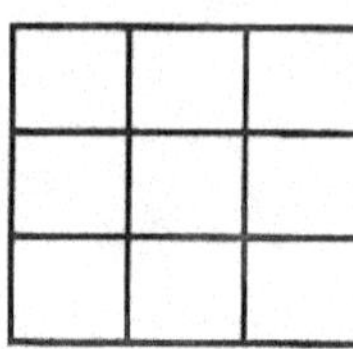

(A) 9 (B) 10 (C) 14 (D) None of these

15. A dice is the best example of ________ ?

(A) Cuboid (B) Cube (C) Cone (D) Sphere

...

ANSWERSHEET

1.	Ⓐ Ⓑ Ⓒ Ⓓ	2.	Ⓐ Ⓑ Ⓒ Ⓓ	3.	Ⓐ Ⓑ Ⓒ Ⓓ	4.	Ⓐ Ⓑ Ⓒ Ⓓ
5.	Ⓐ Ⓑ Ⓒ Ⓓ	6.	Ⓐ Ⓑ Ⓒ Ⓓ	7.	Ⓐ Ⓑ Ⓒ Ⓓ	8.	Ⓐ Ⓑ Ⓒ Ⓓ
9.	Ⓐ Ⓑ Ⓒ Ⓓ	10.	Ⓐ Ⓑ Ⓒ Ⓓ	11.	Ⓐ Ⓑ Ⓒ Ⓓ	12.	Ⓐ Ⓑ Ⓒ Ⓓ
13.	Ⓐ Ⓑ Ⓒ Ⓓ	14.	Ⓐ Ⓑ Ⓒ Ⓓ	15.	Ⓐ Ⓑ Ⓒ Ⓓ	16.	Ⓐ Ⓑ Ⓒ Ⓓ
17.	Ⓐ Ⓑ Ⓒ Ⓓ	18.	Ⓐ Ⓑ Ⓒ Ⓓ	19.	Ⓐ Ⓑ Ⓒ Ⓓ	20.	Ⓐ Ⓑ Ⓒ Ⓓ
21.	Ⓐ Ⓑ Ⓒ Ⓓ	22.	Ⓐ Ⓑ Ⓒ Ⓓ	23.	Ⓐ Ⓑ Ⓒ Ⓓ	24.	Ⓐ Ⓑ Ⓒ Ⓓ
25.	Ⓐ Ⓑ Ⓒ Ⓓ	26.	Ⓐ Ⓑ Ⓒ Ⓓ	27.	Ⓐ Ⓑ Ⓒ Ⓓ	28.	Ⓐ Ⓑ Ⓒ Ⓓ
29.	Ⓐ Ⓑ Ⓒ Ⓓ	30.	Ⓐ Ⓑ Ⓒ Ⓓ	31.	Ⓐ Ⓑ Ⓒ Ⓓ	32.	Ⓐ Ⓑ Ⓒ Ⓓ
33.	Ⓐ Ⓑ Ⓒ Ⓓ	34.	Ⓐ Ⓑ Ⓒ Ⓓ	35.	Ⓐ Ⓑ Ⓒ Ⓓ	36.	Ⓐ Ⓑ Ⓒ Ⓓ
37.	Ⓐ Ⓑ Ⓒ Ⓓ	38.	Ⓐ Ⓑ Ⓒ Ⓓ	39.	Ⓐ Ⓑ Ⓒ Ⓓ	40.	Ⓐ Ⓑ Ⓒ Ⓓ
41.	Ⓐ Ⓑ Ⓒ Ⓓ	42.	Ⓐ Ⓑ Ⓒ Ⓓ	43.	Ⓐ Ⓑ Ⓒ Ⓓ	44.	Ⓐ Ⓑ Ⓒ Ⓓ
45.	Ⓐ Ⓑ Ⓒ Ⓓ	46.	Ⓐ Ⓑ Ⓒ Ⓓ	47.	Ⓐ Ⓑ Ⓒ Ⓓ	48.	Ⓐ Ⓑ Ⓒ Ⓓ
49.	Ⓐ Ⓑ Ⓒ Ⓓ	50.	Ⓐ Ⓑ Ⓒ Ⓓ	51.	Ⓐ Ⓑ Ⓒ Ⓓ	52.	Ⓐ Ⓑ Ⓒ Ⓓ
53.	Ⓐ Ⓑ Ⓒ Ⓓ	54.	Ⓐ Ⓑ Ⓒ Ⓓ	55.	Ⓐ Ⓑ Ⓒ Ⓓ	56.	Ⓐ Ⓑ Ⓒ Ⓓ
57.	Ⓐ Ⓑ Ⓒ Ⓓ	58.	Ⓐ Ⓑ Ⓒ Ⓓ	59.	Ⓐ Ⓑ Ⓒ Ⓓ	60.	Ⓐ Ⓑ Ⓒ Ⓓ
61.	Ⓐ Ⓑ Ⓒ Ⓓ	62.	Ⓐ Ⓑ Ⓒ Ⓓ	63.	Ⓐ Ⓑ Ⓒ Ⓓ	64.	Ⓐ Ⓑ Ⓒ Ⓓ
65.	Ⓐ Ⓑ Ⓒ Ⓓ	66.	Ⓐ Ⓑ Ⓒ Ⓓ	67.	Ⓐ Ⓑ Ⓒ Ⓓ	68.	Ⓐ Ⓑ Ⓒ Ⓓ
69.	Ⓐ Ⓑ Ⓒ Ⓓ	70.	Ⓐ Ⓑ Ⓒ Ⓓ	71.	Ⓐ Ⓑ Ⓒ Ⓓ	72.	Ⓐ Ⓑ Ⓒ Ⓓ
73.	Ⓐ Ⓑ Ⓒ Ⓓ	74.	Ⓐ Ⓑ Ⓒ Ⓓ	75.	Ⓐ Ⓑ Ⓒ Ⓓ	76.	Ⓐ Ⓑ Ⓒ Ⓓ
77.	Ⓐ Ⓑ Ⓒ Ⓓ	78.	Ⓐ Ⓑ Ⓒ Ⓓ	79.	Ⓐ Ⓑ Ⓒ Ⓓ	80.	Ⓐ Ⓑ Ⓒ Ⓓ
81.	Ⓐ Ⓑ Ⓒ Ⓓ	82.	Ⓐ Ⓑ Ⓒ Ⓓ	83.	Ⓐ Ⓑ Ⓒ Ⓓ	84.	Ⓐ Ⓑ Ⓒ Ⓓ
85.	Ⓐ Ⓑ Ⓒ Ⓓ	86.	Ⓐ Ⓑ Ⓒ Ⓓ	87.	Ⓐ Ⓑ Ⓒ Ⓓ	88.	Ⓐ Ⓑ Ⓒ Ⓓ
89.	Ⓐ Ⓑ Ⓒ Ⓓ	90.	Ⓐ Ⓑ Ⓒ Ⓓ	91.	Ⓐ Ⓑ Ⓒ Ⓓ	92.	Ⓐ Ⓑ Ⓒ Ⓓ
93.	Ⓐ Ⓑ Ⓒ Ⓓ	94.	Ⓐ Ⓑ Ⓒ Ⓓ	95.	Ⓐ Ⓑ Ⓒ Ⓓ	96.	Ⓐ Ⓑ Ⓒ Ⓓ
97.	Ⓐ Ⓑ Ⓒ Ⓓ	98.	Ⓐ Ⓑ Ⓒ Ⓓ	99.	Ⓐ Ⓑ Ⓒ Ⓓ	100.	Ⓐ Ⓑ Ⓒ Ⓓ

Chapter 7
PATTERNS

Choose the correct answer

Directions (Q. 1 to Q. 21)

1. 1, 2, 3, 4, 5, 6, _____

(A) 7 (B) 6 (C) 8 (D) 9

2. 18, 20, 22, 24, 26, 28, _______

(A) 27 (B) 29 (C) 30 (D) 32

3. 6, 8, _______

(A) 9 (B) 10 (C) 7 (D) 11

4. 20, 25, 30, 35, 40, ______

(A) 41 (B) 45 (C) 39 (D) 42

5. 4, 8, 12, 16, 20, _____

(A) 24 (B) 28 (C) 21 (D) 22

6. 16, 32, 48, ___

(A) 46 (B) 54 (C) 64 (D) 60.

7. 90, 100, 110, 120, 130, _____

(A) 103 (B) 135 (C) 140 (D) 145

8. 150, 140, 160, 150, 170, _____

(A) 160 (B) 180 (C) 175 (D) 150.

9. 138, 137, 139, 138, 140, _____

(A) 139 (B) 141 (C)138 (D) 137.

10. 642, 641, 643, 642, 644, ______

(A) 643 (B) 641 (C) 649 (D) 645

11. 42, 142, 242, 342, _____

(A) 343 (B) 243 (C) 442 (D) 542

12. 312, 412, 512, 612, 712, _____

(A) 713 (B) 812 (C) 912 (D) None of these

13. 410, 420, 430, 440, ___

(A) 450 (B) 455 (C) 441 (D) 442

14. 800, 820, 840, 860, _______

(A) 861 (B) 870 (C) 880 (D) 862.

15. 444, 449, 454, 459, ______

(A) 460 (B) 464 (C) 559 (D) 564

16. 999, 888, 777, 666, _____

(A) 676 (B) 667 (C) 555 (D) 665

17. 648, 846, 293, 392, 192, ____

(A) 291 (B) 921 (C) 219 (D) 193

18. _____, 400, 390, 380, 370

(A) 401 (B) 410 (C) 441 (D) 411

19. 142, 242, ____, 442, 542, 642

(A) 243 (B) 342 (C) 541 (D) 341

20. 8, 16, 24, 32, 40, _____
    (A) 48 (B) 41 (C) 42 (D) 44
21. 11, 22, 33, 44, _____
    (A) 45 (B) 55 (C) 43 (D) 54

Direction (Q. 22 to Q. 28)

22.

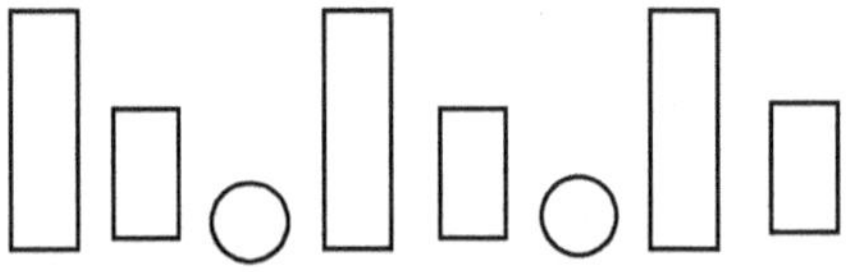

(A)  (B)  (C)  (D)

23.

(A)  (B)  (C)  (D)

24.

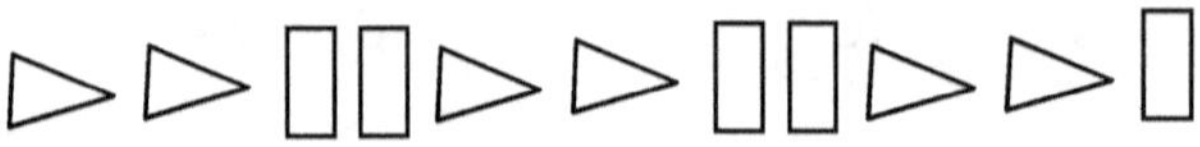

(A) 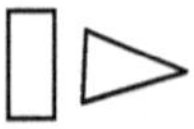 (B) 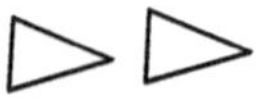 (C) 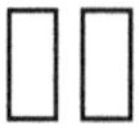 (D)

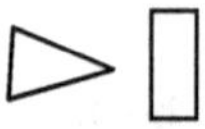

25.

(A)  (B)  (C)  (D) None of these

26. ↑↓↓↑↑↑↓↓↓↓↑↑↑↑ _____

(A) ↑↑ (B) ↑↓ (C) ↓↓ (D) None of these

27.

(A) (B) (C) (D) None of these

28.     _____

(A) (B) (C) (D) None of these

...

ANSWERSHEET

1.	Ⓐ Ⓑ Ⓒ Ⓓ	2.	Ⓐ Ⓑ Ⓒ Ⓓ	3.	Ⓐ Ⓑ Ⓒ Ⓓ	4.	Ⓐ Ⓑ Ⓒ Ⓓ
5.	Ⓐ Ⓑ Ⓒ Ⓓ	6.	Ⓐ Ⓑ Ⓒ Ⓓ	7.	Ⓐ Ⓑ Ⓒ Ⓓ	8.	Ⓐ Ⓑ Ⓒ Ⓓ
9.	Ⓐ Ⓑ Ⓒ Ⓓ	10.	Ⓐ Ⓑ Ⓒ Ⓓ	11.	Ⓐ Ⓑ Ⓒ Ⓓ	12.	Ⓐ Ⓑ Ⓒ Ⓓ
13.	Ⓐ Ⓑ Ⓒ Ⓓ	14.	Ⓐ Ⓑ Ⓒ Ⓓ	15.	Ⓐ Ⓑ Ⓒ Ⓓ	16.	Ⓐ Ⓑ Ⓒ Ⓓ
17.	Ⓐ Ⓑ Ⓒ Ⓓ	18.	Ⓐ Ⓑ Ⓒ Ⓓ	19.	Ⓐ Ⓑ Ⓒ Ⓓ	20.	Ⓐ Ⓑ Ⓒ Ⓓ
21.	Ⓐ Ⓑ Ⓒ Ⓓ	22.	Ⓐ Ⓑ Ⓒ Ⓓ	23.	Ⓐ Ⓑ Ⓒ Ⓓ	24.	Ⓐ Ⓑ Ⓒ Ⓓ
25.	Ⓐ Ⓑ Ⓒ Ⓓ	26.	Ⓐ Ⓑ Ⓒ Ⓓ	27.	Ⓐ Ⓑ Ⓒ Ⓓ	28.	Ⓐ Ⓑ Ⓒ Ⓓ
29.	Ⓐ Ⓑ Ⓒ Ⓓ	30.	Ⓐ Ⓑ Ⓒ Ⓓ	31.	Ⓐ Ⓑ Ⓒ Ⓓ	32.	Ⓐ Ⓑ Ⓒ Ⓓ
33.	Ⓐ Ⓑ Ⓒ Ⓓ	34.	Ⓐ Ⓑ Ⓒ Ⓓ	35.	Ⓐ Ⓑ Ⓒ Ⓓ	36.	Ⓐ Ⓑ Ⓒ Ⓓ
37.	Ⓐ Ⓑ Ⓒ Ⓓ	38.	Ⓐ Ⓑ Ⓒ Ⓓ	39.	Ⓐ Ⓑ Ⓒ Ⓓ	40.	Ⓐ Ⓑ Ⓒ Ⓓ
41.	Ⓐ Ⓑ Ⓒ Ⓓ	42.	Ⓐ Ⓑ Ⓒ Ⓓ	43.	Ⓐ Ⓑ Ⓒ Ⓓ	44.	Ⓐ Ⓑ Ⓒ Ⓓ
45.	Ⓐ Ⓑ Ⓒ Ⓓ	46.	Ⓐ Ⓑ Ⓒ Ⓓ	47.	Ⓐ Ⓑ Ⓒ Ⓓ	48.	Ⓐ Ⓑ Ⓒ Ⓓ
49.	Ⓐ Ⓑ Ⓒ Ⓓ	50.	Ⓐ Ⓑ Ⓒ Ⓓ	51.	Ⓐ Ⓑ Ⓒ Ⓓ	52.	Ⓐ Ⓑ Ⓒ Ⓓ
53.	Ⓐ Ⓑ Ⓒ Ⓓ	54.	Ⓐ Ⓑ Ⓒ Ⓓ	55.	Ⓐ Ⓑ Ⓒ Ⓓ	56.	Ⓐ Ⓑ Ⓒ Ⓓ
57.	Ⓐ Ⓑ Ⓒ Ⓓ	58.	Ⓐ Ⓑ Ⓒ Ⓓ	59.	Ⓐ Ⓑ Ⓒ Ⓓ	60.	Ⓐ Ⓑ Ⓒ Ⓓ
61.	Ⓐ Ⓑ Ⓒ Ⓓ	62.	Ⓐ Ⓑ Ⓒ Ⓓ	63.	Ⓐ Ⓑ Ⓒ Ⓓ	64.	Ⓐ Ⓑ Ⓒ Ⓓ
65.	Ⓐ Ⓑ Ⓒ Ⓓ	66.	Ⓐ Ⓑ Ⓒ Ⓓ	67.	Ⓐ Ⓑ Ⓒ Ⓓ	68.	Ⓐ Ⓑ Ⓒ Ⓓ
69.	Ⓐ Ⓑ Ⓒ Ⓓ	70.	Ⓐ Ⓑ Ⓒ Ⓓ	71.	Ⓐ Ⓑ Ⓒ Ⓓ	72.	Ⓐ Ⓑ Ⓒ Ⓓ
73.	Ⓐ Ⓑ Ⓒ Ⓓ	74.	Ⓐ Ⓑ Ⓒ Ⓓ	75.	Ⓐ Ⓑ Ⓒ Ⓓ	76.	Ⓐ Ⓑ Ⓒ Ⓓ
77.	Ⓐ Ⓑ Ⓒ Ⓓ	78.	Ⓐ Ⓑ Ⓒ Ⓓ	79.	Ⓐ Ⓑ Ⓒ Ⓓ	80.	Ⓐ Ⓑ Ⓒ Ⓓ
81.	Ⓐ Ⓑ Ⓒ Ⓓ	82.	Ⓐ Ⓑ Ⓒ Ⓓ	83.	Ⓐ Ⓑ Ⓒ Ⓓ	84.	Ⓐ Ⓑ Ⓒ Ⓓ
85.	Ⓐ Ⓑ Ⓒ Ⓓ	86.	Ⓐ Ⓑ Ⓒ Ⓓ	87.	Ⓐ Ⓑ Ⓒ Ⓓ	88.	Ⓐ Ⓑ Ⓒ Ⓓ
89.	Ⓐ Ⓑ Ⓒ Ⓓ	90.	Ⓐ Ⓑ Ⓒ Ⓓ	91.	Ⓐ Ⓑ Ⓒ Ⓓ	92.	Ⓐ Ⓑ Ⓒ Ⓓ
93.	Ⓐ Ⓑ Ⓒ Ⓓ	94.	Ⓐ Ⓑ Ⓒ Ⓓ	95.	Ⓐ Ⓑ Ⓒ Ⓓ	96.	Ⓐ Ⓑ Ⓒ Ⓓ
97.	Ⓐ Ⓑ Ⓒ Ⓓ	98.	Ⓐ Ⓑ Ⓒ Ⓓ	99.	Ⓐ Ⓑ Ⓒ Ⓓ	100.	Ⓐ Ⓑ Ⓒ Ⓓ

PAPER I

1. Who am I? Multiply me by any number and you will get 0.

   (A) 4 (B) 0 (C) 3 (D) None of these

2. How many tens are there in 60 seconds?

   (A) 4 (B) 6 (C) 10 (D) None of these

3. In the word' INDIA' what fraction of alphabets are made of vowels ?

   (A) 4/6 (B) 4/5 (C) 3/5 (D) None of these

4. Doreamon has a chocolate which he cuts into 10 equal pieces. Nobita ate 3/10 chocolate and Jiyan ate 5/10 chocolate. Who ate more chocolates?

   (A) Nobita (B) Jiyan (C) None of them (D) Can't say

5. Cost of one mango is rupees 50. To find the cost of one watermelon and one mango what will you do?

   (A) Subtraction (B) Addition

   (C) Multiply (D) Insufficient information.

6) Asmita paid ₹ 20 note for a pen and got ₹ 3.50 back. How much did the pen cost?

   (A) 23.50 (B) 16.50 (C) 20.50 (D) None of these.

7. A calendar is showing 29th as the last date of the current month. Which month can it be?

   (A) December (B) May (C) March (D) February

8. Rohan read a book for 30 minutes. If he finished at 8:00 pm, at what time did he start reading the book ?

   (A) 8:30 pm (B) 8:30 am (C) 7:30 am (D) 7:30 pm

9. When the minute hand is on 8, it shows ______ minutes .

(A) 8 (B) 35 (C) 40 (D) None of these

10. A milkman sold 150 litres of milk on Monday. He sold 20 litres more than Monday on Tuesday. How much did he sell on Tuesday?

(A) 130 litres (B) 170 litre (C) 150 litres (D) None of these

11. A string 12 metres long is cut into 3 equal pieces. How long is each piece?

(A) 4 metres (B) 6 metres (C) 2 metres (D) None of these

12. Monkey, elephant and giraffe were going in an animal parade. Elephant was leading the parade. Giraffe was not at the end. Which animal was in the middle?

(A) Monkey (B) Giraffe (C) Elephant (D) None of these

13. Rishika is making friendship bands using red, blue and green ribbons. She is also using either diamonds or beads. How many different types of bands she can make?

(A) 6 (B) 7 (C) 8 (D) None of these

14. If Y means plus, X means 9, and Z means 3, then xyz =?

(A) 9 (B) 6 (C) 12 (D) None of these

15. In a cinema hall, there are 100 seats. If 23 seats are vacant, how many people are there in the hall?

(A) 123 (B) 100 (C) 77 (D) None of these

16. The minute hand is on 8 and hour hand is between 6 and 7. What time is clock showing?

(A) 8:23 (B) 6:40 (C) 8:30 (D) None of these

17. $6 \times 5 =$ ____ + 6

What is the missing number?

(A) 30 (B) 36 (C) 24 (D) None of these

18. I am an even number and one of the digit is 5. Sum of my digit is seven. Who am I?

(A) 25 (B) 52 (C) 54 (D) None of these

19. Length of a curtain for one window is 4m 50 cm and for another is 5m 30 cm. What is the total length of two curtains?

(A) 9 m 80 cm (B) 98 m 00 cm (C) 9 km 80 m (D) None of these

20. 4 more than 5 times 6 is ______

(A) 30 (B) 20 (C) 24 (D) 34

21.

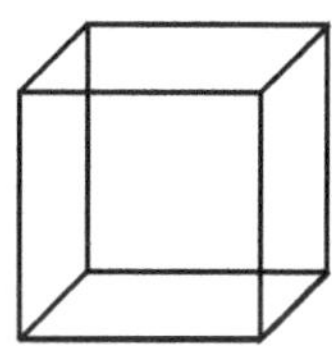

Faces of this figure are

(A) Squares and rectangles (B) Only rectangles

(C) Only squares (D) Both B and C

22. How much amount is shown here?

(A) 283 p 50 ₹ (B) 283 ₹ 50 p (C) 283 ₹ (D) None of these

23. 190 more than the smallest 3-digit number is ______

(A) 90 (B) 200 (C) 290 (D) None of these

24. 4 + 18 + 23 = ___ + 19

(A) 45 (B) 19 (C) 26 (D) None of these

25. Anushka has bought 2 dozen apples. Out of that 4 were spoilt. How many were good?

(A) 12 (B) 24 (C) 20 (D) 40

26. If one '□' means '+' then 6 □ 2 = __

(A) 8 (B) 6 (C) 2 (D) 0

27. 789 – ___ = 495

(A) 1284 (B) 294 (C) 356 (D) None of these

28. Which is not the correct equation?

(A) 20 + 20 + 20 + 202 = 262 (B) 900 – 387 = 513

(C) 285 – 0 = 0 (D) 15 + 15 + 15 + 45 + 23 = 113

29. Place value of underlined digit in $\underline{6}98$ is _____ .

(A) 6 (B) 60 (C) 600 (D) None of these

30. Mr. Shah gave 30 mangoes to his 5 sons. If each son received equal number of mangoes, how many mangoes did each of his son receive?

(A) 150 (B) 6 (C) 26 (D) None of these

31. Ten minutes past one in the afternoon means

(A) 10:01 am (B) 1:10 pm (C) 1:10 am (D) 10:01pm

32. When hour hand travels from 8 to 9, minute hand will ______ .

(A) Move from 8 to 9 (B) Complete two circles

(C) Complete one circle (D) Complete half circle

33. Here is a pattern of numbers.

2233133221

(A) KKHHAHHKKA (B) KHAKHAKH

(C) KKHHAKKHHA (D) None of these

34. 2000 m = _____ km.

(A) 20 (B) 2 (C) 22 (D) None of these

35. I am a solid with no edges or corners. Who am I?

(A) Sphere (B) Cube (C) Cubiod (D) Cone

36. 67 – 66 + 65 – 64 + 63 – 62 + 61 – 60 = _____

(A) 4 (B) 44 (C) 40 (D) None of these

37. John has 16 sweets. Mark has 4 more than John. Mark gives his sweets equally to his 4 friends. How many sweets does each of Mark's friend receive?

(A) 20 (B) 4 (C) 5 (D) None of these

38. Mrs Shauna baked 80 apple pies. She gave away 53 apple pies and put the rest equally into 9 boxes. How many apples pies were there in each box?

(A) 27 (B) 107 (C) 3 (D) None of these

39. I have 4 notes. The total value of my money is rupees 60. Here are 2 notes, and other two notes are missing. Which can be my two missing notes?

(A) 5, 10 (B) 10,10 (C) 20,10 (D) None of these

40. 170, 160, 180, 170, 190, 180, ____

(A) 190 (B) 160 (C) 170 (D) 200

...

ANSWERSHEET

1.	Ⓐ Ⓑ Ⓒ Ⓓ	2.	Ⓐ Ⓑ Ⓒ Ⓓ	3.	Ⓐ Ⓑ Ⓒ Ⓓ	4.	Ⓐ Ⓑ Ⓒ Ⓓ
5.	Ⓐ Ⓑ Ⓒ Ⓓ	6.	Ⓐ Ⓑ Ⓒ Ⓓ	7.	Ⓐ Ⓑ Ⓒ Ⓓ	8.	Ⓐ Ⓑ Ⓒ Ⓓ
9.	Ⓐ Ⓑ Ⓒ Ⓓ	10.	Ⓐ Ⓑ Ⓒ Ⓓ	11.	Ⓐ Ⓑ Ⓒ Ⓓ	12.	Ⓐ Ⓑ Ⓒ Ⓓ
13.	Ⓐ Ⓑ Ⓒ Ⓓ	14.	Ⓐ Ⓑ Ⓒ Ⓓ	15.	Ⓐ Ⓑ Ⓒ Ⓓ	16.	Ⓐ Ⓑ Ⓒ Ⓓ
17.	Ⓐ Ⓑ Ⓒ Ⓓ	18.	Ⓐ Ⓑ Ⓒ Ⓓ	19.	Ⓐ Ⓑ Ⓒ Ⓓ	20.	Ⓐ Ⓑ Ⓒ Ⓓ
21.	Ⓐ Ⓑ Ⓒ Ⓓ	22.	Ⓐ Ⓑ Ⓒ Ⓓ	23.	Ⓐ Ⓑ Ⓒ Ⓓ	24.	Ⓐ Ⓑ Ⓒ Ⓓ
25.	Ⓐ Ⓑ Ⓒ Ⓓ	26.	Ⓐ Ⓑ Ⓒ Ⓓ	27.	Ⓐ Ⓑ Ⓒ Ⓓ	28.	Ⓐ Ⓑ Ⓒ Ⓓ
29.	Ⓐ Ⓑ Ⓒ Ⓓ	30.	Ⓐ Ⓑ Ⓒ Ⓓ	31.	Ⓐ Ⓑ Ⓒ Ⓓ	32.	Ⓐ Ⓑ Ⓒ Ⓓ
33.	Ⓐ Ⓑ Ⓒ Ⓓ	34.	Ⓐ Ⓑ Ⓒ Ⓓ	35.	Ⓐ Ⓑ Ⓒ Ⓓ	36.	Ⓐ Ⓑ Ⓒ Ⓓ
37.	Ⓐ Ⓑ Ⓒ Ⓓ	38.	Ⓐ Ⓑ Ⓒ Ⓓ	39.	Ⓐ Ⓑ Ⓒ Ⓓ	40.	Ⓐ Ⓑ Ⓒ Ⓓ
41.	Ⓐ Ⓑ Ⓒ Ⓓ	42.	Ⓐ Ⓑ Ⓒ Ⓓ	43.	Ⓐ Ⓑ Ⓒ Ⓓ	44.	Ⓐ Ⓑ Ⓒ Ⓓ
45.	Ⓐ Ⓑ Ⓒ Ⓓ	46.	Ⓐ Ⓑ Ⓒ Ⓓ	47.	Ⓐ Ⓑ Ⓒ Ⓓ	48.	Ⓐ Ⓑ Ⓒ Ⓓ
49.	Ⓐ Ⓑ Ⓒ Ⓓ	50.	Ⓐ Ⓑ Ⓒ Ⓓ	51.	Ⓐ Ⓑ Ⓒ Ⓓ	52.	Ⓐ Ⓑ Ⓒ Ⓓ
53.	Ⓐ Ⓑ Ⓒ Ⓓ	54.	Ⓐ Ⓑ Ⓒ Ⓓ	55.	Ⓐ Ⓑ Ⓒ Ⓓ	56.	Ⓐ Ⓑ Ⓒ Ⓓ
57.	Ⓐ Ⓑ Ⓒ Ⓓ	58.	Ⓐ Ⓑ Ⓒ Ⓓ	59.	Ⓐ Ⓑ Ⓒ Ⓓ	60.	Ⓐ Ⓑ Ⓒ Ⓓ
61.	Ⓐ Ⓑ Ⓒ Ⓓ	62.	Ⓐ Ⓑ Ⓒ Ⓓ	63.	Ⓐ Ⓑ Ⓒ Ⓓ	64.	Ⓐ Ⓑ Ⓒ Ⓓ
65.	Ⓐ Ⓑ Ⓒ Ⓓ	66.	Ⓐ Ⓑ Ⓒ Ⓓ	67.	Ⓐ Ⓑ Ⓒ Ⓓ	68.	Ⓐ Ⓑ Ⓒ Ⓓ
69.	Ⓐ Ⓑ Ⓒ Ⓓ	70.	Ⓐ Ⓑ Ⓒ Ⓓ	71.	Ⓐ Ⓑ Ⓒ Ⓓ	72.	Ⓐ Ⓑ Ⓒ Ⓓ
73.	Ⓐ Ⓑ Ⓒ Ⓓ	74.	Ⓐ Ⓑ Ⓒ Ⓓ	75.	Ⓐ Ⓑ Ⓒ Ⓓ	76.	Ⓐ Ⓑ Ⓒ Ⓓ
77.	Ⓐ Ⓑ Ⓒ Ⓓ	78.	Ⓐ Ⓑ Ⓒ Ⓓ	79.	Ⓐ Ⓑ Ⓒ Ⓓ	80.	Ⓐ Ⓑ Ⓒ Ⓓ
81.	Ⓐ Ⓑ Ⓒ Ⓓ	82.	Ⓐ Ⓑ Ⓒ Ⓓ	83.	Ⓐ Ⓑ Ⓒ Ⓓ	84.	Ⓐ Ⓑ Ⓒ Ⓓ
85.	Ⓐ Ⓑ Ⓒ Ⓓ	86.	Ⓐ Ⓑ Ⓒ Ⓓ	87.	Ⓐ Ⓑ Ⓒ Ⓓ	88.	Ⓐ Ⓑ Ⓒ Ⓓ
89.	Ⓐ Ⓑ Ⓒ Ⓓ	90.	Ⓐ Ⓑ Ⓒ Ⓓ	91.	Ⓐ Ⓑ Ⓒ Ⓓ	92.	Ⓐ Ⓑ Ⓒ Ⓓ
93.	Ⓐ Ⓑ Ⓒ Ⓓ	94.	Ⓐ Ⓑ Ⓒ Ⓓ	95.	Ⓐ Ⓑ Ⓒ Ⓓ	96.	Ⓐ Ⓑ Ⓒ Ⓓ
97.	Ⓐ Ⓑ Ⓒ Ⓓ	98.	Ⓐ Ⓑ Ⓒ Ⓓ	99.	Ⓐ Ⓑ Ⓒ Ⓓ	100.	Ⓐ Ⓑ Ⓒ Ⓓ

Paper II

1. In a school bus there are 25 students, 2 teachers, and one driver. Total number of eyes in the bus are ____

   (A) 28 (B) 82 (C) 56 (D) none of these

2. Rohan scored 50 more marks than Yash. If Yash scored 34 marks, how much did Rohan score?

   (A) 54 (B) 84 (C) 16 (D) None of these

3. Find the values of P and Q respectively.

   43 – 9 = P – 7 = Q

   (A) 34,27 (B) 27,34 (C) 34,41 (D) None of these

4. I am more than 84-17 and less than 67 + 23. What number am I ?

   (A) 67 (B) 90 (C) 72 (D) None of these

5. Difference between the greatest three digit number and greatest one digit number is ____

   (A) 999 (B) 9 (C) 990 (D) None of these

6. Which of the following will be the next number in the given series?

   2, 12, 32, 62, 102, 152, ____

   (A) 221 (B) 212 (C) 112 (D) None of these

7. In an aeroplane, the business class can fetch 14 passengers while economy class can fetch 12 passengers. How many passengers can 9 such aeroplanes fetch?

   (A) 26 (B) 234 (C) 243 (D) None of these

8. 638 km + _____ = 946 km – 234 km

The missing distance is _______.

(A) 712 (B) 721 (C) 74 (D) None of these

9. 63 marbles are put equally into 9 boxes. There are _______ marbles in each boxes.

(A) 567 (B) 7 (C) 72 (D) 54

10. What is the missing number given below?

$4 + 4 + 4 + 4 + 4 + 4 + 3 = \_\_ \times 9$

(A) 24 (B) 27 (C) 3 (D) None of these

11. How many months in a year have 30 days?

(A) 7 (B) 5 (C) 4 (D) None of these

12. In which number sentence does 6 make the equation true?

(A) $60 \div \_\_ = 6$ (B) $24 \div \_\_ = 8$

(C) $36 \div \_\_ = 6$ (D) $42 \div \_\_ = 6$

13. Poonam wants to place 6 dots along each side of this given figure. Identity the least number of dots she needs

(A) 6 (B) 12 (C) 24 (D) 36

14. A jar contains 19 sweets, 4 chocolates, 14 candies and 9 lollipops. If Ahan pulls out one thing from the jar, which will least likely come out of it?

(A) Lollipops (B) Candies (C) Sweets (D) Chocolates

15. Observe the following sequences.

9, 18, 27, 36, 45, ____

Which is the 9th number in the sequence?

(A) 54 (B) 55 (C) 81 (D) None of these

16. I am a three digit number between 100 and 999. Also my digits are same and product of my digits is 27. What number am I ?

(A) 666 (B) 999 (C) 333 (D) 222

17.

□ + □ = 14, ○ + □ = 16, then ○ = ____

(A) 7 (B) 9 (C) Both A and B (D) None of these

18. If today is Monday, then what day was it the day before yesterday?

(A) Sunday (B) Friday (C) Tuesday (D) Saturday

19.

562	489	73

?	273	149

Follow the pattern of figure -1 to find the missing number in figure - 2.

(A) 422 (B) 124 (C) 4220 (D) None of these

20.  [aeroplane] and [phone] cost ₹ 847 . If [aeroplane] is for ₹ 578, how much is [phone] ?

(A) 269 (B) 1425 (C) 296 (D) None of these

21. Mohan bought 36 carrots. He tied them into bundles of 6 each. How many bundles of carrot does he have?

(A) 42 (B) 30 (C) 6 (D) none of these

22. How many tens are there in 230?

(A) 30 (B) 10 (C) 3 (D) 20

23. 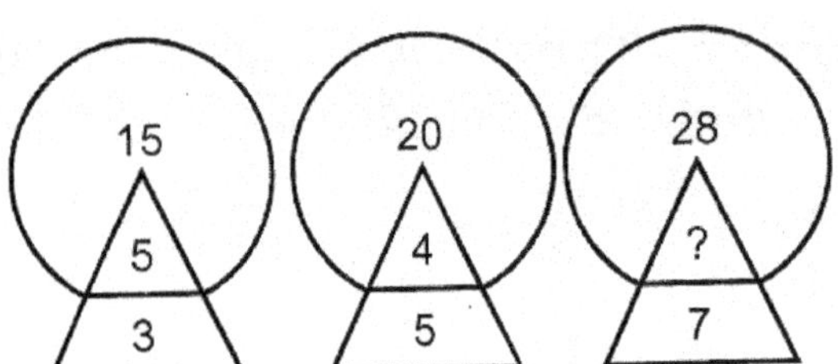

Find the missing number .

(A) 3 (B) 4 (C) 6 (D) 7

24. Sanjay has red and green shirts. He has blue, brown and black pants. In how many ways he can select the outfits ?

(A) 5 (B) 6 (C) 7 (D) 4

25. Find the odd one out.

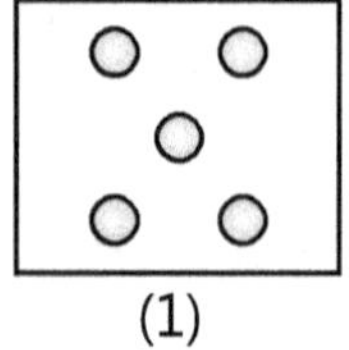
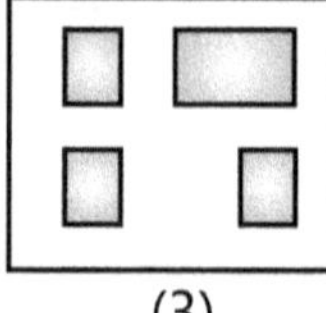
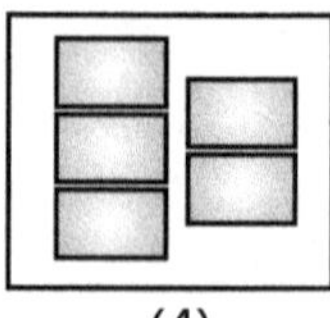

(1) (2) (3) (4)

(A) 1 and 2 (B) only 3 (C) 3 and 4 (D) both a and b

26.

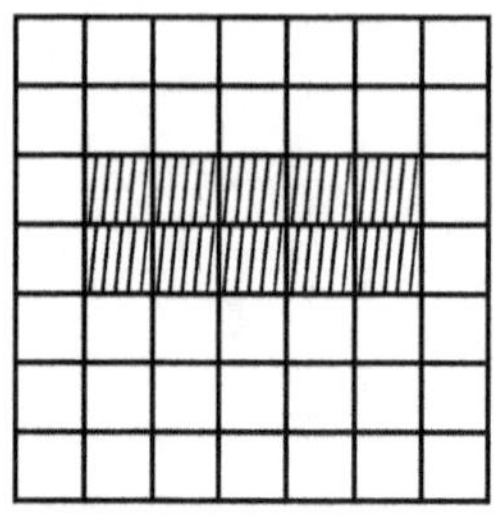

Each square in the grid is 1m long. What is the length of the rectangle made by joining 10 such squares as shown in the figure?

(A) 1m (B) 10m (C) 5m (D) both b and c

Direction for question 27 to 31.

Seema has these notes and coins.

27. To buy a toy of the ₹ 53, she gave one note and one coin. Is it possible.

    (A) No (B) Yes

    (C) Can't say (D) Insufficient information

28. Which coins and notes will Seema give to buy a doll for ₹ 33 and a bat for ₹ 41 ?

    (A) ₹ 50, ₹ 10 ₹ 2, ₹ 1, 50 paise coin, 50 paise coin.

    (B) ₹ 20, ₹ 10, ₹ 1, ₹1

    (C) ₹ 50, ₹ 20, ₹ 2, ₹ 1, 50 paise coin, 50 paise coin

    (D) ₹ 20, ₹ 50, ₹ 1, ₹ 2

29. What is the total amount shown here?

    (A) 100 (B) 90 (C) 89 (D) None of these

30.Seema has Rs 90. Her dad gave her one coin. Now the amount she has is ₹ 100. Which is that coin?

    (A) 5 (B) 10 (C) 20 (D) 50

31. Seema wants to buy a book of ₹ 183, she has 100 rupees. How much more does she need?

    (A) 80 (B) 83 (C) 283 (D) None of these

32. Shriya's Olympiad class starts at 4:15 p.m. It lasts for 45 minutes. At what time class will end?

    (A) 4 p.m. (B) 5 a.m. (C) 5 p.m. (D) 4:45 p.m.

Direction (Q. 33 to 35)

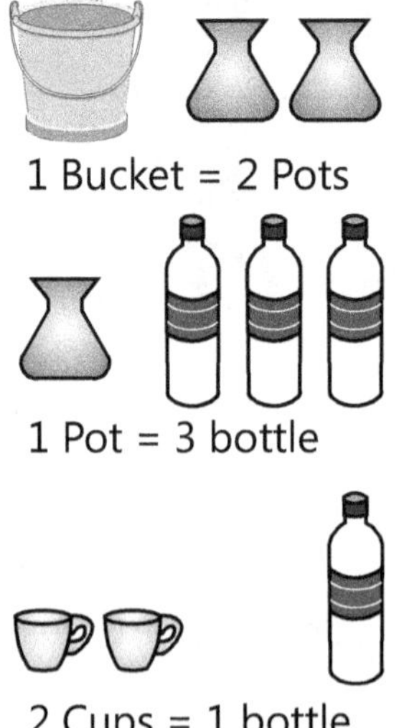

33. Bucket can hold water from _____ bottles.

(A) 4 (B) 3 (C) 5 (D) 6

34. To fill one pot how many cups of water is needed?

(A) 4 (B) 3 (C) 5 (D) 6

35. Whose capacity is the maximum?

(A) Bottle (B) Cup (C) Bucket (D) Pot

36. There were 600 students in the canteen during recess. When the bell rang 280 students returned to class while a few ones entered the canteen. If there were 380 students still in the canteen after recess, how many students entered the canteen when the bell rang ?

(A) 320 (B) 60 (C) 40 (D) None of these

37. Reena has 73 pencils. Rita has 48 pencils more than Reena. How many pencils are there altogether ?

(A) 194 (B) 157 (C) 121 (D) None of these

38. Mohan painted a pole completely red and green. The red part is 35m. The green part 15m shorter than the red part. What is the height of the pole?

    (A) 20 m (B) 50 m (C) 55 (D) None of these

39. There are 20 flowers in a bunch. Ram has 6 bunches and Sham has 4 bunches. How many flowers are there in all?

    (A) 120 (B) 80 (C) 200 (D) None of these

40. Ramsingh has 88 balls. He sold 51 balls. Which of the statements given below is true ?

    (A) He sold less than half of the balls.

    (B) He sold more than half of the balls.

    (C) He sold exactly half his balls.

    (D) He sold one fourth of his ball

...

ANSWERSHEET

1.	Ⓐ Ⓑ Ⓒ Ⓓ	2.	Ⓐ Ⓑ Ⓒ Ⓓ	3.	Ⓐ Ⓑ Ⓒ Ⓓ	4.	Ⓐ Ⓑ Ⓒ Ⓓ
5.	Ⓐ Ⓑ Ⓒ Ⓓ	6.	Ⓐ Ⓑ Ⓒ Ⓓ	7.	Ⓐ Ⓑ Ⓒ Ⓓ	8.	Ⓐ Ⓑ Ⓒ Ⓓ
9.	Ⓐ Ⓑ Ⓒ Ⓓ	10.	Ⓐ Ⓑ Ⓒ Ⓓ	11.	Ⓐ Ⓑ Ⓒ Ⓓ	12.	Ⓐ Ⓑ Ⓒ Ⓓ
13.	Ⓐ Ⓑ Ⓒ Ⓓ	14.	Ⓐ Ⓑ Ⓒ Ⓓ	15.	Ⓐ Ⓑ Ⓒ Ⓓ	16.	Ⓐ Ⓑ Ⓒ Ⓓ
17.	Ⓐ Ⓑ Ⓒ Ⓓ	18.	Ⓐ Ⓑ Ⓒ Ⓓ	19.	Ⓐ Ⓑ Ⓒ Ⓓ	20.	Ⓐ Ⓑ Ⓒ Ⓓ
21.	Ⓐ Ⓑ Ⓒ Ⓓ	22.	Ⓐ Ⓑ Ⓒ Ⓓ	23.	Ⓐ Ⓑ Ⓒ Ⓓ	24.	Ⓐ Ⓑ Ⓒ Ⓓ
25.	Ⓐ Ⓑ Ⓒ Ⓓ	26.	Ⓐ Ⓑ Ⓒ Ⓓ	27.	Ⓐ Ⓑ Ⓒ Ⓓ	28.	Ⓐ Ⓑ Ⓒ Ⓓ
29.	Ⓐ Ⓑ Ⓒ Ⓓ	30.	Ⓐ Ⓑ Ⓒ Ⓓ	31.	Ⓐ Ⓑ Ⓒ Ⓓ	32.	Ⓐ Ⓑ Ⓒ Ⓓ
33.	Ⓐ Ⓑ Ⓒ Ⓓ	34.	Ⓐ Ⓑ Ⓒ Ⓓ	35.	Ⓐ Ⓑ Ⓒ Ⓓ	36.	Ⓐ Ⓑ Ⓒ Ⓓ
37.	Ⓐ Ⓑ Ⓒ Ⓓ	38.	Ⓐ Ⓑ Ⓒ Ⓓ	39.	Ⓐ Ⓑ Ⓒ Ⓓ	40.	Ⓐ Ⓑ Ⓒ Ⓓ
41.	Ⓐ Ⓑ Ⓒ Ⓓ	42.	Ⓐ Ⓑ Ⓒ Ⓓ	43.	Ⓐ Ⓑ Ⓒ Ⓓ	44.	Ⓐ Ⓑ Ⓒ Ⓓ
45.	Ⓐ Ⓑ Ⓒ Ⓓ	46.	Ⓐ Ⓑ Ⓒ Ⓓ	47.	Ⓐ Ⓑ Ⓒ Ⓓ	48.	Ⓐ Ⓑ Ⓒ Ⓓ
49.	Ⓐ Ⓑ Ⓒ Ⓓ	50.	Ⓐ Ⓑ Ⓒ Ⓓ	51.	Ⓐ Ⓑ Ⓒ Ⓓ	52.	Ⓐ Ⓑ Ⓒ Ⓓ
53.	Ⓐ Ⓑ Ⓒ Ⓓ	54.	Ⓐ Ⓑ Ⓒ Ⓓ	55.	Ⓐ Ⓑ Ⓒ Ⓓ	56.	Ⓐ Ⓑ Ⓒ Ⓓ
57.	Ⓐ Ⓑ Ⓒ Ⓓ	58.	Ⓐ Ⓑ Ⓒ Ⓓ	59.	Ⓐ Ⓑ Ⓒ Ⓓ	60.	Ⓐ Ⓑ Ⓒ Ⓓ
61.	Ⓐ Ⓑ Ⓒ Ⓓ	62.	Ⓐ Ⓑ Ⓒ Ⓓ	63.	Ⓐ Ⓑ Ⓒ Ⓓ	64.	Ⓐ Ⓑ Ⓒ Ⓓ
65.	Ⓐ Ⓑ Ⓒ Ⓓ	66.	Ⓐ Ⓑ Ⓒ Ⓓ	67.	Ⓐ Ⓑ Ⓒ Ⓓ	68.	Ⓐ Ⓑ Ⓒ Ⓓ
69.	Ⓐ Ⓑ Ⓒ Ⓓ	70.	Ⓐ Ⓑ Ⓒ Ⓓ	71.	Ⓐ Ⓑ Ⓒ Ⓓ	72.	Ⓐ Ⓑ Ⓒ Ⓓ
73.	Ⓐ Ⓑ Ⓒ Ⓓ	74.	Ⓐ Ⓑ Ⓒ Ⓓ	75.	Ⓐ Ⓑ Ⓒ Ⓓ	76.	Ⓐ Ⓑ Ⓒ Ⓓ
77.	Ⓐ Ⓑ Ⓒ Ⓓ	78.	Ⓐ Ⓑ Ⓒ Ⓓ	79.	Ⓐ Ⓑ Ⓒ Ⓓ	80.	Ⓐ Ⓑ Ⓒ Ⓓ
81.	Ⓐ Ⓑ Ⓒ Ⓓ	82.	Ⓐ Ⓑ Ⓒ Ⓓ	83.	Ⓐ Ⓑ Ⓒ Ⓓ	84.	Ⓐ Ⓑ Ⓒ Ⓓ
85.	Ⓐ Ⓑ Ⓒ Ⓓ	86.	Ⓐ Ⓑ Ⓒ Ⓓ	87.	Ⓐ Ⓑ Ⓒ Ⓓ	88.	Ⓐ Ⓑ Ⓒ Ⓓ
89.	Ⓐ Ⓑ Ⓒ Ⓓ	90.	Ⓐ Ⓑ Ⓒ Ⓓ	91.	Ⓐ Ⓑ Ⓒ Ⓓ	92.	Ⓐ Ⓑ Ⓒ Ⓓ
93.	Ⓐ Ⓑ Ⓒ Ⓓ	94.	Ⓐ Ⓑ Ⓒ Ⓓ	95.	Ⓐ Ⓑ Ⓒ Ⓓ	96.	Ⓐ Ⓑ Ⓒ Ⓓ
97.	Ⓐ Ⓑ Ⓒ Ⓓ	98.	Ⓐ Ⓑ Ⓒ Ⓓ	99.	Ⓐ Ⓑ Ⓒ Ⓓ	100.	Ⓐ Ⓑ Ⓒ Ⓓ

EXPLANATION

Chapter 1 : Number Sense

1. B. 458

2. A. Seven hundred and ninety three.

3. C. 602

   6 hundred means 6 in hundreds place and 2 means 2 in ones place. Nothing in tens place.

   H T O

   6 0 2

4. D. 800

   In 846, number 8 is in hundreds place so 800.

5. A. Tens.

6. B. 3 is in ones place.

7. C. 888

   800 means 8 in hundreds place, 80 means 8 in tens place and 8 means 8 in ones place.

8. D. 7

9. C. 942

   H T O

   9 4 2

10. A. 40

    546 = 500 + x + 6

    Expanded form of 546 is 500 + 40 + 6 Replace x with 40.

11. B. 9

    192 = 1 hundred + ____ tens + 2 ones.

    192 = 100 + 90 + 2

    90 means 9 tens

12. C.

13. B. 3

    900 + 40 + 3

14. B. 149

    To make the smallest three digit number arrange the number in ascending order.

    Arrange 4 1 9 in ascending order. It is 149.

15. A. 923. Read the numbers carefully.

16. C. 764

17. C. Read the numbers carefully.

18. B. 2000 + 300 + 6

    Th, H T O

    2, 3 0 6

    Nothing in tens place, so we write 0 in tens place.

19. A.

8 tens	2 ones

    – 6 tens = [ ]

    Means 82 – 60 = 22

20. D. 416

Read the numbers carefully.

21. A

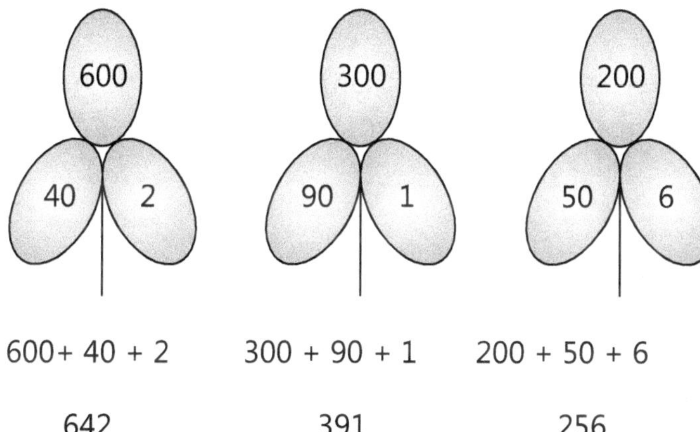

600+ 40 + 2   300 + 90 + 1   200 + 50 + 6

642   391   256

22. D. 101

Smallest three digit number is 100. One more than 100 is 100 + 1 = 101.

23. B. 99

Largest two digit number is 99.

24. A. 10

Smallest two digit number is 10.

25. B. 999

Largest three-digit number is 999. (highest, greatest, biggest, largest means the same)

26. C. 100

Smallest three digit number is 100 (smallest, least, lowest means the some).

27. B. 9

Largest one- digit number is 9.

28. C. 38

    The number says that, "I am a two digit number". (All the numbers are two digit.)

    Then it says,"I have 8 in ones place". (88, 38, 28, 78 have 8 in ones place.)

    Then it says,"I am less than 40, I am more than 30". (Means the number is between 30 and 40. Only 38 comes between 30 and 40)

29. A. 359

    The number says that,"I am a 3 digit number". (All the numbers are three digit numbers.)

    Then it says, "I have 5 in tens place". (153, 359, 451 have 5 in tens place)

    Then it says,"I am less than 360 and more than 350". (Means the number is between 350 and 360. Only 359 is between 350 and 360 and with 5 in tens place)

30. C. 760- 756

    Option A. 468- 466 = 2

    Option B. 394-392 = 2

    Option C. 760 - 756 = 4

    Option D. 214- 212 = 2

31. D.

    Option A. 455- 450 = 5

    Option B. 870-865 = 5

    Option C. 220 - 215 = 5

    Option D. 284- 186 = 98

32. A.

    2 hundred eighty six means 286

33. C.

    287, 288, 289, 290

34. A. 50 and 30

    It's a balancing scale where both the sides should have same number. 50 and 30 means 50 + 30 = 80 on right hand side and 80 on left hand side is given.

35. A. 52 and 40

    It's a balancing scale where both the sides should have the same number. 52 and 40 means 52 + 40 = 92 on right hand side and 92 on left hand side is already given.

36. B. 474

37. A. 666

38. B. 06.

    In the number 486, 6 is in ones place. 06 means 6.

39. B. 90

    In the number 392, 9 is in tens place. So 9 tens = 90.

40. C. 248

    Arrange as the smallest three digit number means arrange the digits in ascending order.

41. A. <

    Eight hundred and two [<] 828

    (802)

42. A.

More than 16 tens means more than 160. Only 168 is more than 160.

43. B. 202

More than 20 tens means more than 200. Only 202 is more than 200.

44. B. 316

Number more than 300 but less than 400, means the number is between 300 and 400. Only 316 is between 300 and 400

45. B. 400

399 comes before 400

46. B. 444

400 + 40 + 4 = 444

47. C. 424

There are four beads in hundreds place so 400.

There are two beads in tens place so 20.

here are four beads in ones place so 4.

48. C.

Observe the numbers carefully. Compare hundreds place then tens place and then ones place of each number and put the correct sign.

49. B. Observe the numbers carefully.

50. B. A pencil

You can measure objects shorter than 20 cm with your scale.

51. C. both (A) & (B)

500 ones means 500. Option A. 50 tens = 500.

Option B. 5 hundred = 500.

52. A. 800

800 ones means 800 only.

53. A. 60

6 tens means 60

60 tens means 600

6 ones means 6

54. B. 40

4 tens means 40

44 ones means 44

55. A. 80

Expanded form of 486 = 400 + 80 + 6.

So replace B with 80.

56. C. 300

Expanded form of 392 = 300 + 90 + 2

Replace A with 300

57. C. 10

Largest one digit number is 9. One more than 9 means 9 + 1 = 10.

58. B. 100

Largest two digit number = 99. One more than 99 means 99 + 1 = 100.

...

Chapter 2 : Computation Operation

1. B. 406- 220.

   Number of stamps Reema has = 406. It is 220 more than Seema.

   So to find out how many stamps Seema has, we need to subtract.

2. C. 518- 346.

   Number of stamps Maya has = 518. It is 346 more than Jaya. So to find out how many stamps Jaya has we need to subtract.

3. D. None of these

   Number of papers Radhika has = 814. It is 179 more than Anamika. So to find out how many papers Anamika has we need to subtract. Option C. shows subtraction, but the number is different.

   It should have been 814- 179 but it is 814- 178

4. C. 121

   Rule : If any of the addend is missing we subtract the another addend from the sum.

   ☐ Addend 1

   + 422 Addend 2

   543 = Sum of two numbers

   543 – 422 = 121

5. C. 427

   Rule : If any of the addend is missing we subtract the another addend from the sum.

	$\square$	Addend 1
+	473	Addend 2

900 = Sum of two numbers

900 – 473 = 427

6. C. 755

Rule : If any of the addend is missing we subtract the another addend from the sum.

	$\square$	Addend 1
+	141	Addend 2

896 = Sum of two numbers

896 – 141 = 755

7. B. 3

Option A. 4 + 4 + 4 = 12 or 4 × 3 = 12 (incorrect)

Option B. 3 + 3 + 3 = 9 or 3 × 3 = 9 (correct)

Option C. 2 + 2 + 2 = 6 or 2 × 3 = 6 (incorrect)

Option D. 5 + 5 + 5 = 15 or 5 × 3 = 15 (incorrect)

Another way

✿ + ✿ + ✿ =9. Flower is added 3 times. Remember multiplication is easier than repeated addition.

So 3 × ? = 9 . 3 × 3 = 9

8. C. 5

Option A. 4 + 4 + 4 + 4 = 16 or $4 \times 4 = 16$ (incorrect)

Option B. 2 + 2 + 2 + 2 = 8 or $2 \times 4 = 8$ (incorrect)

Option C. 5 + 5 + 5 + 5 = 20 or $5 \times 4 = 20$ (correct)

Another way

☐ + ☐ + ☐ + ☐ = 20 (instead of adding the same number 4 times we multiply it) Remember multiplication is easier than repeated addition.

$4 \times ? = 20$. $4 \times 5 = 20$

9. C. 4

Option A. 8 + 8 = 16 or $8 \times 2 = 16$ (incorrect)

Option B. 2 + 2 = 4 or $2 \times 2 = 4$ (incorrect)

Option C. 4 + 4 = 8 or $4 \times 2 = 8$ (correct)

10. C. 20

Rule : If the dividend is missing we multiply divisor and quotient.

Divide the number by 4 and result is 5, means dividend is missing, 4 is a divisor and result 5 is a quotient.

____ ÷ 4 = 5

So $4 \times 5 = 20$

Let's check 20 ÷ 4 = 5

11. C. 18

Rule : If the dividend is missing we multiply divisor and quotient.

Divide the number by 3 and result is 6, means dividend is missing, 3 is a divisor and result 6 is a quotient.

___ ÷ 3 = 6

So 3 × 6 = 18

Let's check **18** ÷ 3 = 6

12. C. 45

Rule : If the dividend is missing we multiply the divisor and the quotient.

Divide the number by 5 and result is 9, means dividend is missing, 5 is a divisor and result 9 is a quotient.

___ ÷ 5 = 9

So 5 × 9 = 45

Let's check 45 ÷ 5 = 9

13. C. 3

Rule : If multiplicand is missing we divide the product by multiplier . If multiplier is missing we divide the product by multiplicand.

Multiply a number by 6 and the number you get is 18 means.

Multiplicand is missing.

6 is a multiplier.

18 is a product

___ x 6 = 18

So 18 ÷ 6 = **3** OR 3 × 6 = 18

14. B. 6

Rule : If multiplicand is missing we divide the product by multiplier. If multiplier is missing we divide the product by the multiplicand.

Multiply a number by 5 and the number you get is 30 means.

Multiplicand is missing.

5 is a multiplier.

30 is a product.

$\_\_\_ \times 5 = 30$

So $30 \div 5 = 6$ OR $6 \times 5 = 30$

15. A. 5

Rule : If multiplicand is missing we divide the product by multiplier . If multiplier is missing we divide the product by the multiplicand.

Multiply a number by 2 and the number you get is 10 means.

Multiplicand is missing.

2 is a multiplier.

10 is a product.

$\_\_\_ \times 2 = 10$

So $10 \div 2 = 5$ OR $5 \times 2 = 10$

16. C. 2

$20 \times ? = 10 + 30$. First solve the right hand side of the equal to sign.

$20 \times ? = 40$

$20 \times 2 = 40$

17. C. 4

$5 \times ? = 15 + 5$. First solve the right hand side of the equal to sign.

$5 \times ? = 20$

$5 \times 4 = 20$

18. B. 8

$2 \times ? = 9 + 7$. First solve the right hand side of the equal to sign.

$2 \times ? = 16$

$2 \times 8 = 16$

19. C. 3

$? \times 7 = 15 + 6$. First solve the right hand side of the equal to sign.

$? \times 7 = 21$

$3 \times 7 = 21$

20. B. 3

$30 \div ? = 2 \times 5$. First solve the right hand side of the equal to sign.

$30 \div ? = 10$.

Rule : In a division sum if the divisor is missing, we divide dividend by quotient.

So $30 \div 10 = 3$

$30 \div 3 = 10$

21. C. 2

$40 \div ? = 4 \times 5$. First solve the right hand side of the equal to sign.

$40 \div ? = 20$.

Rule : In a division sum if the divisor is missing, we divide dividend by the quotient.

So $40 \div 20 = 2$

$40 \div 2 = 20$

22. D. $8 - 4 = 4$

$4 \times 8 = 32$ not 36.

$4 \div 8 = 2$ is not possible. Always greater number (dividend) is divided by the smaller number (divisor)

$4 + 8 = 12$ not 8

$8 - 4 = 4$ (correct)

23. B. B

6×3	$125 + 6$	$85 \div 5$	16×7
A	B	C	D
18	131	17	112

B is the maximum (means greatest) = 131.

24. B. B

9×8	$200 + 12$	$82 \div 2$	$201 - 3$
A	B	C	D
72	212	41	198

B is the maximum (means greatest) = 212.

25. D. $490 - 246$

Total number of students in a school		= 490
Number of girls in a school	−	= 246
Number of boys in a school		244

From the total number of students remove number of girls to get the number of boys.

26. D. 840- 492

Total number of passengers in a train	= 840
Number of men in the train	− 492
Number of women in the train	348

From the total number of passengers remove number of men to get number of women.

27. C. 340 pages

Number of pages needed for writing	= 800
Number of pages he had	− 460
Number of pages to be bought	340

Key words for subtraction : how many more, how many less, how many left, difference .

From the total number of pages that are needed remove the pages that he had.

28. C.

Observe carefully.

Option A : balls are distributed equally but there are 9 balls .

Option B : 12 balls are distributed equally but there are 2 children .

Option C : 12 balls are equally distributed among 4 children.

$12 \div 4 = 3$. So each child will get 3 balls. (1 box represents 1 child)

29. C.

Option A : there are 8 balloons but they are not distributed equally.

Option B : there are only 7 balloons.

Option C : there are 8 balloons equally distributed among 2 children.

$8 \div 2 = 4$. So each child will get 4 balloons. (1 box represents one child)

30. B. 85

To find out how many cakes he baked, we need to add the cakes he sold and the cakes left.

Number of cakes he sold	= 80
Number of cakes left	+ 5
Total number of cakes he baked	85

31. C. 36

Total number of eggs	= 200
Number of eggs broken	– 164
Number of unbroken eggs	36

From the total eggs remove the broken eggs to find out how many unbroken eggs were left.

32. B. 885

396 + 489 = 885 (sum means addition)

33. B. 592

348 more than 244 means

348 + 244 = 592

34. B. 300

70 tens means 700, 10 hundred means 1,000 . Now read the question again.

What must be added to 700 to make 1,000 ?

700	Addend 1
+ ____	Addend 2
1,000	Sum

Rule : If any of the addend is missing we subtract the another addend from the sum.

So 1,000 – 700 = 300

Let's check

$$\begin{array}{r} 700 \\ +\ 300 \\ \hline 1{,}000 \end{array}$$

35. B.

60 tens means 600 and 90 tens means 900.

Now read the question again.

What must be added to 600 to make 900 ?

600 Addend 1

+ ____ Addend 2

900 Sum

Rule : If any of the addend is missing we subtract the another addend from the sum.

So 900 – 600 = 300

Let's check

$$\begin{array}{r} 600 \\ +\ 300 \\ \hline 900 \end{array}$$

36. B. 60 tens

20 tens means 200 and 80 tens means 800.

Now read the question again.

What must be added to 200 to make 800 ?

200	Addend 1
+ ____	Addend 2
800	Sum

Rule : If any of the addend is missing we subtract the another addend from the sum.

So 800- 200 = 600

Let's check

$$\begin{array}{r} 200 \\ +\ 600 \\ \hline 800 \end{array}$$

37. B. 10- 4 = 6

There are 10 ball. 4 balls are cancelled. So 6 balls are left.

10 – 4 = 6

38. B. 11- 3 = 8

There are 11 triangles. 3 triangles are cancelled. So 8 triangles are left.

11 – 3 = 8

39. A. 108

Number of stamps Radhika has = 208. It is 100 more than Radha. So to find out how many stamps Radha has we need to subtract.

208 – 100 = 108

40. B. 35

Number of pens Mohan has = 50. It is 15 more than Sohan. So to find out how many pens Sohan has we need to subtract.

50 – 15 = 35

41. C. 40 -12

Number of story books Ramesh has = 40. It is 12 more than Sham. So to find out how many story books Sham has we need to subtract.

42. A. 300

Rule : If any of the addend is missing we subtract the another addend from the sum.

☐ Addend 1

+ 200 Addend 2

500 = Sum of two numbers

500 – 200 = 300

Let's check

300 + 200 = 500

43. C. 272

Rule : If any of the addend is missing we subtract the another addend from the sum.

☐ Addend 1

+ 178 Addend 2

450 = Sum of two numbers

450 – 178 = 272

Let's check

272 + 178 = 450

44. A. 4

Always starting solving from the right hand side or ones place.

So 3+ 1 = 4, 4 + 4 = 8, 5 + 1 = 6

45. B. 6

Always starting solving from the right hand side .

So 3 + 4 = 7, 2 + 6 = 8, 3 + 6 = 9

46. A. 2

Option A : 2 + 2 + 2 = 6 OR 2 × 3 = 6 (correct)

Option B : 3 + 3 + 3 = 9 OR 3 × 3 = 9 (incorrect)

Option C : 4 + 4 + 4 = 12 OR 4 × 3 = 12 (incorrect)

Another way

Flower is added 3 times.(Instead of adding the same number 3 times we multiply.) **Remember multiplication is easier than repeated addition.**

3 × ___ = 6

3 × **2** = 6

47. A. 4

Option A : 4 + 4 + 4 = 12 OR 4 X 3 = 12 (correct)

Option B : 3 + 3 + 3 = 9 OR 3 X 3 = 9 (incorrect)

Option C : 5 + 5 + 5 = 15 OR 5 x 3 = 15 (incorrect)

Another way

+ + + = 12.

Flower is added 3 times. (Instead of adding the same number 3 times we multiply.) **Remember :Multiplication is easier than repeated addition.**

$3 \times \_\_\_ = 12$

$3 \times \underline{\mathbf{4}} = 12$

48. A. 6

Always starting solving from the right hand side or ones place.

$9 - \_\_\_ = 3$, $9 - 6 = 3$ OR (Rule : If subtrahend is missing we subtract the difference from minuend. Here 9 is minuend and 3 is difference.) 9 - 3 = **6**.

Let's check : $9 - \underline{\mathbf{6}} = 3$

$4 - 3 = 1$, $8 - 3 = 5$

49. A. 3

Always starting solving from the right hand side or ones place.

$8 - 1 = 7$,

$5 - \_\_\_ = 2$ $(5 - \boxed{3} = 2)$

$5 - 4 = 1$

50. C. 4×5

There are 5 boxes, each box has 4 triangles. So to find out how many triangles are there we either add 4 triangles 5 times or we multiply 4×5.

Remember : Multiplication is easier than repeated addition.

OR

Option A : 4×6 (incorrect) as there are 5 boxes not 6 boxes

Option B : 7×6 (incorrect) there are neither 7 boxes or triangles nor 6 boxes or triangles.

51. A. 5

Rahul is putting 30 balls equally in 6 boxes. To find out how many balls are there in each box we divide

Number of balls = 30

Number of boxes = 6

Each box has 5 balls.

52. B. $10 \div 2 = 5$

There are 10 triangles. Each group has two triangles. To find out number of groups we will divide 10 by 2

53. B. 8×2

Read the question carefully. We know one jar has 2 beads and there are 8 such jars. To find out how many beads are there in all we multiply.

Number of jars Ram has = 8

Number of beads each jar has = 2

So $8 \times 2 = 16$

54. C. 546 - 249

Total number of students in the school = 546

– Number of boys – 249

From the total number of students 546, remove number of boys 249 to get the number girls.

55. B. $3 + 8 = 12$

We have to search for incorrect statement.

Option A: $3 \times 8 = 24$ (correct)

Option B: $3 + 8 = 12$ (incorrect) $3 + 8 = 11$ not 12

Option C: $8 \times 2 = 16$ (correct)

Option D: $8 + 2 = 10$ (correct)

56. B. 270

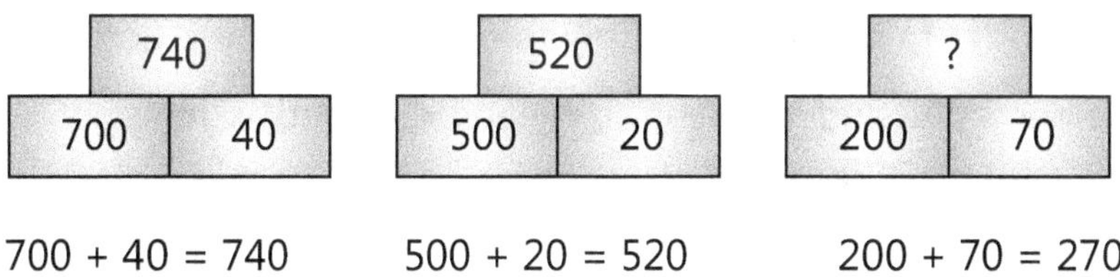

700 + 40 = 740 500 + 20 = 520 200 + 70 = 270

57. C. ÷

24 ÷ 6 = 4

Option A: 24 × 6 = 144 (not 4)

Option B: 24 + 6 = 30(not 4)

Option C: 24 ÷ 6 = 4 (correct)

Option D: 24 – 6 = 18 (not 4)

58. C.

3 × 9	30 ÷ 5	35 × 4	100 + 5
A	B	C	D
27	6	140	105

59. A. 18

Rule : If the dividend is missing we multiply the divisor and the quotient.

Divide the number by 2 and the result is 9, means dividend is missing, 2 is a divisor and result 9 is a quotient.

___ ÷ 2 = 9

So 2 × 9 = 18

Let's check 18 ÷ 2 = 9

60. C. 24

Rule : If the dividend is missing we multiply the divisor and the quotient.

Divide the number by 4 and result is 6, means dividend is missing, 4 is a divisor and the result 6 is a quotient.

___ ÷ 4 = 6

So 4 × 6 = **24**

Let's check **24** ÷ 4 = 6

61. D. 25

It's 5 times table.

62. D. 9

Rule : If multiplicand is missing we divide the product by the multiplier. If multiplier is missing we divide the product by the multiplicand.

Multiply a number by 5 and the number you get is 45 means

multiplicand is missing.

5 is the multiplier.

45 is a product

___ × 5 = 45

So 45 ÷ 5 = **9** OR **9** x 5 = 45

63. B. 5

Rule: If multiplicand is missing we divide the product by the multiplier. If multiplier is missing we divide the product by the multiplicand.

Multiply a number by 4 and the number you get is 20 means.

multiplicand is missing.

4 is the multiplier.

20 is the product

___ × 4 = 20

So 20 ÷ 4 = **5** OR **5** x 4 = 20

64. B. 7

$10 \times ? = \underline{\mathbf{30 + 40}}$. First solve the right hand side of the equal to sign.

$10 \times ? = 70$

$10 \times \underline{\mathbf{7}} = 70$

65. C. 10

$5 \times ? = \underline{\mathbf{20 + 30}}$. First solve the right hand side of the equal to sign.

$5 \times ? = 50$

$5 \times \underline{\mathbf{10}} = 50$

66. A. 10

Taking 200 away from 210 means remove 200 from 210. OR subtraction 210 – 200 = 10.

67. C. 2

6 hundred means 600.

Taking away 600 from 602 means remove 600 from 602. 602 – 600 = 2.

68. 3×5

3 is added 5 times. **Multiplication is easier than repeated addition.**

69. D. None of these

4 is added 5 times. **Multiplication is easier than repeated addition**.

So $4 \times 5 = 20$.

70. B. 445

100 more than sum of 144 and 201 (sum means addition) To the sum of 144 and 201 add 100 . OR add 144, 201, 100

H T 0

1 4 4

+ 2 0 1

+ 1 0 0

4 4 5

71. B. 10

How many fives means 5 times table. $5 \times$ ___

Sum of 25 and 25 means $25 + 25 = 50$

So. $5 \times$ ___ $= 50$

$5 \times \underline{\mathbf{10}} = 50$

72. C. 8

How many fives means 5 times table. $5 \times$ ___

Sum of 15 and 25 means $15 + 25 = 40$

So, $5 \times$ ___ $= 40$

$5 \times \underline{\mathbf{8}} = 50$

73. A. 528

100 more than sum of 182 and 346(sum means addition) To the sum of 182 and 346 add 100 . OR add 182, 346, 100

H T 0

1 8 2

+ 3 4 6

+ 1 0 0

6 2 8

74. B. 10

10 groups of 3 makes 30

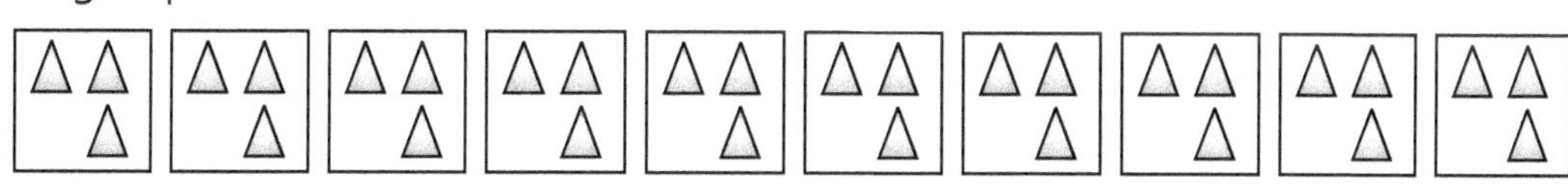

10 × 3 = 30

75. C. 6

6 groups of 4 is same as 24

6 × 4 = 24

76. B. 200 + 142

We are in search of an option whose sum will be 342.

Option A : 284 + 340 = 624 (incorrect), Option B : 200 +142 = 342 (correct), Option C : 1000 – 934 = 66 (incorrect)

77. D. None of these

We are in search of an option whose sum will be 439.

Option A : 128 + 300 = 428,

Option B : 563 + 124 = 687,

Option C : 342 – 234 =108.

78. A. +

7 _ 8 = 20 – 5. First solve the right hand side of the equal to sign.

7 _ 8 = 15

7 + 8 = 15

Option B. 7- 8 is not possible (incorrect)

Option C. 7 x 8 = 56 (incorrect)

Option D. 7 ÷ 8 not possible (incorrect)

79. B.

    21 ____ 3 = 6×3. First solve the right hand side of the equal to sign.

    $21 - 3 = 18$

    $21 - 3 = 18$

    Option A. $21 + 3 = 24$ (incorrect)

    Option C. $21 \div 3 = 7$ (incorrect)

    Option D. $21 \times 3 = 63$ (incorrect)

80. C. 4

    $40 \div ? = 5 \times 2$. First solve the right hand side of the equal to sign.

    $40 \div ? = 10$

    Rule : If the divisor is missing we divide the dividend by the quotient.

    $40 \div 10 = 4$

    $40 \div 4 = 10$

81. A. 1

    $30 \div ? = \underline{6 \times 5}$. First solve the right hand side of the equal to sign.

    $30 \div ? = 30$

    $30 \div 1 = 30$

    Division rule : If any number is divided by 1, the answer is the number itself.

82. B. $4 \times 6 = 24$

    Option A. $4 + 4 + 4 + 4 + 4 = 16$. ($4 \times 5 = 20$) multiplication is easier than repeated addition.

    Option C. 18- 4 = 12 (18- 4 = 14)

    Option D. $40 \div 4 = 8$ ($40 \div 4 = 10$)

83 B. 6 2

+ 3 2

On adding, sum should be 94 .

(A)	(B)	(C)	(D)
3 2	6 2	9 4	3 2
+ 9 4	+ 3 2	+ 6 2	+ 3 2
1 2 6	9 4	15 6	6 4

84. B. 8

There are total 20 balls. Radha gives 3 balls to her 4 friends. So 3 x 4 = 12

Friend 1 →

Friend 2 →

Friend 3 →

Friend 4 →

Now out of 20 balls, 12 balls less.

2 0

\- 1 2

0 8

85. A. 15 – 3 = 12

Read the question twice and carefully.

After she ate 3

Cookies left + 12

So total cookies 15

Out of total 15 cookies Rishika ate 3 cookies. So 15 – 3 = 12 cookies left.

86. C. 14 – 6 = 8

Read the question twice and carefully.

After she ate	6
Chocolates left	+ 8
So total chocolates=	14

Out of the total 14 chocolates Radhika ate 6 chocolates. So 14 – 6 = 8 chocolates left.

87. C. 32

There were 8 frogs.

Each frog had 4 legs.

To find out how many legs are there we multiply $4 \times 8 = 32$.

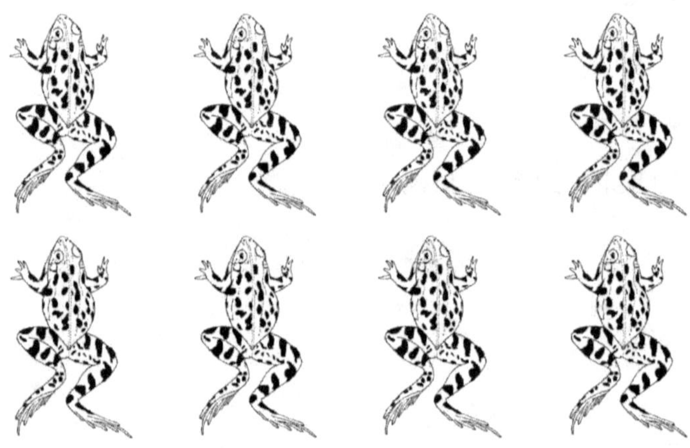

Multiplication is easier than repeated addition.

88. B. 8 + 8 + 8 + 8 = 32

Option A: 8 x 4 = 72 (incorrect) . $8 \times 4 = 32$

Option B: 8 + 8 + 8 + 8 = 32 Or $8 \times 4 = 32$(correct)

Option C: $64 \div 8 = 6$ (incorrect). $64 \div 8 = 8$

Option D: 90 – 8 = 62 (incorrect). 90 – 8 = 82

89. C. Multiplication

In the number machine when you put in 8 and 4, out comes 32 means $8 \times 4 = 32$

In the number machine when you put in 6 and 4, out comes 24 means $6 \times 4 = 24$

In the number machine when you put in 9 and 5, out comes 45 means $9 \times 5 = 45$

In the number machine when you put in 7 and 1, out comes 7 means $7 \times 1 = 7$

In the number machine when you put in 5 and 4, out comes 20 means $5 \times 4 = 20$

So the rule is to multiply.

Try out addition $8 + 4 = 12$, we want 32

Try out subtraction $8 - 4 = 4$ we want 32

Try out division $8 \div 4 = 2$ we want 32

90. A. Addition

In the number machine when you put in 6 and 2, out comes 8 means $6 + 2 = 8$

In the number machine when you put in 10 and 8, out comes 18 means $10 + 8 = 18$

In the number machine when you put in 5 and 6, out comes 11 means $5 + 6 = 11$

In the number machine when you put in 2 and 5, out comes 7 means $2 + 5 = 7$

In the number machine when you put in 5 and 4, out comes 20 means $5 + 4 = 9$.

So the rule is to add.

Try out subtraction $6 - 2 = 4$, we want 8

Try out multiplication $6 \times 2 = 12$, we want 8

Try out division $6 \div 2 = 4$, we want 8

91. A. 53

$$\begin{array}{r} \\ +\ 22 \\ \hline \end{array}$$

We are in search of an option whose sum will be 75

$$\begin{array}{r} 75 \\ -22 \\ \hline 53 \end{array}$$

So 22 + 53 = 75. On adding 53 and 22 we get 75

(A)	(B)	(C)	(D)
$\begin{array}{r} 53 \\ +\ 22 \\ \hline 75 \end{array}$	$\begin{array}{r} 22 \\ +\ 75 \\ \hline 97 \end{array}$	$\begin{array}{r} 22 \\ +\ 21 \\ \hline 43 \end{array}$	$\begin{array}{r} 22 \\ +\ 22 \\ \hline 44 \end{array}$

92. B. 18

Read the question carefully twice.

Number of balloons blew away	=	6
Number of balloons left	=	+ 12
Number of balloons he started with		18

93. B. 8

Read the question carefully twice.

After your friend gave you 12 pencils and now you have 20. So to find out how many pencils you had before your friend gave you, we subtract.

Total number of pencils you have now		20
Number of pencils your friend gave	–	12
Number of pencils you had before		08

94. B. 101

95 + 38 = 133 and 133 − 32 = 101

95. B. 31

How many fewer triangles than circles he drew? Means how many less triangles than circles he drew?

(Key words for subtraction: how many more, how many less, difference, how many left.)

Number of circles he drew	80
Number of triangles he drew	− 49
Number of less triangles than circles	31

...

Chapter 3 : Fractions

1. A. $\frac{6}{14}$

We have to find out the fraction of the shaded parts of the figure.

There are total 14 parts (including-shaded parts). So denominator will be 14. Out of that 6 parts are shaded so numerator will be 6.

So $\frac{6}{4}$ parts of the fraction is shaded.

2. A. 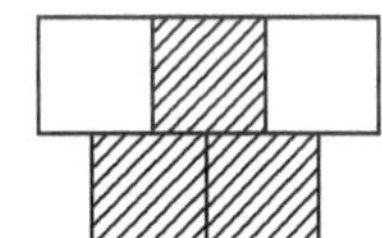

$\frac{3}{5}$ Shaded means 3 parts shaded out of the total 5 equal parts.

Option B.  $\frac{1}{4}$

Here one part is shaded out of 4 equal parts. So 1/4

Option C. 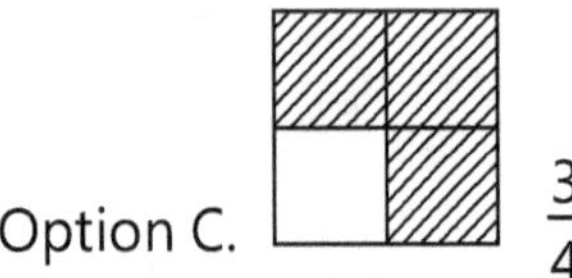 $\frac{3}{4}$

Here three parts are shaded out of 4 equal parts. So 3/4

3. B. i & iv

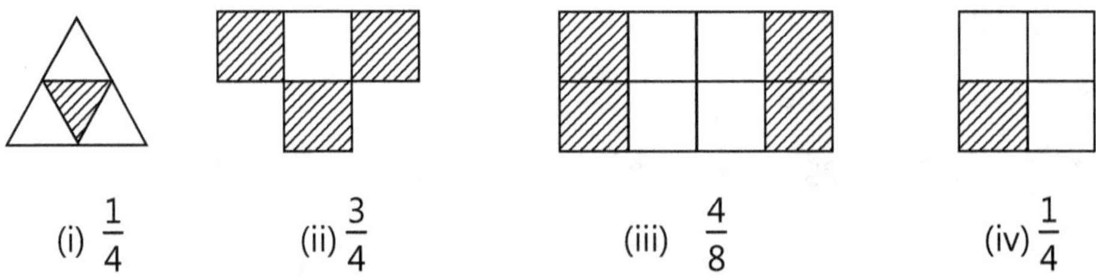

Fig (i) and fig (iv) are shaded equally $\frac{1}{4}$.

4. C. 4

Rule : Any fraction which has same numerator and denominator makes one whole.

E.g. : $\frac{3}{3}$ = 1 whole $\frac{2}{2}$ = 1 whole $\frac{4}{4}$ = 1 whole

Rule to add fractions : We add only numerators not the denominator

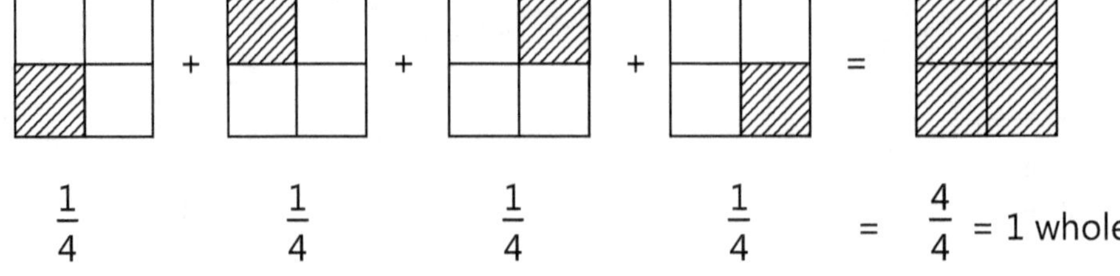

So, $\frac{1}{4}+\frac{1}{4}+\frac{1}{4}+\frac{1}{4}=\frac{4}{4}$ = 1 whole

5. C. 2

Rule : Any fraction which has same numerator and denominator makes one whole.

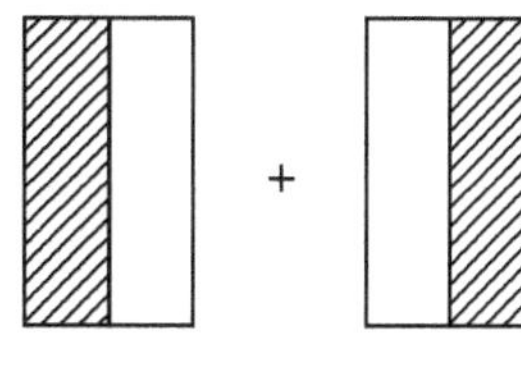

$\frac{1}{2} + \frac{1}{2} = \frac{2}{2} = 1$ whole

$\frac{1}{2} + \frac{1}{2} = \frac{2}{2} = 1$ whole

6. A. 3

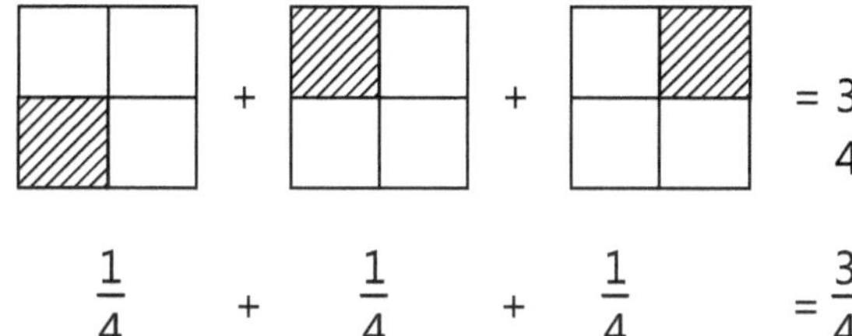

$\frac{1}{4} + \frac{1}{4} + \frac{1}{4} = \frac{3}{4}$

7. D. $\frac{11}{13}$

When the denominators of all the fractions are same we compare only the numerators. We will compare 7, 2, 10, 11.

$\frac{7}{13}$ $\frac{2}{13}$ $\frac{10}{13}$ $\boxed{\frac{11}{13}}$

8. D. $\frac{8}{14}, \frac{7}{14}, \frac{4}{14}$

When the denominators of all the fractions are same we compare only the numerators. We arrange the numerators from largest to smallest.

Only option D is arranged from largest to smallest.

9. B. B

$\frac{4}{5}$ of its contents shaded means.

From total 5 parts, 4 parts are shaded.

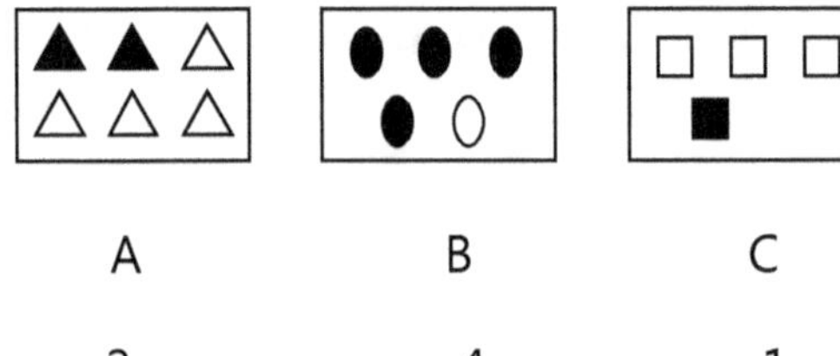

A B C

$\frac{2}{6}$ $\frac{4}{5}$ $\frac{1}{4}$

10. B. x ⊗ ⊗

x x

$\frac{2}{5}$ of its content circled means 2 parts are circled out of 5 parts.

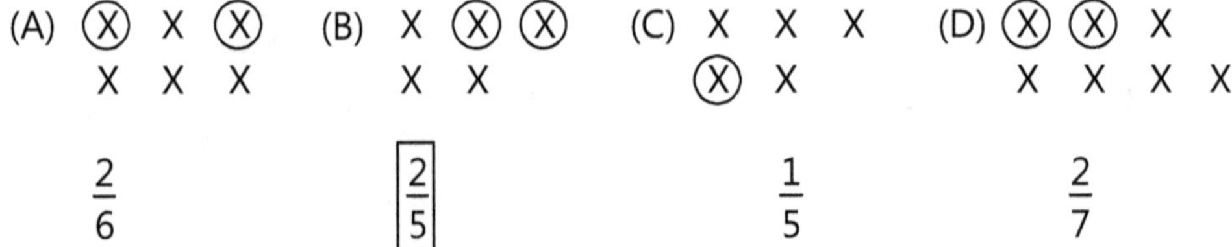

11. C. $\frac{3}{4}$

We have to find a fraction for the shaded part.

12. D. $\frac{5}{8}$

When the denominators of all the fractions are the same we compare only the numerators. We will compare 3, 4, 1, 5.

(A) $\frac{3}{8}$ (B) $\frac{4}{8}$ (C) $\frac{1}{8}$ (D) $\frac{5}{8}$

13. C. $\frac{7}{9}$

While adding fractions, we add only numerators not denominators

$\frac{4}{9} + \frac{3}{9} = \frac{7}{9}$

14. C. $\frac{10}{13}$

While adding fractions, we add only numerators not denominators

$\frac{4}{13} + \frac{6}{13} = \frac{10}{13}$

15. B. $\frac{4}{10}$

Number of pieces Rahul ate = 4, so numerator will be 4

Total number of pieces of pizza = 10, so denominator will be 10.

Rahul has eaten $\frac{4}{10}$ pizza.

16. A. $\frac{1}{6}$

Total number of pieces of the cake = 6, so denominator will be 6.

She has given each part to her friends means each friend got 1 piece.

We have to find the fraction of cake each friend got. 1 is numerator.

So $\frac{1}{6}$ cake each friend got.

17. C. $\frac{1}{10}$

Total number of pieces of the cake = 10, so denominator will be 10.

She has given each part to her friends means each friend got 1 piece.

We have to find the fraction of cake each friend got. 1 is numerator.

So $\frac{1}{10}$ cake each friend got.

18. C. $\frac{5}{8}$

$\frac{3}{8} + ? = 1$ whole

Rule : Any fraction which has same numerator and denominator makes one whole.

$\frac{3}{8}$ and _____ = 1 whole means, $\frac{3}{8}$ + which number will give you $\frac{8}{8}$ OR 1 whole $\frac{3}{8} + \boxed{\frac{5}{8}} = \frac{8}{8} = 1$ whole

19. C. $\frac{5}{12}$

$\frac{5}{12} + ? = 1$

Rule : Any fraction which has same numerator and denominator makes one whole.

$\frac{5}{12}$ and ___ = 1 whole means, $\frac{7}{12}$ + which number will give you 1 whole OR $\frac{12}{12}$.

$\frac{5}{12} + \boxed{\frac{7}{12}} = \frac{12}{12} = 1$ whole

20. A. $\frac{2}{9}$

Vijay drew $\frac{3}{9}$ of a circle green means 3 parts out of 9 parts are green.

So green's fraction is $\frac{3}{9}$

$\frac{4}{9}$ yellow means 4 parts out of 9 parts are yellow.

So yellow's fraction is $\frac{4}{9}$

To find blue we add $\frac{3}{9}$ and $\frac{4}{9}$ and subtract from the total 9 part

$$\frac{3}{9}+\frac{4}{9}=\frac{7}{9} \text{ then } \frac{9}{9}-\frac{7}{9}=\boxed{\frac{2}{9}}$$

21. A. $\frac{7}{12}$

Total number of pieces of a cake = 12 . Denominator = 12

Number of pieces given to Ram $\frac{3}{12}$

Number of pieces given to Geeta $\frac{2}{12}$

Rest of the pieces Sangita had. So to find how many pieces Sangita had we add $\frac{3}{12}$ and $\frac{2}{12}$ and subtract from 12

$$\frac{3}{12}+\frac{2}{12}=\frac{5}{12} \text{ then } \frac{12}{12}-\frac{5}{12}=\boxed{\frac{7}{12}}$$

22. A. $\frac{8}{12}$

Total number of pieces of a puzzle = 12 (denominator)

Number of pieces Radha has = 4

To make the puzzle she needs 8 more pieces (12 – 4 = 8)

So, $\frac{8}{12}$

23. A. $\frac{4}{7}$

Total number of equal pieces of cake = 7 (denominator)

Number of pieces Joe ate is 3 so $\frac{3}{7}$.

Out of 7 pieces he ate 3 pieces, so 7- 3 = 4 (pieces left).

So, $\frac{4}{7}$

24. B. $\frac{2}{8}$

Kamal gave $\frac{4}{8}$ to his sister

Kamal ate $\frac{2}{8}$

8 denominator means total 8 pieces are there . Out of 8, (4 + 2) = 6 pieces less.

So only 2 pieces are left $\frac{8}{8}-\frac{6}{8}=\frac{2}{8}$

25. A. $\frac{5}{15}$

Total number of fruits = 15 (denominator)

Number of bananas = 6

Number of apples $=\frac{4}{10}$

To find fraction for mangoes 15 – 10 = 5

$$\frac{15}{15}-\frac{10}{15}=\frac{5}{15}$$

26. C. $\frac{5}{9}$

Bina drew $\frac{3}{9}$ of a picture green means 3 parts out of 9 parts are green.

So green's fraction is $\frac{3}{9}$.

$\frac{1}{9}$ red means 1 part out of 9 parts are red.

So red's fraction is $\frac{1}{9}$.

To find uncoloured part we add $\frac{3}{9}$ and $\frac{1}{9}$ and subtract from the total 9 part

$\frac{3}{9} + \frac{1}{9} = \frac{4}{9}$ then $\frac{9}{9} - \frac{4}{9} = \frac{5}{9}$.

27. A. Meena

Compare only the numerators.

28. B. Mona

Compare only numerators

29. A. $\frac{3}{6}$

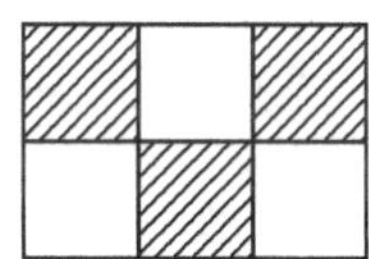

3 parts out of the total 6 equal parts are **NOT** shaded.

30. B. $\frac{3}{6}$

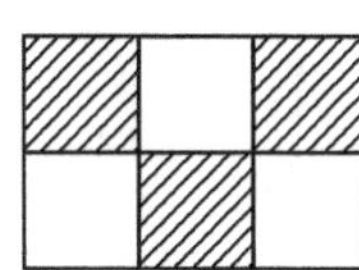

3 parts out of the total 6 equal parts are shaded .

31. C. 6

There are 6 equal parts.

32. D. 4

Out of 7 pieces, 3 pieces Anvita ate. 7 – 3 = 4

So 4 pieces are left

33. B. $\frac{4}{7}$

Total number of pieces = 7

Number of pieces eaten by Anvita = $\frac{3}{7}$

So fraction of bread left = $\frac{7}{7} - \frac{3}{7} = \frac{4}{7}$

34. B. $\frac{3}{7}$

Anvita ate 3 parts out of 7 parts.

35. C. $\frac{4}{7}$

$\frac{3}{7}$ + ? = 1 whole

Rule: Any fraction which has same numerator and denominator makes one whole.

$\frac{3}{7}$ and ___ = 1 whole means, $\frac{3}{7}$ + which number will give you $\frac{7}{7}$ OR 1 whole

$\frac{3}{8} + \boxed{\frac{4}{7}} = \frac{7}{7}$ = 1 whole

36. A. $\frac{2}{6}$

We compare only numerators.

37. A. $\frac{7}{9}$

We compare only numerators.

38. C.

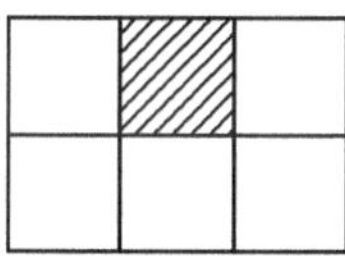

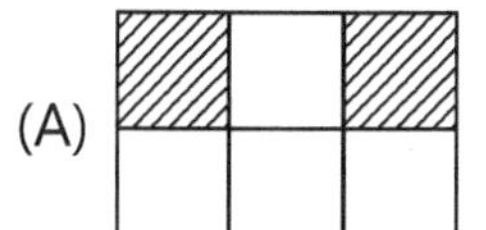 $= \frac{2}{6}$

(B) $= \frac{3}{6}$

(C) $= \frac{1}{6}$

(D) $= \frac{4}{6}$

$\frac{1}{6}$ is the smallest. We compare only the numerators.

39. B

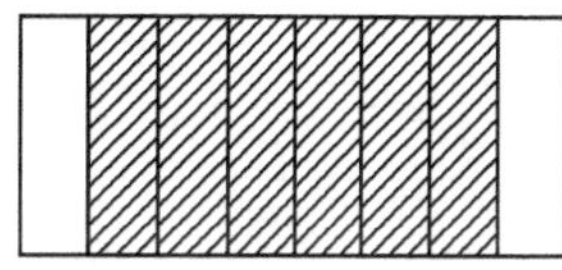

(A)

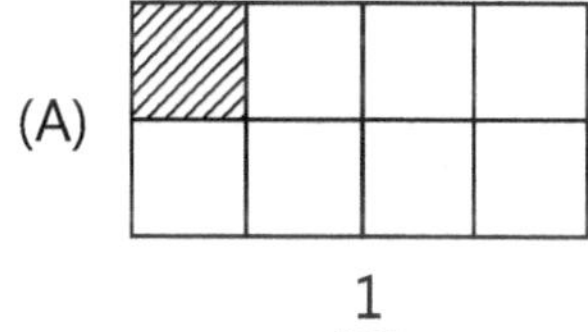

$\frac{1}{8}$

(B)

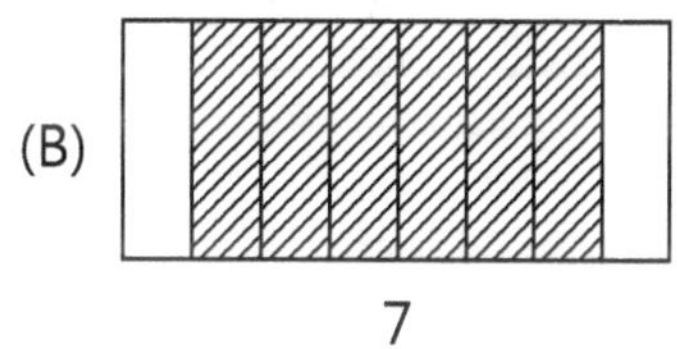

$\frac{7}{8}$

(C)

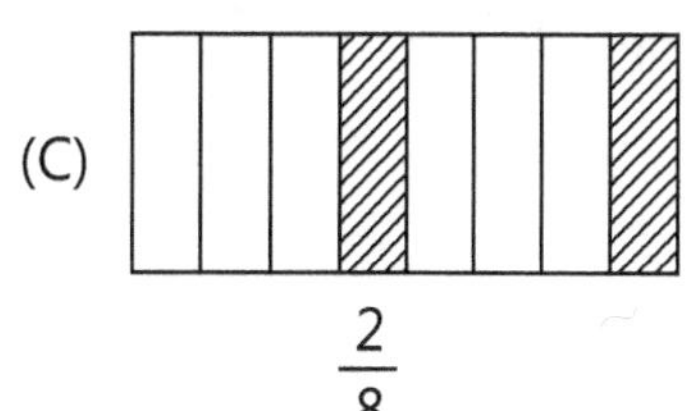

$\frac{2}{8}$

(D)

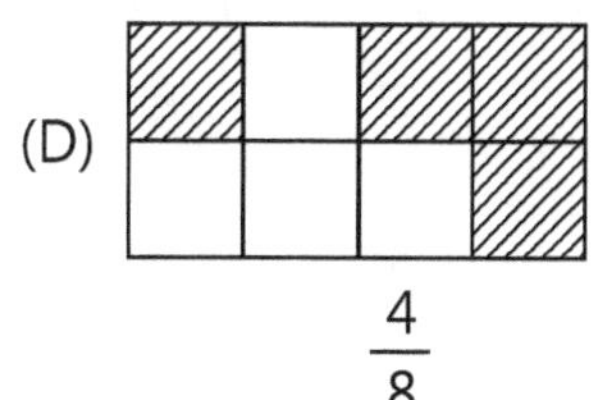

$\frac{4}{8}$

$\frac{7}{8}$ is the largest. We compare only the numerators.

40. A. $\frac{9}{10}$

$\frac{4}{10}+\frac{5}{10}=\frac{9}{10}$

We add only numerators and not denominators.

41. C. 9

9 is denominator so $\frac{2}{9}$ is the same as 2 out of **9** equal parts of a whole.

42. B. 6

6 is numerator so $\frac{6}{13}$ is the same as **6** out of 13 equal parts of a whole.

43. C. 2

2 is numerator, so $\frac{2}{7}$ is the same as **2** out of 7 equal parts of a whole.

44. C. $\frac{2}{9}+\frac{5}{9}$

(A) $\frac{3}{6}+\frac{1}{6}=\frac{4}{6}$ (B) $\frac{3}{9}+\frac{5}{9}=\frac{8}{9}$ (C) $\frac{2}{9}+\frac{5}{9}=\frac{7}{9}$

45. B. Half

46. A. One quarter

47. B. 5/11

There are total 11 shapes (squares and circles together). Out of that, squares are 5. So $\frac{5}{11}$.

48. C. $\frac{2}{5}$

There are a total of 5 shapes (rectangles and stars together). Out of that, stars are 2. So $\frac{2}{5}$.

49. A. 1

$\frac{1}{2} + \frac{1}{2} = \frac{2}{2} = 1$

Rule : Any fraction which has same numerator and denominator makes one whole.

50. B. $\frac{2}{4}$

$\frac{1}{4} + \frac{1}{4} = \frac{2}{4}$ (which is 1/2 you will learn this in next class)

While adding fractions, we add only numerators not denominators.

51. C. $\frac{3}{4}$

$\frac{1}{4} + \frac{1}{4} + \frac{1}{4} = \frac{3}{4}$

While adding fractions, we add only numerators not denominators.

52. B. 4

$\underline{13} + \underline{4} = \underline{17}$

53. D. 6

4 + 6 = 10.

Replace x with 6

$\frac{4}{13} + \frac{6}{13} = \frac{10}{13}$

54. A. 2

10 – 2 = 8

Replace a with 2

$\frac{10}{17} - \frac{2}{17} = \frac{8}{17}$

55. B. 5

$$5 + 5 = 10$$

$$\frac{5}{11} + \frac{5}{11} = \frac{10}{11}$$

56. A. 2

2 halves make 1 whole.

Rule : Any fraction which has same numerator and denominator makes one whole.

$$\frac{1}{2} + \frac{1}{2} = \frac{2}{2} = 1 \text{ whole}$$

57. D. 4

Rule : Any fraction which has same numerator and denominator makes one whole.

E.g. : $\frac{3}{3} = 1$ whole $\quad \frac{2}{2} = 1$ whole $\quad \frac{4}{4} = 1$ whole

Rule to add fractions : We add only numerators not the denominator.

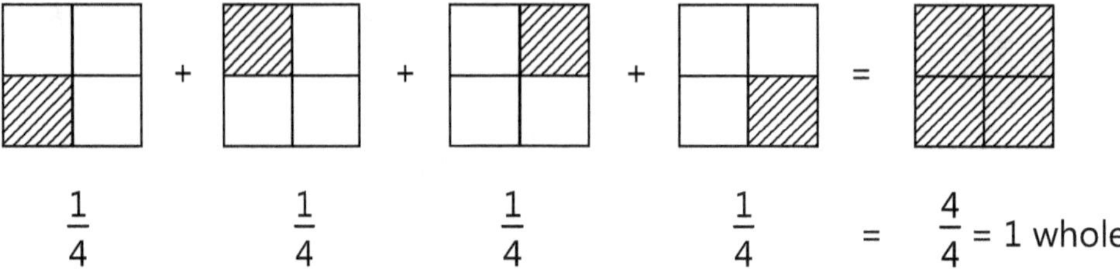

$$\frac{1}{4} \quad \frac{1}{4} \quad \frac{1}{4} \quad \frac{1}{4} \quad = \quad \frac{4}{4} = 1 \text{ whole}$$

So, $\frac{1}{4} + \frac{1}{4} + \frac{1}{4} + \frac{1}{4} = \frac{4}{4} = 1$ whole

58. C. $\frac{7}{7}$

Any fraction which has same numerator and denominator makes one whole.

So $\frac{7}{7}$ = 1 whole.

59. D. $\frac{11}{11}$

Any fraction which has the same numerator and denominator makes one whole.

So $\frac{11}{11}$ = 1 whole.

60. A. >

$\frac{7}{8} > \frac{3}{8}$

...

Chapter 4 : Length, Mass and Volume

1. A. A

   Observe carefully the length of each pencil.

   Length of pencil C is [3 to 7] = 4 cm

   Length of pencil B is [4 to 10] = 6 cm

   Length of pencil A is [1 to 4] = 3 cm

   So pencil A is the smallest.

2. B. B

   Observe carefully the length of each pencil.

   Length of pencil C is [3 to 7] = 4 cm

   Length of pencil B is [4 to 10] = 6 cm

   Length of pencil A is [1 to 4] = 3 cm

   So length of pencil B is the largest.

3. C. 6 cm

4. A. 1 cm

   Length of pencil C = 4 cm

   Length of pencil A = 3 cm

   So pencil A is 1 cm shorter than pencil C

5. B. 2 cm

   Length of pencil B = 6 cm

   Length of pencil C = 4 cm

   So pencil B is 2 cm longer than pencil C

6. B. 153

   Radha is 142 cm tall.

   Sham is 11 cm longer than Radha. To find the height of Sham, we add.

Radha's height	142 cm
Sham's height 11 cm longer than Radha	+ 11 cm
Sham's height	153 cm

7. C. 102 cm

   Mona's ribbon's length is 80 cm. Sona's ribbon's length is 22 cm longer than Mona's. To find the length of Sona's ribbon we add

   80 cm

   + 22 cm

   102 cm

8. A. 6 m. Observe carefully. You can use a scale. Keep the scale horizontally on the tip of the pencil.

9. D. None of these

   Height of the block is 9 m.

10. B. 3 m

    Height of the block is 9 m

    Height of the pencil is 6 m

    So the block is 3 m longer than the pencil.

11. D. None of these

    Height of the block is 9 m

    Height of the pencil is 6 m

    So pencil is 3 m less than the pencil.

12. B. Its height is more than 7 m.

    Block's height is 9 m which is more than 7 m

13. B. 155 m

Total length of the ribbon	200 cm
Length of one piece of ribbon	– 45 cm
Length of the other piece	155 cm

14. B. 70 kg

    Shopkeeper has 7 bags. Weight of one bag is 10 kg. So weight of 10 bags will be $7 \times 10 = 70$.

15. C. 40m + 38m

    Jai cycled from his home to school and then to the library.

16. D. None of these

    The actual distance between his home and library is 45 m. None of the options show 45m.

17. C. 38 m

    Observe carefully.

18. A. 40 m

    The distance between Jai's home and school is 40 m.

19. C. 4 m

20. A. 26 litres

Total quantity of milk	100 litres
- Quantity of milk used	– 74 litres
Quantity of milk left with him	26 litres.

21. B. 5 cm

The length of the pin is 5 cm.

22. A. 8 cm

The length of the pencil is 8 cm.

23. B. 3 cm

The length of the pencil is 8 cm

The length of the pin is 5 cm

Pencil is longer than pin by 3 cm

24. C. C

25. D. Fig.

26. B. 3 kg

4 cakes together weigh 12 kg. To find weight of 1 cake.

$4 \times ? = 12$. $4 \times \underline{\mathbf{3}} = 12$

OR

$12 \div 4 = ?$. $12 \div 4 = \underline{\mathbf{3}}$

27. A. 3 kg.

Weight of 2 balls is 6 kg. So weight of 1 ball will be 3 kg.

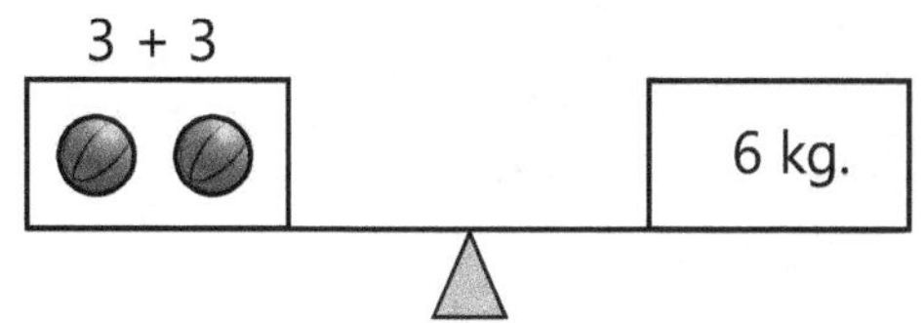

Option B. 4 + 4 = 8, Option C . 6 + 6 = 12

28. C. 5 kg

Weight of 2 balls is 10 kg. So weight of 1 ball will be 5 kg.

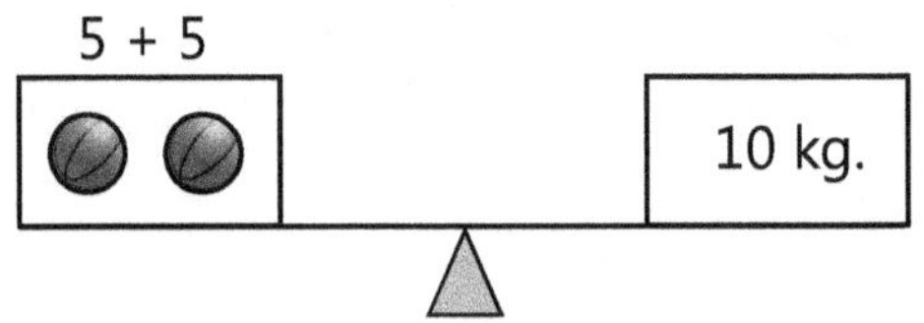

Option A. 10 + 10 = 20, Option B. 6 + 6 = 12

29. A. 4 kg

Weight of 3 balls is 12 kg. So weight of 1 ball will be 12 ÷ 3 = ___

12 ÷ 3 = 4 OR 3 × ___ = 12, 3 × **4** = 12

4 + 4 + 4

12 kg.

30. A.

100 + 100 + 100 =300

100 100 100

+ + = 300g.

Option B. 300 + 300 + 300 = 900 g (incorrect)

Option C. 150 + 150 + 150 = 450 g (incorrect)

Option D. 250 + 250 + 250 = 750 g (incorrect)

31. B. 200 g

200 200 200

+ + = 600 g.

Option A. 100 + 100 + 100 = 300 g

Option C. 300 + 300 + 300 = 900 g

32. A. 4 litres

3 glasses hold 12 litres so one glass can hold 12 ÷ 3 = 4

33. C. 2 kg

Weight of 5 mangoes is 10 kg. To find the weight of 1 mango we divide.

10 ÷ 5 = **2** OR 5 × **2** = 10

34. B. 3 kg

Weight of 4 potatoes is 12 kg. To find the weight of 1 potato we divide.

12 ÷ 4 = **3** OR 4 × **3** = 12

35. D. Rice

36. A. 5 kg

37. B. Tea

38. B. Salt

39. A. 5 kg.

Weight of tea is 10 kg

Weight of salt is 5 kg

Tea is 5 kg heavier than salt.

40. C. 1 kg

Weight of sugar is 6 kg

Weight of salt is 5 kg

Sugar is 1 kg heavier than salt.

41. C. Cup

42. A. Barrel

Barrel is a big container for liquids with round sides and flat ends.

43. C. 2 litres

Observe the level of water in the bottle.

44. D. 60 litres

Total quantity of water in the tank	120 litres
Quantity of water drained out (removed)	– 60 litres
Quantity of water left	60 litres

45. B. Y

Observe carefully

X contains 300 ml

Y contains 700 ml

Z contains 500 ml

Y contains more than 600 ml

46. D. Z

X contains 300 ml

Y contains 700 ml

Z contains 500 ml

So, Y and Z contain more than 400 ml

47. B. Z

Z contains 500 ml. 500 millilitres means half a litre.

48. C. 300 ml

1 litre means 1,000 ml

Y contains 700 ml . To make Y 1 litre or 1,000ml more 300 ml of water is needed. 700 + [300] = 1000

49. B. 200 ml

X contains 300 ml

Z contains 500 ml

300 + [200] = 500

200 ml of water should be added to X to make is equal to Z (500 ml).

50. B. 300 ml

Z contains 500 ml. To make cylinder Z 200 ml we should take out 300 ml of water. 500 – [200] = 300

51. D. Both A and C

Read all the options carefully.

Option A : 1 litre and option C: 1000 ml. Both mean the same .

52. D. 90 litres

Total quantity of paint	200 litres
Paint used	– 110 litres
Paint left	90 litres

53. D. 48 litres

Seema drinks 4 litres of water daily. So in 12 days she drinks.

$$\begin{array}{r} 12 \\ \times 4 \\ \hline 48 \end{array}$$

54. B. barrel

Bucket holds 11 litres

Barrel holds 14 litres

55. C. Vase

Bottle can hold 5 litres

Vase can hold 2 litres

56. B. Barrel

Barrel holds 14 litres

...

Chapter 5 : Time and Money

1. B. 3

   The short hand is the hour hand.

2. A. 40 minutes

   The minute hand is pointing at number 8. So $8 \times 5 = 40$ minutes.

3. B. 40 min past 3.

   Time in the clock is 3: 40 which can be also said as 40 mins past 3.

4. D. Both B and C

   Read all the options carefully.

   Clock is showing 1:30. We can say half past 1 or 30 min past 1.

5. A. 45 min past 4

   Clock shows the time 4:45. 4:45 can also be written as 45 min past 4.

6. B. 6 : 10

   Short hand (hour hand) is on 6 and minute hand is on 2. ($2 \times 5 = 10$). So 6 : 10.

7. B. 20

   Time in the clock is 9:20 OR 20 min past 9. This time is 20 min after 9 O'clock.

8. A. A.M

   The time from 12 midnight to 12 noon is noted as A.M. (Anti Meridian) and the time from 12 noon to 12 midnight as P.M.(Post Meridian) . Morning 6:00 comes between 12 midnight to 12 noon. So morning 6 o'clock is 6:00 A.M.

9. C.

10. C. P.M.

The time from 12 midnight to 12 noon is noted as A.M. (Anti Meridian) and the time from 12 noon to 12 midnight as P.M. (Post Meridian). Afternoon 3 comes between 12 noon to 12 midnight. So 3 P.M

11. D. P.M .

The time from 12 midnight to 12 noon is noted as A.M. (Anti Meridian) and the time from 12 noon to 12 midnight as P.M. (Post Meridian). Night 8:30 comes between 12 noon to 12 midnight. So 8:30 P.M.

12. B. 9:00

10:00 comes after 9:00.

13. B. 5:00. 6:00 comes after 5:00

14. A. 30 min

The programme was from 5:20 to 5:50. To find out how long the programme lasted we subtract.

```
  5:50
– 5:20
  ----
  0:30
```

15. B. 50 min

Rani studied from 4:05 to 4:55. To find out how long did she study we subtract.

```
  4:55
– 4:05
  ----
  0:50
```

16. B. 45 min

Mohan left home at 6:00 in the morning and reached school at 6:45. To find out how long he took to reach home we subtract.

$$\begin{array}{r} 6{:}45 \\ -\ 6{:}00 \\ \hline 0{:}45 \end{array}$$

17. C. 3 hrs

Tina went to see the movie at 4:15 pm and came back at 7:15 pm. To find out how long the movie lasted we subtract.

$$\begin{array}{r} 7{:}15 \\ -\ 4{:}15 \\ \hline 3{:}00 \end{array}$$

18. C. 1 hr 30 min

Rina started walking to the beach at 6:00 pm. She went back home at 7:30 pm. To find out how long she walked we subtract.

$$\begin{array}{r} 7{:}30 \\ -\ 6{:}00 \\ \hline 1{:}30 \end{array}$$

OR

6:00 to 7:00 = 1 hour

7:00 to 7:30 = 30 min. So 1 hr 30 min.

19. D. 11:30

Class started at 11:00. It lasted for half an hour means 30 mins. So 11:00 + 30 min = 11:30

$$\begin{array}{r} 11{:}00 \\ +\ \ {:}30 \\ \hline 11{:}\ 30 \end{array}$$

20. D. 6:50 am

Rohit started jogging at 6:00 am. He jogged for 50 min which means he stopped after 50 min. So 6:00 + 50 min = 6:50

$$\begin{array}{r} 6{:}00 \\ +\ \ {:}50 \\ \hline 6{:}50 \end{array}$$

It will be am not pm

21. C. 4:35 pm

Reema started studying at 4:10 pm and she studied for 25 min. To find out when did she stop we add. 4:10 + 25 min

$$\begin{array}{r} 4{:}10 \\ +\ \ 25 \\ \hline 4{:}35 \end{array}$$

It will be pm not am.

22. B. 2 hr 30 min

Movie started
1:00

Movie ended
3:30

The movie started at 1:00 and ended at 3:30.

1:00 to 2:00 = 1 hour

2:00 to 3:00 = 1 hour

3:00 to 3:30 = 30 min.

So 2 hours and 30 min.

23. D. Both A and B.

Read the question and the options carefully.

Kavita reached a mall at 9:30 am. She shopped there for 1 hour and left the mall, means she left after 1 hour. So she left at 10:30.

9:30 + 1 hour = 10:30

OR

30 min past 10. Both means the same.

Option A : 10:30 and option B : 30 min past 10. Option D says both A and B

24. A. 4:20 pm

Ram went to his Olympaid classes at 3:00 pm. The class was for 1 hr 20 min.

His class got over at 3:00 + 1:20 = 4:20 pm

3:00 pm

+ 1:20 pm

4:20 pm

25. A. 10:20 am

Rule : When the clock is running fast we will subtract to find the actual time. When the clock is slow we add to find the actual time.

The clock is showing 10:35 am. It is 15 min fast. So to find the actual time we subtract.

10:35 am

− :15

10: 20 am

26. B. 11:20 pm

Rule : When the clock is running fast we subtract to find the actual time. When the clock is slow we add to find the actual time.

The clock is showing 11:40 am. It is 20 min fast . So to find the actual time we subtract.

11:40 am

– :20

11: 20 pm

Option D : 11:20 am (incorrect)

27. B. 2:40 pm

Rule : When the clock is running fast we will subtract to find the actual time. When the clock is slow we add to find the actual time.

The clock is showing 2:30 pm. It is 10 min slow . So to find the actual time we add

2:30 pm

\+ : 10

2:40 pm

28. B. 3:53 am

The clock is showing 3:35 am. It is 18 min slow. So to find the actual time we add

3:35 am

\+ : 18

3: 53 am

Option C : 3:53 pm (incorrect)

29. B. 6:15 pm

15 min after 6:00 is 6:15 pm

6:00

+ : 15

6: 15 pm

Option C : 6:15 am (incorrect)

30. A. 2:20 am

20 min after 2 am is 2:20 am

2:00 am

+ :20

2: 20 am

Option B : 2:20 pm (incorrect)

31. A. 12:18 pm

18 min after 12 noon is 12:18 pm

Time after 12 noon is noted as PM

12:00 noon

+ : 18

12:18 pm

Option B : 12:18 am (incorrect)

32. C. 12:20 am

20 min after 12 midnight is 12:20 am

Time after 12 midnight is noted as am

12:00 noon

+ :20

12:20 am

Option D : 12: 20 pm (incorrect)

33. B. 60 min

34. A. 180 min

1 hour = 60 min . So 3 hours will be $3 \times 60 = 180$ min

35. C. 60

1 minute = **60** seconds

36. C.

1:00

3 hours before 4 am is 1am

4 am

- 3

1 am

37. A. 3:30 hrs

Seema watched her favourite programme from 4 pm to 7:30 p.m. We have to find out how long did the programme last.

Time between 4 to 7:30 is

4 to 5 = 1 hour

5 to 6 = 1 hour

6 to 7 = 1 hour

3 hours

7 to: 7:30 = 30 min (half an hour)

So 3 hrs and 30 min. We can write it as 3:30 hrs.

38. D. 1:30

Bina went in the swimming pool at 6:30 am and came out of 8:00 am.

Time between 6:30 to 8 is

6:30 to 7:30 = 1 hour

7:30 to 8:00 = 30 min (half an hour)

So 1 hour and 30 min. We can write it as 1:30

39. B. 2

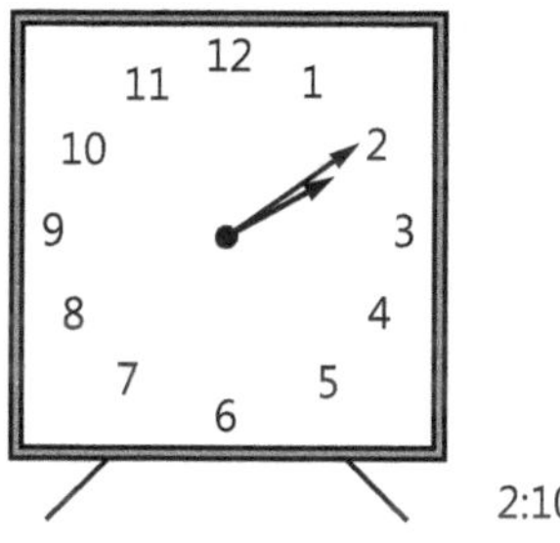

2:10

At 2:10 hour hand will be on 2.

Even minute hand will be on 2.

40. A. 4

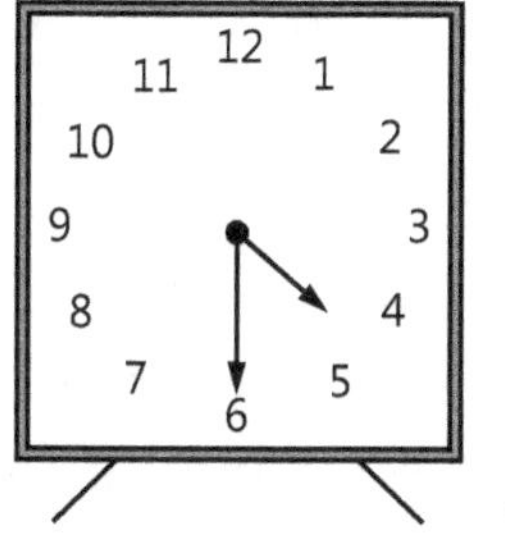

4:30

At 4:30 hour hand will be on 4.

41. B. 9 and 10

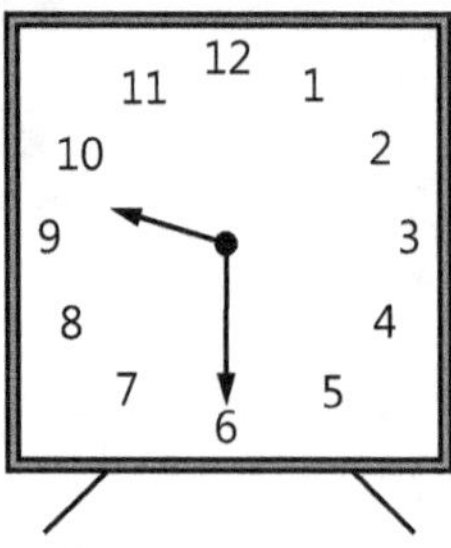

At 9:30 hour hand will lie between 9 and 10.

42. A. 6 and 7

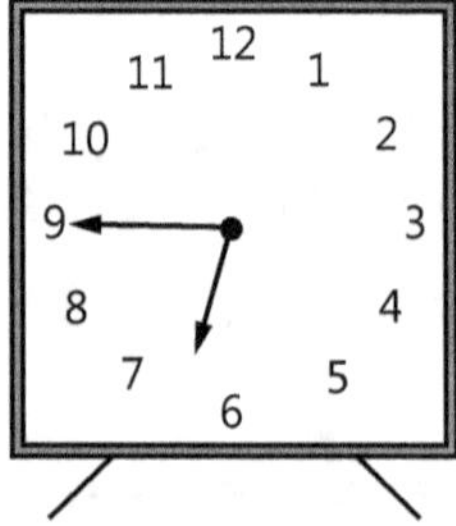

At 6:45 hour hand will lie between 6 and 7 .

43. C. 7 and 8

7:35

At 7:35 hour hand will lie between 7 and 8 .

44. B. 3 hours

Leena starts her homework at 1 pm and finishes at 5 pm. So 1 to 5 there are 4 hours, but she takes an hour off for lunch. So 4 - 1 = 3 hours. She studies for 3 hours everyday.

45. C. 4 hours

Rajeshwari starts her homework at 6 am and finishes at 11 am. So 6 to 11 there are 5 hours, but she takes an hour off for breakfast. 5 – 1 = 4 hours. She studies 4 hours everyday.

46. B. 12:30 pm

1 hour after 11:30 will be 12:30, but here we will cross 12 noon. So am will change to pm

The time from 12 midnight to 12 noon is noted as A.M. (Anti Meridian) and the time from 12 noon to 12 midnight as P.M. (Post Meridian).

47. C. 3:20 pm

Rahul's school starts at 10.20 am. The school works for 5 hours. So school will get over at 3:20, but here we will cross 12 noon. So am will chang to pm.

The time from 12 midnight to 12 noon is noted as A.M. (Anti Meridian) and the time from 12 noon to 12 midnight as P.M.(Post Meridian) .

48. B. 90 min

Rohan takes 30 minutes to complete 1 round of the park. To complete 3 rounds. He will take $30 \times 3 = 90$ min

$$\begin{array}{r} 30 \\ \times 3 \\ \hline 90 \end{array}$$

49. D. Both B and C

Meena takes 20 minutes to complete 1 round of the park. To complete 3 rounds.

She will take $20 \times 3 = 60$ min

60 minutes = 1 hour

Read all the options carefully.

Option B: 60 min and Option C : 1 hour. Both means the same. Option D says both B and C.

50. D. both B and C

Monisha takes 60 minutes to complete 1 round of the park. To complete 2 rounds.

She will take $60 \times 2 = 120$ min

1 hour = 60 min

2 hours = $60 \times 2 = 120$ min.

So 2 hours = 120 min

Read all the options carefully.

Option B : 120 minutes and option C : 2 hours. Both means the same. Option D says both B and C.

51. B. 100 p

52. B. 200

₹ $2 \times 100 = 200$ p

53. A. 600

₹ $6 \times 100 = 600$ p

54. A. 3

300 p = 3 ₹

55. B. 07

700 p = 7 ₹ (07 means 7)

56. C. ten notes of ₹ 10

Rule. Multiplying by 10 means simply adding a 0

Multiplying by 100 means adding two zeros (00)

Option (A) twenty notes of Rs. 10. → $20 \times 10 = 200$ (incorrect)

Option (B) five notes of Rs. 10 → $5 \times 10 = 50$ (incorrect)

Option (C) ten notes of Rs. 10 → $10 \times 10 = 100$ (correct)

Option (D) ten notes of Rs. 100 → $10 \times 100 = 1000$ (incorrect)

57. A. 32 ₹

₹ 20
+ ₹ 12
₹ 32

58.B. ₹ 48

₹ 14
+ ₹ 34
₹ 48

59. A.

Option (A) 25p + 25p + 25p + 25p = 100p =1 rupee (correct)

Option (B) 10p + 10p + 10p = 30p (incorrect)

Option (C) 50p + 10p = 60p (incorrect)

Option (D) 30p + 30p = 60p (incorrect)

60. B. 4

You need four, 10 ₹ notes to make 40 ₹

$10 \times \_ = 40$

$10 \times \boxed{4} = 40$

61. C. 7

You need seven, 5 ₹ notes to make 35 ₹

$5 \times \_\_ = 35$

$5 \times \underline{\mathbf{7}} = 35$

62. A. 4

You need four, 2 ₹ notes to make 8 Rs.

$2 \times \_\_ = 8$

$2 \times \boxed{4} = 8$

63. C. 7

You need seven, 2 ₹ notes to make 14 ₹

$2 \times \_\_ = 14$

$2 \times \boxed{7} = 14$

64. B. book

Book is the most expensive item.

Observe carefully.

Cost of the ball is 10 ₹. Cost of the book is 40 ₹

Cost of pencil box is 25 ₹. Cost of 1 dozen erasers is 20 ₹

(1 dozen erasers = 12 erasers)

65. D. ball

Ball is the cheapest

Observe carefully.

Cost of the ball is 10 ₹. Cost of the book is 40 ₹

Cost of pencil box is 25 ₹. Cost of 1 dozen erasers is 20 ₹

(1 dozen erasers = 12 erasers)

66. C. Ball

With 10 ₹ Manish can only buy a ball worth ₹ 10, because all other items cost more than 10 ₹. So he cannot buy anything else.

67. C. Pencil box and 1 dozen ereasers

With ₹ 45 Raj can buy Pencil box and 1 dozen erasers.

Option (A) Ball and book

Ball 10 ₹

Book + 40 ₹

50 ₹ (incorrect)

Option (B) Book and pencil box

Book 40 ₹

Pencil box + 25 ₹

65 ₹ (incorrect)

Option (C) Pencil box and 1 dozen erasers

Pencil box 25 ₹

1 dozen erasers + 20 ₹

45 ₹ (correct)

68. A. ₹ 95

To find out how much money is needed to buy all four items, we add all the items.

Cost of the ball is	10 ₹
Cost of the book is	+ 40 ₹
Cost of pencil box is	+ 25 ₹
Cost of 1 dozen erasers is	+ 20 ₹
Total amount	95 ₹

69. B. ☐ 50 ₹

To buy a book of ₹ 36 we either need 36 ₹ or more than 36 ₹.

Only option B. 50 ₹ is more than 36 ₹.

70. A. 10

$10 \times \_\_ = 100$

$10 \times \underline{\mathbf{10}} = 100$

71. C. 5

20 + 20 + 20 + 20 + 20 (multiplication is better than repeated addition)

$20 \times \_ = 100$

$20 \times \underline{\mathbf{5}} = 100$

$(2 \times 5 = 10, \quad 20 \times 5 = 100)$

To get 20 X 5, first multiply $2 \times 5 = 10$ and then place 0 after it = 100

72. C. 40

Cost of the toys = 560, but Harish gave ₹ 600 (which is more than 560) to the shopkeeper. So the shopkeeper will return the extra money that Harish has given him.

Total amount Harish gave to the shopkeeper	600
Cost of the toys	– 560
Amount the shopkeeper will return	40

73. B. 190

Cost of the books = 310, but Hema gave 500 ₹ note to the shopkeeper. So the shopkeeper will return the extra money that Hema has given him.

Amount that Hema gave to the shopkeeper	500
Cost of the books	– 310
Amount the shopkeeper will return	190

74. B. ₹ 75

Cost of the toy car is ₹ 425.

Jigar paid ₹ 500.

The shopkeeper will return the extra money that Jigar has given him.

Amount that Jigar paid	500
Cost of the toy car	– 425
Amount the shopkeeper will return	75

75. A. ₹ 180

Cost of the school bag ₹ 320

Khushi paid ₹ 500

Khushi paid more money. The shopkeeper will return the extra money that Khushi has given him.

Amount that Khushi paid	500
Cost of the school bag	– 320
Amount the shopkeeper will return	80

76. B. 02

Two notes of 50 ₹ will make ₹ 100.

₹ 50

+ ₹ 50

₹100 OR $50 \times 2 = 100$

Option A : $5 \times 50 = 250$ (incorrect) To get 5×50, first multiply $5 \times 5 = 25$ and then place 0 after it = 250

Option C : $10 \times 50= 500$ (incorrect) Multiplying by 10 means simply adding a 0.

Option D : $1\times50 = 50$ (incorrect)

77. B. 4

₹ 50

+ ₹ 50

+ ₹ 50

+ ₹ 50

₹ 200

OR $50 \times 4 = 200$. Multiplication is better then repeated addition.

Option A : $5 \times 50= 250$ (incorrect) To get 5×50, first multiply $5 \times 5 = 25$ and then place 0 after it = 250

Option C : $2 \times 50 = 100$ (incorrect) To get 2×50, first multiply $2 \times 5 = 10$ and then place 0 after it = 100

78. A. ₹ 60

Every month Sushmita saves ₹ 5. We have to find out how much did she save at the end of the year .

There are 12 months in a year.

So at the end of the year she saves 12 x 5 = 60 ₹

79. C. ₹ 60

Radha saves ₹ 2 from her pocket money daily. We have to find out how much did she save at the end of the April month.

There are 30 days in April.

So at the end of the month she saves ₹ $2 \times 30 = 60$ ₹.

80. C. 150 ₹

Riya saves ₹ 5 everyday. We have to find out how much did she save at the end of the September month .

There are 30 days in September.

So at the end of the month she saves ₹ 5 × 30 = 150 ₹.

81. C. 120 ₹

Mohan saves ₹ 10 every month from his pocket money. We have to find out how much did he save at the end of the year .

There are 12 months in a year.

So at the end of the year he saves 12 x 10 = 120 ₹.

82. C. Brush your teeth.

83. A. 600

One pair of shoes cost ₹ 200.

So 3 similar pairs of shoes will cost ₹ 200 x 3 = 600 ₹.

84. A. ₹ 560

Cost of one shirt = 140 ₹

Cost of 4 shirts will be = 140 × 4 = 560 ₹

85. B. ₹ 340.

One pair of shoes cost ₹ 200

Cost of one shirt = 140 ₹

One pair of shoes and a shirt will cost

$$\begin{array}{r} 200 \\ +\ 140 \\ \hline 340 \end{array}$$

...

Chapter 6 : Geometry

1. D. both B and C.

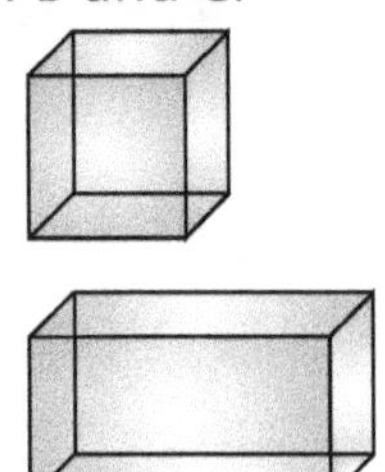

All the sides in a cube are equal and every face is a square. It has 6 faces, 12 edges, 8 corners.

In a cuboid the opposite sides of each face are equal. Every face is a rectangle. It has 6 faces (flat) 12 edges, 8 corners.

2. B. 9

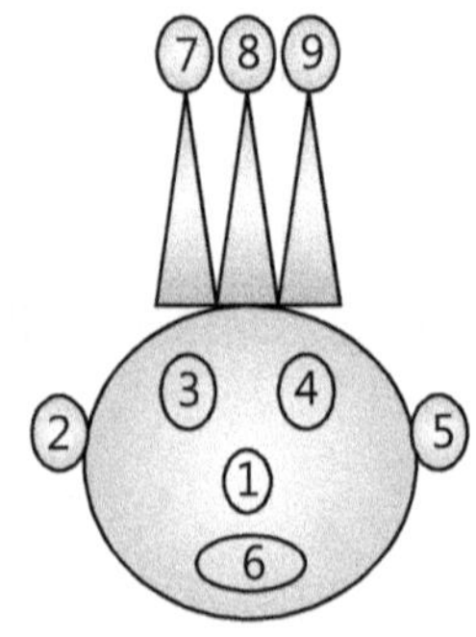

3. D. 13

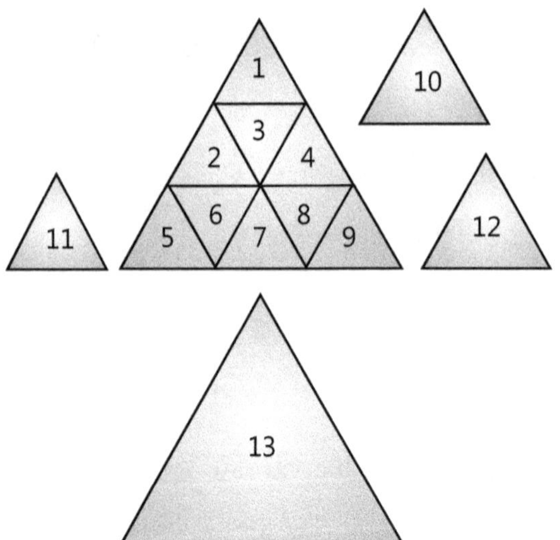

10 is made up of 1, 2, 3, 4.

11 is made up of 2, 5, 6, 7.

12 is made up of 4, 8, 7, 9.

13 is the big triangle made up of 1, 2, 3, 4, 5, 6, 7, 8, 9.

4. A. 29

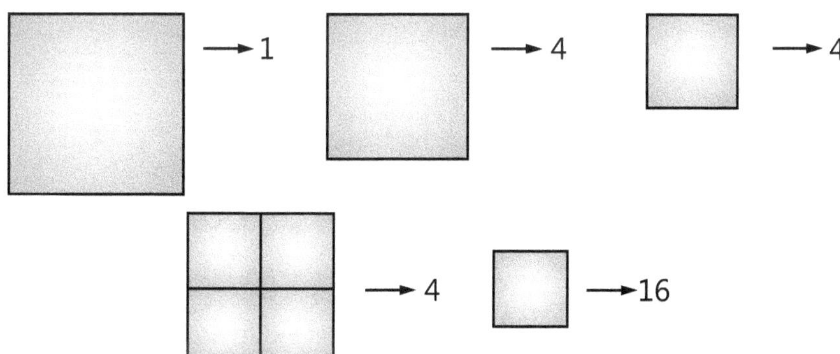

5. A. 4

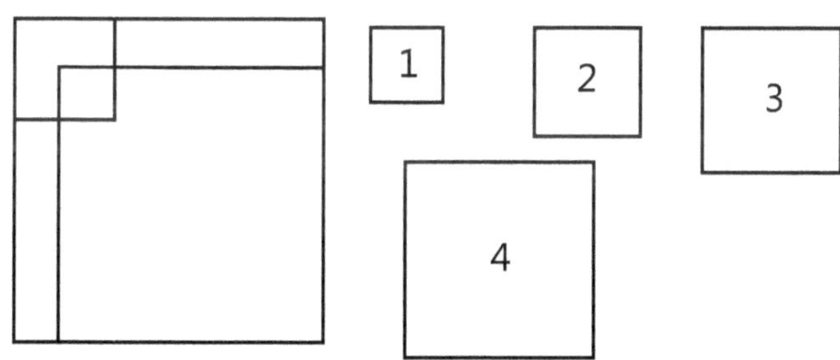

6. B. 2

A cone has a plane surface and a curved surface. It has one corner. It has 2 faces.

7. A. 3. A cylinder has 3 faces, 2 plane or flat faces and one curved face.

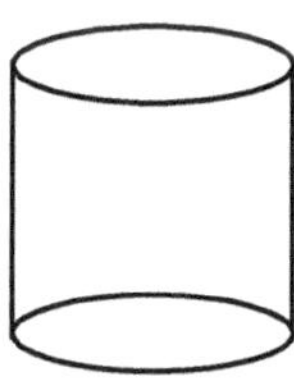

8. B. 4

Solid A cone has 2 faces and solid B cube has 6 faces.

So solid B has 4 more faces then solid A.

9. B. 6

10. C. Triangle

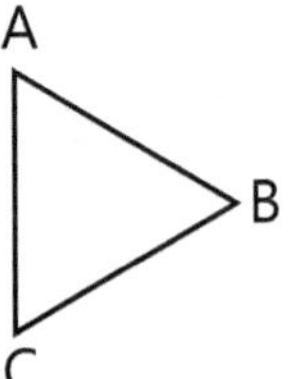

A

B

C

11. A.

12. B.

13. B. 3.

2 semicircles make one circle . There are 6 semicircles.

2 semicircles	= 1 circle
+ 2 semicircles	= 1 circle
+ 2 semicircles	= 1 circle
6 semicircles	= 3 circles

14. C. 14

15. B. cube

...

Chapter 7 : Patterns

1. A. 7

2. C. 30

   +2 +2 +2 +2 +2 +2

   18, 20, 22, 24, 26, 28, 30

   Pattern is add 2.

3. B. 10

   +2 +2

   6, 8, 10

   Pattern is to add 2.

4. B. 45

   +5 +5 +5 +5 +5

   20, 25, 30, 35, 40, 45

   Pattern is to add 5.

5. A. 24

   +4 +4 +4 +4 +4

   4, 8, 12, 16, 20, 24

   Pattern is to add 4 OR 4 times table.

6. C. 64

   +16 +16 +16

   16, 32, 48, 64

   Pattern is to add 16 OR 16 times table.

7. C. 140

+10 +10 +10 +10 +10

90, 100, 110, 120, 130, 140

Pattern is to add 10.

8. A. 160

–10 +20 –10 +20 –10

150, 140, 160, 150, 170, 160

Subtract 10 and add 20 is the pattern.

9. A. 139

–1 +2 –1 +2 –1

138, 137, 139, 138, 140, 139

Subtract 1 and add 2 is the pattern.

10. A. 643

–1 +2 –1 +2 –1

642, 641, 643, 642, 644, 643

Subtract 1 and add 2 is the pattern.

11. C. 442

+100 +100 +100 +100

42, 142, 242, 342, 442

Pattern is to add 100.

12. B. 812

+100 +100 +100 +100 +100

312, 412, 512, 612, 712, 812

Pattern is to add 100.

13. A. 450

+10 +10 +10 +10

410, 420, 430, 440, 450

Pattern is to add 10.

14. C. 880

+20 +20 +20 +20

800, 820, 840, 860, 880

Pattern is to add 20.

15. B. 464

+5 +5 +5 +5

444, 449, 454, 459, 464

Pattern is to add 5.

16. C. 555

17. A. 291

Pattern is to write the number in reverse order.

648 its reverse order is 846

293 its reverse order is 392

192 its reverse order is **291**

648, 846, 293, 392, 192, **291**

18. B. 410

____, 400, 390, 380, 370

Start from the right hand side.

Pattern is to add 10 and write answer on the left side.

+10 +10 +10 +10

410, 400, 390, 380, 370

19. B. 342

+100 +100 +100 +100, +100

142, 242, 343, 442, 542, 642

Pattern is to add 100.

20. A. 48

+8 +8 +8 +8 +8

8, 16, 24, 32, 40, 48

Pattern is to add 8 OR 8 times table.

21. B. 55

+11 +11 +11 +11

11, 22, 33, 44, 55

Pattern is to add 11 OR 11 times table.

22. B.

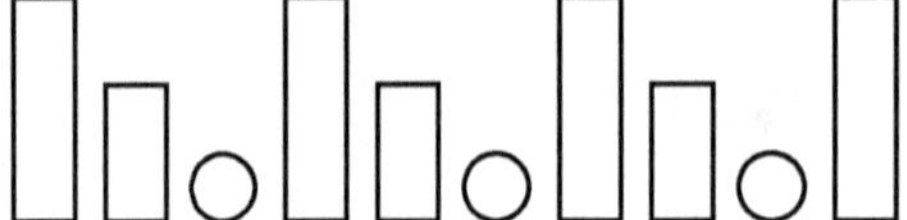

Big rectangle, small rectangle, circle, big rectangle, small rectangle, circle, big rectangle, small rectangle, **circle, big rectangle**.

23. B.

24. A

25. A

26. B

One arrow pointing up, two arrows pointing down, threes pointing up, four arrows down, so five arrows point up but there are only four arrows that are pointing up .next will be one arrow upward and next downward.

27. C

Observe the figure carefully.

28. B

...

Model Paper I

1. B. 0

   Multiplication rule: Any number multiplied by zero answer is zero.

2. B. 6.There are 6 tens in sixty. 6x10 = 60

3. C. 3/5 .There are 3 vowels. **I** N D **I A**. There are total 5 letters so 3/5.

4. B. Jiyan . 5/10 is more than 3/10

5. D. Insufficient information. We know cost of one mango is 50 rupees. To find the cost of 1 mango and 1 watermelon we need to know the cost of 1 watermelon.

   Cost of watermelon is not given. Information is insufficient.

6. B. 16.50

She paid	20	OR	20.00
Shopkeeper returned her	– 3.50		– 3.50
So the cost of pen	16.50		16.50

   Write the numbers carefully while subtracting. There is a point which separates rupees and paise.

7. D. February. Month of February has 29 days after every 4 years (leap year) so 29th is the last day of the month.

8. D. 7.30 pm. As Rohan finished at 8:00 pm he must have started 30 minutes before 8 : 00 which is 7:30 pm.

9. C. 40. When the minute hand is on 8, it means 40 minutes. $8 \times 5 = 40$.

10. B. 170 litres

Milk sold on Monday	150 litres
On Tue he sold 20 litres more than Monday	+ 20 litres
Milk sold on Tue is	170 litres

11. A. 4 metres. Length of the string is 12 m. He cuts it into 3 equal parts. So 12 divided by 3 is 4.

12. B. giraffe.

    1st elephant

    2nd giraffe

    3rd monkey

    Elephant was leading means he was at 1st place. Giraffe was not at the end means, it was at the 2nd place. And monkey was the last.

13. A. 6

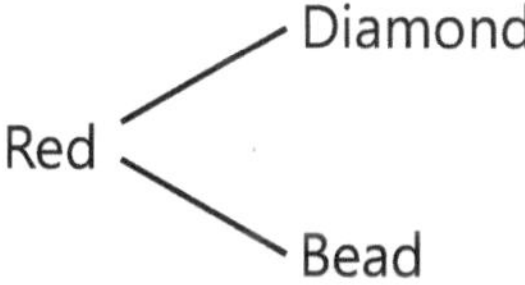

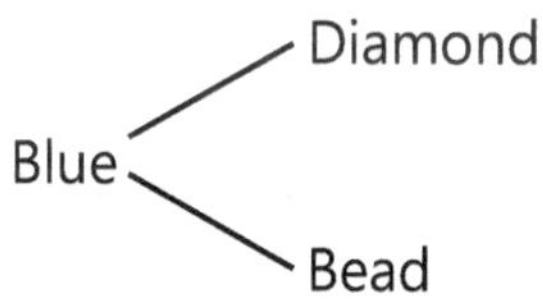

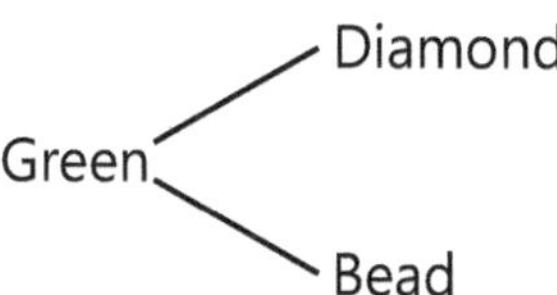

So 6 different ways.

14. C. 12

Y means plus, X means 9, and Z means 3,

X Y Z

9 + 3 = 12

15. C. 77

Total no of seats	100
No of seats vacant (empty, nobody is sitting)	– 23
No of people (seats that are not empty)	77

16. B. 6:40

When the hour hand is between 6 and 7 it means 6 'o clock is going on. When the minute hand is on 8 it means 40 minutes.

17. C. 24

$6 \times 5 =$ ____ + 6

$6 \times 5 = 30$ left hand side of equal to sign, so we need 30 on the right hand side also. So 30 – 6 = 24. OR $\boxed{24}$ + 6 we get 30.

18. B. 52

Option B and C are even numbers. Now both have 5 as one of their digits, but sum of their digits is seven. So 52. 5 + 2 = 7.

19. A. 9m 80 cm

Length of one curtain	4 m 50 cm
Length of another curtain	+ 5 m 30 cm
Total length of two curtains	9 m 80 cm

20. D. 34

4 more than 5 times 6 means

5 times 6 means

$5 \times 6 = 30$ and 4 more means $30 + 4 = 34$

21. C. Only squares. Faces of a cube are always square shaped.

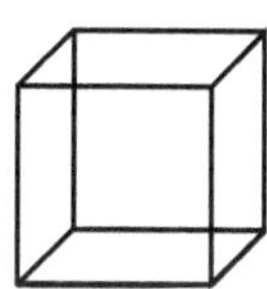

22. B. 283 ₹ 50 p

$$\begin{array}{r} 100 \\ +\ 100 \\ +\ 50 \\ +\ 20 \\ +\ 10 \\ +\ 2 \\ \underline{+\ 1} \\ 283 \end{array}$$

283 rupees and 50 paisa.

23. C. 290

190 more than the smallest 3-digit number. Smallest three digit number is 100 and 190 more than 100 is $190 + 100 = 290$.

24. C. 26

$4 + 18 + 23 = \_\_\_\_ + 19$

$45 \quad = \boxed{26} + 19$

Sum of numbers on the left hand side of the equal to sign is 45 so we need 45 on the right hand side also. $\_\_\_ + 19 = 45$. So $45 - 19 = \boxed{26}$.

25. C. 20

One dozens means 12, so two dozens means $12 \times 2 = 24$. Out of that 4 were spoilt so $24 - 4 = 20$.

26. A. 8 . If one '☐' means '+' then 6 ☐ 2 = ___

$$6 + 2 = 8$$

27. B. 294.

789 – ___ = 495

When subtrahend is missing we subtract the minuend and difference.

$789 - 495 = 294$

28. C. $285 - 0 = 0$

Subtraction rule : If 0 is subtracted from any number answer is that number itself.

$285 - 0 = 285$

29. C. 600

30. B. 6

30 mangoes distributed among 5 sons. So $30 \div 5 = 6$.

31. B. 1:10 pm

Ten minutes past one means ten minutes after 1 O' clock. 1:10. After 12 noon is post-meredian. So 1:10 pm.

32. C. Complete one circle

When hour hand travels from 8 to 9, it means one hour so the minute hand travels one complete round. i.e. 60 minutes.

33. A. KKHHAHHKKA

    Observe carefully.

34. B. 2

    1000m = 1 km

    20000m = 2 km

35. A. Sphere

36. A. 4

    When there are more than one sign in the sum please use BODMAS rule

    B – Bracket (u will learn in higher standards)

    O – Of

    D – Division

    M – Multiplication

    A – Addition

    S – Subtraction

    So we add all the numbers having + sign

    67 + 65 + 63 + 61 = 256

    Now subtract one by one numbers having - sign

    256 – 66 = 190

    190 – 64 = 126

    126 – 62 = 64

    64 – 60 = 4

37. C. 5

No of sweets John has = 16

Mark has 4 more than John, so 16 + 4 = 20

No of sweets Mark has = 20

Mark distributed 20 sweets equally to 4 friends

20 ÷ 4 = 5

38. C. 3

No of apple pies baked	=	80
No of apple pies given away	= –	53
No of apple pies left	=	27

27 apple pies were kept equally in 9 boxes. So 27 ÷ 9 = 3

In each box there were 3 apple pies.

39. C. 20, 10

Total amount that I have is 60 rupees.

10 + 20 = 30

So 30 more we need to make it 60.

20 + 10 = 30

40. D. 200

–10 +20 –10 +20 –10 +20

170, 160, 180, 170, 190, 180, 200

...

ANSWERSHEET

1.	Ⓐ Ⓑ Ⓒ Ⓓ	2.	Ⓐ Ⓑ Ⓒ Ⓓ	3.	Ⓐ Ⓑ Ⓒ Ⓓ	4.	Ⓐ Ⓑ Ⓒ Ⓓ
5.	Ⓐ Ⓑ Ⓒ Ⓓ	6.	Ⓐ Ⓑ Ⓒ Ⓓ	7.	Ⓐ Ⓑ Ⓒ Ⓓ	8.	Ⓐ Ⓑ Ⓒ Ⓓ
9.	Ⓐ Ⓑ Ⓒ Ⓓ	10.	Ⓐ Ⓑ Ⓒ Ⓓ	11.	Ⓐ Ⓑ Ⓒ Ⓓ	12.	Ⓐ Ⓑ Ⓒ Ⓓ
13.	Ⓐ Ⓑ Ⓒ Ⓓ	14.	Ⓐ Ⓑ Ⓒ Ⓓ	15.	Ⓐ Ⓑ Ⓒ Ⓓ	16.	Ⓐ Ⓑ Ⓒ Ⓓ
17.	Ⓐ Ⓑ Ⓒ Ⓓ	18.	Ⓐ Ⓑ Ⓒ Ⓓ	19.	Ⓐ Ⓑ Ⓒ Ⓓ	20.	Ⓐ Ⓑ Ⓒ Ⓓ
21.	Ⓐ Ⓑ Ⓒ Ⓓ	22.	Ⓐ Ⓑ Ⓒ Ⓓ	23.	Ⓐ Ⓑ Ⓒ Ⓓ	24.	Ⓐ Ⓑ Ⓒ Ⓓ
25.	Ⓐ Ⓑ Ⓒ Ⓓ	26.	Ⓐ Ⓑ Ⓒ Ⓓ	27.	Ⓐ Ⓑ Ⓒ Ⓓ	28.	Ⓐ Ⓑ Ⓒ Ⓓ
29.	Ⓐ Ⓑ Ⓒ Ⓓ	30.	Ⓐ Ⓑ Ⓒ Ⓓ	31.	Ⓐ Ⓑ Ⓒ Ⓓ	32.	Ⓐ Ⓑ Ⓒ Ⓓ
33.	Ⓐ Ⓑ Ⓒ Ⓓ	34.	Ⓐ Ⓑ Ⓒ Ⓓ	35.	Ⓐ Ⓑ Ⓒ Ⓓ	36.	Ⓐ Ⓑ Ⓒ Ⓓ
37.	Ⓐ Ⓑ Ⓒ Ⓓ	38.	Ⓐ Ⓑ Ⓒ Ⓓ	39.	Ⓐ Ⓑ Ⓒ Ⓓ	40.	Ⓐ Ⓑ Ⓒ Ⓓ
41.	Ⓐ Ⓑ Ⓒ Ⓓ	42.	Ⓐ Ⓑ Ⓒ Ⓓ	43.	Ⓐ Ⓑ Ⓒ Ⓓ	44.	Ⓐ Ⓑ Ⓒ Ⓓ
45.	Ⓐ Ⓑ Ⓒ Ⓓ	46.	Ⓐ Ⓑ Ⓒ Ⓓ	47.	Ⓐ Ⓑ Ⓒ Ⓓ	48.	Ⓐ Ⓑ Ⓒ Ⓓ
49.	Ⓐ Ⓑ Ⓒ Ⓓ	50.	Ⓐ Ⓑ Ⓒ Ⓓ	51.	Ⓐ Ⓑ Ⓒ Ⓓ	52.	Ⓐ Ⓑ Ⓒ Ⓓ
53.	Ⓐ Ⓑ Ⓒ Ⓓ	54.	Ⓐ Ⓑ Ⓒ Ⓓ	55.	Ⓐ Ⓑ Ⓒ Ⓓ	56.	Ⓐ Ⓑ Ⓒ Ⓓ
57.	Ⓐ Ⓑ Ⓒ Ⓓ	58.	Ⓐ Ⓑ Ⓒ Ⓓ	59.	Ⓐ Ⓑ Ⓒ Ⓓ	60.	Ⓐ Ⓑ Ⓒ Ⓓ
61.	Ⓐ Ⓑ Ⓒ Ⓓ	62.	Ⓐ Ⓑ Ⓒ Ⓓ	63.	Ⓐ Ⓑ Ⓒ Ⓓ	64.	Ⓐ Ⓑ Ⓒ Ⓓ
65.	Ⓐ Ⓑ Ⓒ Ⓓ	66.	Ⓐ Ⓑ Ⓒ Ⓓ	67.	Ⓐ Ⓑ Ⓒ Ⓓ	68.	Ⓐ Ⓑ Ⓒ Ⓓ
69.	Ⓐ Ⓑ Ⓒ Ⓓ	70.	Ⓐ Ⓑ Ⓒ Ⓓ	71.	Ⓐ Ⓑ Ⓒ Ⓓ	72.	Ⓐ Ⓑ Ⓒ Ⓓ
73.	Ⓐ Ⓑ Ⓒ Ⓓ	74.	Ⓐ Ⓑ Ⓒ Ⓓ	75.	Ⓐ Ⓑ Ⓒ Ⓓ	76.	Ⓐ Ⓑ Ⓒ Ⓓ
77.	Ⓐ Ⓑ Ⓒ Ⓓ	78.	Ⓐ Ⓑ Ⓒ Ⓓ	79.	Ⓐ Ⓑ Ⓒ Ⓓ	80.	Ⓐ Ⓑ Ⓒ Ⓓ
81.	Ⓐ Ⓑ Ⓒ Ⓓ	82.	Ⓐ Ⓑ Ⓒ Ⓓ	83.	Ⓐ Ⓑ Ⓒ Ⓓ	84.	Ⓐ Ⓑ Ⓒ Ⓓ
85.	Ⓐ Ⓑ Ⓒ Ⓓ	86.	Ⓐ Ⓑ Ⓒ Ⓓ	87.	Ⓐ Ⓑ Ⓒ Ⓓ	88.	Ⓐ Ⓑ Ⓒ Ⓓ
89.	Ⓐ Ⓑ Ⓒ Ⓓ	90.	Ⓐ Ⓑ Ⓒ Ⓓ	91.	Ⓐ Ⓑ Ⓒ Ⓓ	92.	Ⓐ Ⓑ Ⓒ Ⓓ
93.	Ⓐ Ⓑ Ⓒ Ⓓ	94.	Ⓐ Ⓑ Ⓒ Ⓓ	95.	Ⓐ Ⓑ Ⓒ Ⓓ	96.	Ⓐ Ⓑ Ⓒ Ⓓ
97.	Ⓐ Ⓑ Ⓒ Ⓓ	98.	Ⓐ Ⓑ Ⓒ Ⓓ	99.	Ⓐ Ⓑ Ⓒ Ⓓ	100.	Ⓐ Ⓑ Ⓒ Ⓓ

Model Paper 2

1. C. 56

No of students	25
No of teachers	2
No of driver	1
Total no of people	28

We have to find out number of eyes .So $28 \times 2 = 56$.

2. B. 84

Marks scored by Yash = 34

Rohan scored 50 more marks than Yash = $\underline{50} + 34 = 84$

3. A. 34, 27

$43 - 9 = P - 7 = Q$

$43 - 9 = 34\ (P) - 7 = 27$

(be careful while subtracting) P and Q respectively means we first write the value of P and then Q.

4. C. 72

I am more than 84-17 means 67

Less than 67 + 23 means 90

So the number has to be between 67 and 90

72 is between 67 and 90. between 67 and 90

5. C. 990

Greatest three digit number	= 999
Greatest one digit number	– 9
Difference	990

6. B. 212

+10 +20 +30 +40 +50 +60

2, 12, 32, 62, 102, 152, 212

7. B. 234

No of passengers in business class	= 14
No of passengers in economy class	=12
Total number of passengers	= 26

We have to find how many passengers can 9 such aeroplanes fetch. So $26 \times 9 = 234$

8. C. 74

638 km + _____ = 946 km – 234 km

946 – 234 = 712

638 + ____ = 712

So to find addend we subtract 712-638 (be careful, while subtracting always smaller number is subtracted from greater number)

So 712 – 638 = 74

9. B. 7

63 marbles are put equally into 9 boxes. To find the number of marbles in each box we divide $63 \div 9 = 7$.

10. C. 3

$$4 + 4 + 4 + 4 + 4 + 4 + 3 = \_\_\_ \times 9$$

$$27 = \_\_\_ \times 9$$

$$27 = \boxed{3} \times 9$$

11. C. 4

April, June, September, November

12. C. $36 \div \_\_\_ = 6$

$36 \div \boxed{6} = 6$

13. C. 24

Poonam wants to place 6 dots along each side of this given rectangle. A rectangle has 4 sides. 6 dots on each side .So 6 x 4 = 24

14. D. Chocolates

A jar contains 19 sweets, 4 chocolates, 14 candies and 9 lollipops. Number of chocolates are least, so chocolates are least likely to come out.

15. C. 81

It is 9's table.

$9 \times 9 = 81$

16. C. 333

All the options are three digit numbers and all of them have the same digit. Product of my digits is 27. Product means multiplication. $3 \times 3 \times 3 = 27$.

17. B. 9

$\square + \square = 14$, $\bigcirc + \square = 16$, then $\bigcirc = \_\_\_\_$

$\boxed{7} + \boxed{7} = 14$, $16 - 7 = 9$ $\quad$ ⑨ $+ \boxed{7} = 16$

So $\bigcirc = 9$

18. D. Saturday

If today is Monday, yesterday was Sunday and day before yesterday (Sunday) is Saturday.

19. A. 422

562	(489)	73

?	(273)	149

$489 + 73 = 562$

So $149 + 273 = 422$

20. A. 269

Cost of aeroplane and phone together is 847. Cost of aeroplane is 578. We have to find the cost of phone.

Cost of aeroplane and phone	847
Cost of aeroplane	– 578
Cost of phone	269

21. C. 6

No of carrots = 36. 36 carrots to be tied in bundle of 6 each means each bundle should have 6 carrots. So we divide.

$36 \div 6 = 6$

22. C. 3

Number 230 has 3 tens (30)

So 3 tens makes 30

23. B. 4

$5 \times 3 = 15$, $4 \times 5 = 20$, so $7 \times 4 = 28$

24. B. 6

Two shirts and three pants, so 3 x 2 = 6

Another way

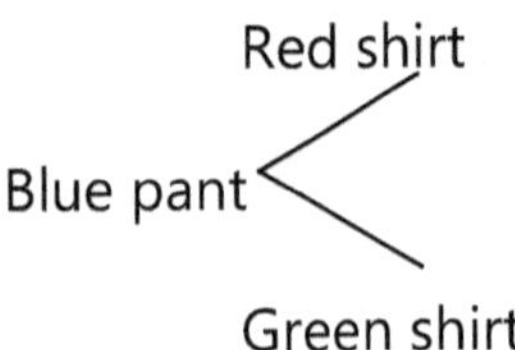

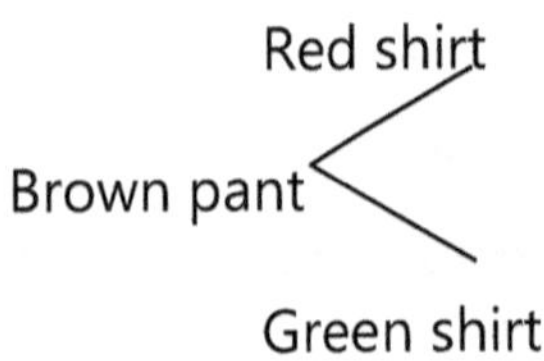

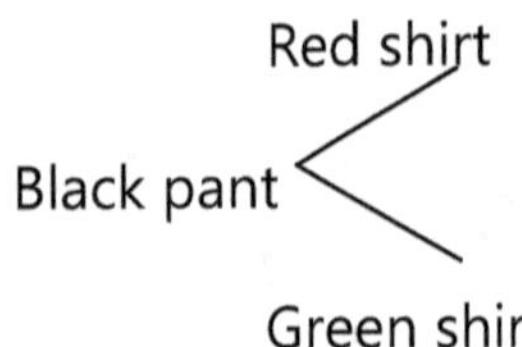

25. B. Only 3

Observe the figure carefully. In Fig. 3 one big rectangle is there, rest all have same size of shapes.

26. C. 5

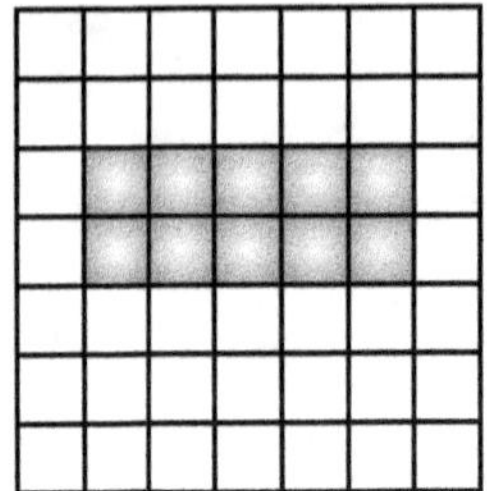

Length is 5 m as each square grid is 1 m long.

27. A. No

₹ 50 + ₹ 1 +₹ 2 = 53 ₹ One note and one coin cannot make ₹ 53.

₹ 50 + ₹ 1 + ₹ 1+ ₹ 1 = 53 ₹

₹ 50 + ₹ 1 + ₹ 1+ 50 p + 50 p = 53 ₹

28. C. ₹ 50, ₹ 20, ₹ 2, ₹ 1, 50 paise coin, 50 paise coin.

50 + ₹ 20 + ₹ 2 + ₹ 1 = ₹ 73

50 paise + 50 paise =100 paise = 1 ₹

So ₹ 73 + 1 = ₹ 74

29. B. 90

50 + ₹ 20 + ₹ 10 + ₹ 5 + ₹2 + ₹ 1+ ₹ 1+50p +50 p (1 rupee) = 90

30. B. 10

Total amount that Seema has is ₹ 90. Her dad gave her one coin and now she has 100 rupees.

So 90 + **10** = 100. Her dad gave her 10 ₹ coin.

31. B. 83

Cost of the book	₹ 183
Seema has	– ₹ 100
Seema needs	₹ 83

32. C. 5 p.m.

4:15 p.m the class starts and lasts for 45 minutes. So 4:15 + 45 = 5 p.m.

33. D. 6

1 pot = 3 bottles, so 2 pots = 6 bottles

1 bucket = 2 pots = [6 bottles]

34. D. 6

1 bottle = 2 cups

2 bottles = 4 cups

3 bottles = 6 cups

1 pot = 3 bottles = 6 cups

35. C. Bucket

36. B. 60

Total no of students in the canteen	=	600
No of students returned to the class	=	– 280
Students left in the canteen	=	320

If there were 380 students still in the canteen after recess, means a few students entered the canteen when bell rang.

320 + ___ = 380 (380 – 320 = 60)

320 + [60] = 380

So 60 students entered the canteen.

37. A. 194

No of pencils Reena has = 73

Rita has 48 pencils more than Reena. So Rita has 48 + 73 = 121.

We have to find out how many pencils are there altogether.

No of pencils Reena has	=	73
No of pencils Rita has	+ =	121
Altogether		194

38. C. 55

Red part = 35 m

Green part is 15 m shorter than red part, so 35 – 15 = 20

We have to find the height of the pole.(Red part + green part)

Red part	= 35m
Green part +	= 20m
Height of the	55m

39. C. 200

No. of bunches Ram has	= 6
No. of bunches Sham has	= +4
Total no. of bunches	= 10
Total no. of flowers in each bunch	= 20

So $20 \times 10 = 200$ flowers

40. B. He sold more than half of the balls.

Ramsingh has 88 balls. He sold 51 balls. Half of 88 is 44 (88 ÷ 2 = 44).

So he sold more than half balls.

❐❐❐

Notes

www.ingramcontent.com/pod-product-compliance
Lightning Source LLC
LaVergne TN
LVHW061222100826
845148LV00004B/829
* 9 7 8 9 3 5 1 6 4 5 3 8 2 *